AGAINST
ALL
WAVES

AGAINST

ALL

WAVES

CHELSEA RAY

Published by Chelsea Ray (Independently published)
First Edition August 2025

ISBN: 979-8-9992820-1-9 (Paperback)
ISBN: 979-8-9992820-0-2 (Hardcover)

Developmental editing by Melissa Frain
Copy and line editing by Cristen Cagle
Formatting by Nearly Novel Book Design
Cover design by Vivien Gintner
Printed in the United States of America
For more information, visit: www.chelsearaywriting.com

*To my husband who proved a kiss
can take your breath away.*

CHAPTER 1

SIX YEARS AGO

Eager ocean waves thrash against the ship, ready to feed on anything for the taking. No sailor or pirate wants to journey through the Sea of Orlosha. But we have no choice. This is the fastest route to land. To finally have food in my stomach again. To buy supplies that *The Turbulence* greatly needs to reclaim its splendor. For once in my life the thought of standing on solid ground is a blessing.

I curse silently as a burst of wind barrels into the ship, howling against the sails and ripping open the patch I worked tirelessly to repair. Our ship can't take much more of this. The deck creaks like its barely hanging on by a thread. As if at any moment it will cave in. I swear the same storm has been stalking us like a cat playing with its prey before devouring it whole. Today may be the day the Sea of Orlosha's curse claims us.

Stories say it was the home of mermaids, but once their scales became another treasure for men, it became a graveyard haunted by mysterious creatures. At thirteen, I've already learned men ruin everything. They take and destroy and leave you without a mother.

Another wave thrashes against *The Turbulence*, causing me to almost lose my footing without pushing some of my weight on my brother, Gus. He stands firm next to me, his hard face showing no

1

emotion as he gives me one hard flick of his wrist.

"Steady your feet and stand tall, Elle. We don't want the captain to give you another reason for being so delicate," he says from the side of his mouth, bringing out his sunken cheeks and making him look older than fifteen.

I grit my teeth, hating him for using the word delicate to describe me. I wouldn't be fumbling all over the place if the captain didn't call us onto the wet and slippery deck. I'm the toughest female pirate around, even if I'm mostly likely the only one that exists.

But Gus isn't wrong. The captain and the crew look for any flaw of mine and use it against me. I can't show any type of weakness. My hands and legs ache from the past eight hours of fighting against the wind, trying to keep the sails steady. All I want is to fall asleep in my hammock below and hope we make it through these waters alive. But when the captain calls, the crew does not make him wait. With the dark clouds threatening to drench us once more, I hope this won't be long.

When I see Blevins, his one eye swollen and blood dripping down his chin with his hands tied behind his back, my heart drops. Gyn, the first mate, nudges Blevins towards the edge of the ship as the captain follows behind with an evil grin. His intense dark green eyes find mine, waiting for any jolt of reaction. I stand tall like my brother warned me and force my face to stay neutral. I hope it is at least. Telling myself to keep breathing in and out slowly, I relax every muscle, including my eyebrows that want to narrow and my lips that want to harden as Blevins grunts and thrashes away from the narrow plank.

Blevins is going to die and there is nothing I can do about it.

Blevins, who has been part of the crew for as long as I can remember, is one of the more civil crew members. But only in secret. Being the youngest on this ship and a girl has made me fight for everything. I've always been the last to eat or drink. Last to sleep. Last to get off the ship when we arrive at a port. All to prove I'm as capable as the others and not 'Bad Luck' as the crew likes to spit out from their mouths.

I've been told by the captain it's the only way to make me stronger. But Blevins has made a point to make sure I've had enough food and drink. Every so often I'd find a few pieces of bread or dried cheese underneath my pillow. He always gave me the boost to continue on to the next day.

At first, I had thought it was Gus showing some type of brotherly affection until Blevins made a comment that my mother helped him survive a fever many years ago and he owed it to her to keep me alive. Sometimes I feel like there is more to it, but I've been too afraid to ask. The one main rule on this ship is to never speak of my mother because if the captain ever found out, blood would be spilled.

The wind howls, flailing my light blonde hair behind me and bringing the smell of more rain approaching. Hunger gnaws at my stomach, mingling with the fear of Blevins's situation. Moments ago, I found beans under my pillow. Those three beans are all I've had the past day. At this moment, I regret touching them. For now, it only means death.

"This is a warning and a reminder to all," the captain growls, giving me one hard glare before focusing on the rest of the gathering crew. Despite his one leg, he invokes terror with a single look. "It seems Blevins thinks he has more privileges than the rest of us to the remaining food. This is my ship and if anyone thinks of taking from it, there will be repercussions."

Gus stiffens and I glance over the ship's railing, noticing a sharp fin slicing through the rolling waves.

The captain gestures to Gyn with a nod. "We have a code and if it's broken you will pay. Blevins, you will walk the plank and let the sea decide your fate."

My body tightens as Gyn pulls out his cutlass sword and points it toward Blevins's chest. A man who took the liberty to steal what is left of the edible food . . . for me.

"Walk," Gyn snarls, his crooked nose more pronounced as the top of his lip curves up.

Blevins looks beyond Gyn, not focused on Gus, but on me. His gray eyes are full of fear, and a plea. As if the girl on this ship is the one to cave and somehow save his life. My pulse rises, biting the inside of my cheek. *Just don't cry.*

He doesn't deserve this. The one man that has shown kindness toward me when he didn't have to. The one man that spoke of my mother with a gleam of love in his eyes for a short second before turning back to the pirate that most are on this ship.

The plank creaks as Blevins steps toward the edge. I only hope he drowns before he is ripped apart by the teeth of that creature below.

But as he gets closer to the edge, I step forward, not wanting to lose another part of something that has been good to me. Lightning strikes above like a warning to stay quiet, but I can't.

"No!" I shout, regretting it as the captain's back straightens and his head turns slowly toward me. Shivers race up and down my arms.

"Gyn, stop," the captain says too calmly. "It seems Bad Luck wants to do the honor." The captain pulls his sword from its sheath around his waist. "Come here, girl."

Several pirates chuckle under their breath as I walk toward the captain. They're always savor the moment when I become the main joke or focus on the ship. I hear a faint grunt of irritation come from Gus.

The wind picks up as rain pelts down. I try to keep my stance steady as if it's a perfect sunny day when really acid is rising up my throat, threatening to come out. My arms give me away as they shake uncontrollably. Never have I been the one to force a man to walk the plank or take someone's life.

The captain grips my arm with more force than needed and shoves his sword into my hand. "If you want to keep calling this your home, finish the job or I'll punish you instead," he says, his tone deeper and colder than before.

I look up at the captain, the one I once called father, Velis Whitlock, hoping to see any remorse. Warning flares in his eyes, so I slowly raise the sword. It is almost too heavy to lift. My whole body shakes as the sword stops at Blevins's chest.

"Walk," I stutter before swallowing back my bile and pushing the tip of the weapon to his body.

Blevins shakes his head, gaze no longer fearful, but filled with sadness. "Gabrielle would never forgive me if I allowed you to do this."

I pause. For two long years I haven't heard her name spoken out loud. As if my mother is a ghost haunting my dreams or this very ship. How can one name bring back this loneliness I've been trying to ignore crawling back up from deep inside?

Shocked gasps echo from the crew. He brought her up. He said her name. The worst thing he could do, and he did it. There is no turning back because either I force him off this plank or the captain will do worse. But before I do anything, Blevins closes his eyes and jumps into the violent sea.

"NO!" I scream, reaching for him with my free hand. There is nothing left to grasp but the wind.

The captain roars and snatches the sword from my hands. Belvins is already gone. The monster's tail slaps the water as it dives for its fresh prey.

"Tie her up. Three lashings!" The captain spits, veins popping out from his neck. Gyn grabs my arm, dragging me to the ship's mast. I cry out as rope wraps tightly around my wrists, pushing me flush with the pole. Forcing myself to look back at the captain, I search for any affection or regret. But he paces back and forth, his brown hair flying wild in the wind like a mad man. How can my mother's name cause so much hatred?

"But he went off the plank!" I wail as Gyn tightens my bonds. My back is exposed to everyone. I close my eyes and lean my head onto the pole, hoping this will go fast. He said three lashes, and these three lashings are for those three beans. Or to punish me for being who I am.

My mother's daughter.

A crack joins the thunder as sharp pain rivets from my back all the way to my toes. I grunt loudly but tell myself to keep my screams within. To show that I can take this like any other man. This feels like another test from the captain, my father, but right now, I feel like what I am. A girl who wants her mother back. To not feel so alone. To feel loved and cared for again but only the word abandoned whispers in my mind.

As the second crack opens my skin, I'm reminded what love causes.

Pain.

Crack.

Suffering.

Warmth travels down my back, the pain bringing me to my knees, popping my shoulders out of place.

Gus is un-tying my hands. "It's okay. It's over," he whispers shakily.

I keep my eyes shut, not wanting to see the crew, nor the captain, staring at me judgmentally. I focus on each drop of rain hitting my skin instead of the roaring hot pain against my back.

"Back to work!" The captain yells as Gus helps me down the stairs toward my hammock. But he turns and opens his closet-sized room. He has a small, feathered mattress on the floor with a tiny cabinet in the corner. Being the captain's son, he has some perks.

I groan as he helps me lay face-down on the mattress.

"I'll be right back," he says, shutting the door behind him.

When he returns, he rips what's left of my shirt off. I see the blood splattered on it and turn my head toward the wall, wanting to forget. Pain flares across my back as he cleans my wounds. Silent tears fall down my cheeks.

"You need to learn to control those tears. They'll hinder you." He lays a warm rag atop the wounds, sits beside me, and leans against the wall.

Though I want to cry more, I force myself to stop. If only he understood that no matter what I do, it always backfires in one way or another. In defeat, I whisper, "I'll try."

Sighing, he takes my boots off and lays a blanket up to my waist. "This room is yours now. You need it more than I do." Something cold touches my shoulder. "And I want you to have this."

I face him, studying the short bronze dagger he's holding. The weapon has a full cross guard that looks like vines with flowers designed around it.

"Where did you get that?" I ask in complete surprise. It's beautiful, and like nothing I've seen before.

"Illira found it on a sunken ship. It's time for you to have your own." He pauses. "For protection."

I grab it, even though the movement creates pain, and bring it close to my chest. A gift from my brother I'd happily take.

"Thank you," I whisper.

"Get some sleep," he says, standing up to leave. He stiffens uncomfortably in his tight navy shirt that's now a size too small for his teenage growing figure. I remind myself to buy some fabric if we make it back onto land.

Before he walks out of the room, I ask, "Why don't you wear it anymore?"

He stops, back facing me as he leans against the doorway. "You know why I don't," he says with pain in his voice, looking anywhere but at me.

"You're wrong, Gus. She had to have her reasons for leaving. I know she loved us." I whisper, hoping no one's around to hear who I'm speaking about.

"She's gone." He pauses and takes a loud deep breath. "And you shouldn't be wearing that necklace. It will only anger the captain if he sees it. You're lucky he didn't when—" He rolls his neck. "You have to let her go."

More tears threaten to fall. "But how?"

"You will have to figure that out on your own, but it needs to be done sooner than later." He shuts the door behind him leaving me to weather this internal storm alone.

He is right. The only way I'm going to survive here is to let the memory of my mother go.

CHAPTER 2

SIX YEARS LATER

I run my finger against the chain of my necklace, reminding myself why I am here. Here, in this old worn-out tavern, waiting for a man. Something I said I'd never do.

The numbness from my back side travels down my leg, only making me angrier by the second. The wooden chair creaks and groans as I attempt to find a more comfortable position. Hopefully it doesn't break the next time I move.

Golden hues dance along the aged buildings as the sun disappears, leaving the hint of its warmth behind on the brick roads. Did I really wait here until dusk? I lean my hands on the wobbly high table. It's more a long slab of wood, laid on top of three stakes. Slowly, I push myself out of the seat, my legs feeling unsteady while my head spins in a haze.

"Do ya want another drink? You've been here for most of the day," the bartender asks before crouching over and coughing into her sleeve. When she looks back at me her gray eyes are bloodshot, her breathing not as consistent as it should be.

My reply to the woman is giving her a slight grin and taking a huge gulp, savoring the warmth of the gin down my throat before banging it back down for another. Might as well.

She fills my drink without hesitation, not allowing me to change my mind even if I want to. The woman has been serving me drink after drink for the past who knows how long. I've caught her multiple times watching me in the dimly lit corner, and right when I'm on my last sip she's already asking if I want another.

I don't blame her. I'm going through more coins than others in this dump. I really should be more lenient with my money, so I don't attract unwanted visitors. But the frail little girl with skin that looks like it's never been touched by the sun's warmth who appears periodically to tug on the woman's skirt encourages me to keep indulging myself.

The front door opens, and I hold my breath thinking maybe, just maybe, my luck has changed. That the man I've been patiently waiting for has finally arrived to fulfill his side of our bargain. But it's only a rowdy group of clearly drunk men. They greet the barkeeper as Greta, asking for bread and cheese before sitting at a round table behind me.

My stomach growls hungrily but my nerves are in full force, making it impossible to eat. I tell myself I will only wait a little bit longer. It's getting late and soon my prowling brother, Gus, will start looking for me. Hopefully the captain keeps him busy doing his dirty work or whatever it is he has him do while we're on land.

The difference between my brother and I is that he still wants our father's approval while I gave that up a long time ago. Sadly, I can't trust Gus with my secret, or it will ruin everything I've been working toward for the past six years.

Unfortunately, I don't have much to show for it. I overheard an older man at a tavern the crew visited a few months ago on Gailling Island, complaining about the food being served. At first, I ignored his outburst and thought nothing of it until he brought up some cinnamon muffins with honeysuckle that would melt your soul. Something just clicked and felt right. Anyone can make cinnamon biscuits, but I'd never met anyone that made honeysuckle muffins other than one person.

My mother.

By that point, it wasn't time to be lazy, and I decided to wait until my brother and the rest of the crew left before confronting him.

He was quite friendly after I paid for a few more drinks for him. He talked about a blonde middle-aged woman handing out baskets of honeysuckle muffins to all the ships at a port he was visiting. I asked if he knew where this port was, but my face must have shown a sign of vulnerability because after that he only finished his drink, some of it dripping down his lip, stating he "couldn't remember."

So, I gave him every coin I had left in my pocket only to learn she was some cook. I debated if I should beat it out of him when he still wouldn't tell me where this port was other than calling it "the land of healing" and making absolutely no sense.

He was probably senile, but I made a deal that I would meet him at a place of his choosing with a bag of gold coins. This dump was his choosing, and I worked hard to convince the captain that Yurma Island was worth visiting. Based on the smell of rotten eggs, old buildings falling apart, and half made shacks, I'll likely receive repercussions later.

But this will be all worth it. I need some answers. Without them it only causes me to hinder myself as a pirate. I cannot be the best without this nagging feeling inside that she's out there somewhere. What causes a sour taste in my mouth is thinking of her taking care of another family when she should have been taking care of her own.

The entrance door flings open again, making me jump, but when I look toward the entrance there is only the dark sky and the wind howling between buildings.

The weight of the golden coins in my pocket becomes heavy. I feel foolish. Naive. Used. Disgusted with myself for trusting a man. This is another thing I can put on my list of failures.

The disgusting stench of day's old sweat wafts toward me, along with a brute's footsteps. He slams into my shoulder and hollers for Greta. I roll my eyes, annoyed that some of my drink had splattered on my hand and not so white shirt.

Greta is back in the corner of the bar. The young girl with the same silver hair as the barkeeper is back, leaning on her mother's leg with tear-filled eyes. Greta leans down, whispering as she points behind the bar. The girl nods and disappears.

Greta walks slowly back to the table, wincing as she picks up a bottle of Gin and asks in a monotone voice, "Want another, Fin?"

"No." He leans forward, grabbing a piece of her sleeve and rubbing it with his thumb. "Thought ya'd like to meet upstairs," he says, giving her a wink. "I even have some of that special medicine that everyone's been talkin' about."

Greta perks up, her gray eyes looking more alive. "How?"

He moves in closer, his nose almost touching hers. "In the shipping yard. Had to slit a few throats but was able to grab a few before it was taken to higher ground, past those gates."

Higher ground. Gates. He must be talking about the trail I saw earlier today that travels above this town. A few guards patrol two giant black gates with a brick fence that travels for miles. Clearly, it's to keep people down below from sneaking in. The buildings I could see were immaculate with fresh paint and well-maintained gardens. It's as if they were being separated from a completely different world and given no second thought of how the ones below were fairing.

This hasn't been the first time I've heard of the rich or more privileged building a community that separates from the less fortunate. I've even seen it at the ports when food and prices are set so only the rich can afford them, leaving others with barely anything. Thank the sea gods my home is not on land but free to sail the wide open.

"The rich folk have already kept everything else from us. But I got somethin' precious of theirs right here in my pocket and I'll kill again to get more of it," he says, patting his hip.

Greta bites the bottom of her lip. "Show me first and then I'll go," she whispers, sounding more like a plea.

He spits by his feet, barely missing my boots, and releases her sleeve. "You callin' me a liar? I can sell this for good coin rather than wasting my time here," he says, taking a step back. "I'm sure ya daughter would cure right away with this."

Greta's eyes widen with fear. "Ok! Just give me a second," she says, disappearing behind the bar.

I feel the weight of the man's eyes land on me, cueing me to leave.

But a hard smack hits right on my rear, followed by a whistle. "Wowee, look at those sea legs. I'd love to be between those thighs."

Already in a foul mood, I scowl at the grimy man and decide I'll carve his eyes out first.

"Oh, would you, hmm?" Finishing the last swig of my gin, I lick my lips with the remainder, enticing him to take another step toward me. His breath smells like liquor, smoke, and decay as he smiles at me with one front tooth missing. "Maybe I should even out your teeth."

He leans forward to grab my shoulder. I take his fingers and ring them back as a warning. "Don't touch me, you filthy rat."

"Oh, feisty, are we? I do like a bit of pain to spice things up," he slurs. His other hand drifts toward my thigh and I swing my mug right into his mouth while kneeing him in the groin. "I warned you. Fool."

He thuds to the ground. Blood runs out of his mouth and a tooth lies beside him. I spit on his face while he groans loudly, and then I place my broken mug on the table. I'm about to leave but stop when Greta reappears. This disgusting man is probably lying about having medicine in his pocket, but it's worth checking.

The sound of chairs pulling out behind me warns me that I should leave. Instead, I glare at the two drunk men at the round table and roll up my sleeves. "I wouldn't make any rash decisions boys." I raise my arm, showing the back of my wrist with a black tattoo in the shape of a ship. "Or the crew of *The Turbulence* won't be too happy."

"One of Velis's pirates," slurs one of the men. He grabs the rest of the bread that's left on the table. "We were just leavin'," he says and staggers out, the other man following on his heels. I smirk to myself. The crew wouldn't give a rat's ass what would happen to me. They'd egg it on, but my brother . . .

Thinking of Gus reminds me I need to leave. He is probably steps away from this tavern by now, knowing I'm always for a good gin or mead.

Cringing, I dig into the drunkard's pocket, hoping I touch nothing but what I'm looking for. The small bottle is surprisingly cool to the touch. When I pull it out, it's a liquid substance the color of bright sapphire. It's nothing like I've seen before. I roll the bottle in my hand, examining the strip of leather on the top of it, and notice some type of engraving.

This can't be real. I must have drank too much because I'm now seeing things. I squeeze my eyes shut and reopen them, focusing back on the bottle but it's still there.

The symbol on the medicine bottle is a half-moon with three stars, a replica of my necklace.

Greta hastily moves around the bar. "Please, don't take it." Her voice quivers. "Please," she begs, looking down at her feet. "I don't have much, but I can give you the coin I have."

The fear in her voice makes me wince. I can't ignore the sting of pain running through me, that Greta thinks I'd keep this. Clearly, she and her daughter need this medicine. This is why I don't like to throw my tattoo around. It's not like I need any friends on land, but once others know I'm a pirate, I'm only seen as a threat or someone fearsome. But isn't that the point? Shouldn't I want others to fear me?

"Here." I give her the bottle, wishing she will stop acting like I am some heartless wench. But shouldn't I be? Anyone else in the crew would take this medicine. They wouldn't give it a second thought, even when actual sick ones were right in front of them.

"Thank you," Greta says, finally looking at me with tears in her eyes.

I nod but keep my eyes on the bottle in her hands. Is the symbol just a coincidence? Or even though the man never came, have I been given some sort of sign that I'm still on the right path? "Do you know who sells these bottles?"

"I've heard it's from an island many call the "land of healing" but that is all I know," she says, coughing into her elbow. "It's hard to get. I heard this medicine can cure anything, even when you're close to death."

My excitement dwindles. This land of healing must have an actual name.

The slimeball below my feet grabs my ankle but I jam my bootheel into his nose. The deep sleazy snore and slumped head lets me know he will be out for a while.

I turn toward the door and drop my bag of golden coins onto the table for Greta to take. "You should leave. He won't be too happy when he wakes."

"I've never met a pirate like you," she says.

The statement makes me stop. Unsure if I should be happy or mad with what she just said, I look over my shoulder. Greta is grasping the bag of coins close to her chest making my heart feel a sense of warmth but also hatred because no matter how many times I've tried, I can't stop this feeling that maybe I'll never live up to being the pirate I'm told I should be.

CHAPTER 3

ELLE

The stars and bright moon light my path towards *The Turbulence*. With each step, I become angrier and angrier, thinking about the man that never came. My mind races, heat rushing up my body and through my veins, flushing my cheeks. I kick a rock across the uneven ground, wanting to scream and release the rising frustration.

Sliding down a brick wall, I wrap my arms around my knees, hiding my face. This isn't what I imagined would happen today. Not even close. Instead, here I sit on the cold and uneven ground, losing it and barely able to breathe. Why am I allowing this old hag to control my life?

The sound of waves splashing against the rocky shore comfort me. But I stay hidden in the shadows. All the weight of what today could have become blows through like a treacherous storm ready to pull me deep into the sea. "Maybe this is all a mistake," I whisper to myself.

The hope I'd had when I arrived this morning has simmered into nothingness. Someone must know where this "land of healing" is but the symbol that matches my own necklace can't be ignored. My breathing rapidly increases.

I need to stop allowing my heart to make these choices. To be the pirate I've been raised to be and forget the mother who has clearly forgotten me.

Wetness glides down my cheeks and I swat the tears away. "Stop crying, you're better than this," I spit out. "Just breathe."

I take a deep breath, forcing myself to stand and shake off the nonsense. Soon my goal will be achieved one way or another. If I can think of one good quality I've gained from my father, it would be never giving up. That man, as terrible as he is, always achieves his goals in any way possible. What I'm currently portraying is only weakness and no pirate on *The Turbulence* is weak or gives up.

Laughter from a couple down the street catches my attention. A man and woman gaze into each other's eyes, barely visible beneath the lone oil lamp hanging above them, no doubt saying sweet nothings that will lead to something I hope won't be on the streets.

His hand glides down her cheek and he sinks down to one knee. A scream of delight escapes the woman's lips as he pulls out a box. I roll my eyes, shaking my head. If only she knew how things would end. I want to yell at her to run as she jumps into his arms. They both seem happy, but I doubt it will last for the two. It never does.

As I come closer to the dock, a knot forms in my stomach as my brother runs toward me with a deep scowl. "Where have you been? I've been searching all over for you!" Grabbing my arm, he pinches my skin.

"Well, I'm here. What are you so frantic about?" I snatch my arm away before he leaves a bruise.

Gus crosses his arms. "*He* has someone."

"Who's this someone?" I say, mimicking Gus's stance.

Gus shakes his head with disbelief. "I knew you were hiding something from me. Why didn't you just tell me! Now you're in some deep shit and I don't know how I'm gonna protect you from this."

I gaze up to the dock and with the night's cold sea breeze, my hands start to shiver. I keep my stance tall as I walk back on the ship. My crewmates are standing on the top deck and giving me more death looks than normal. One of them spits at my feet, a grumble of "bad luck" leaving his lips.

At the end of the ship stands a familiar old man. His gray hair is longer than I remember but the long scar from the top of his mouth down to his chin is more distinct under the moonlight. His hands are bound behind his back, blood trickles from the corners of his mouth, and fear glazes his eyes.

Maybe everyone is right.

I am bad luck.

The man that holds my future in his hands is now standing before me gagged and beaten to a pulp. His legs shake. Sweat mixed with blood drips down his head. Heavy footsteps approach from the shadows below deck, paralyzing me. My back cringes with a past pain, this moment reminding me too much of my last lashing.

The entire crew remains in place, hoping to be ignored by the captain as he slowly passes them by, the hiss and rattle of his wheezing growing louder with each slow step. As I try to wiggle my toes to bring back life flow into my feet, I hesitate as I'm met with a cold piercing stare. I steady myself, clenching my fists, ready and willing to take punishment like the brave pirate I am.

How did he find out? How did he know this is the man I've been waiting for? My stomach feels sick knowing that somehow my brother has something to do with this.

Standing unsteady, the captain towers over me, his hot breath reeking of whiskey. "So nice of you to join us. Look who I found!"

It's complete silence on the ship, other than the flocks of birds flying above and thunder rumbling a mile away. My chest is heavy and I'm trying to focus on each breath that flows out of my nose.

"Do you take me as an idiot!?" he hollers, spit hitting my face.

"Father . . . I—"

Pain pierces my cheek and my vision becomes hazy, causing me to fall to my knees from the force of his slap. I focus on the ship's deck, trying to steady myself even though my whole head feels like it's burning. Getting back up as quickly as I can would be the best option to prove the pain is nothing, but my shaking legs won't allow it.

"Oh, you must be guilty. I haven't heard you call me Father in years," he growls.

My brother steps toward us with wide eyes and a tight lip. "Captain . . ."

My father hunches his shoulders and, without turning around, raises his finger as a warning. I slowly shake my head, hinting for my brother to stand down and let me take this.

"I knew you wouldn't listen. You're a useless, lying whore . . . just like her." His steps recede and I gain the courage to look up. My father holds a knife in his hand, and he's gripping it with intent. He turns, standing next to the man who is thrashing his head back and forth trying to get loose. With a flash of red tint in his eyes, my father slices the man's neck. He cleans his knife on the man's sleeve before he pushes him overboard into the deep sea.

I hold my breath, wondering if I'll be next. But he puts his knife back in its sheath. Rain falls and the crew remain in place, waiting for orders.

"This is your last warning. If I ever hear a whisper of you searching for her again . . ." He peers at my brother and back at me. "You won't like the consequences," he warns. "Now, everyone back to work! A storm's a comin' and we'll be more prepared this time. If we lose anything off this ship, you'll be going with it!"

I stand slowly, knowing that the one man that could help me find my mother is now fish bait. A death caused by my stupidity and in search of a woman I will never find. The truth crawls up my back and whispers in my ear that I have failed.

"And one other thing," the captain says, approaching like a distant thunder, carrying an underlying threat.

Pausing in my haste to return to my cabin and grieve in private, I swallow a sob as the captain's cold callous hand grabs my neck. His nails dig into my skin, pulling my necklace off and tearing the top of my shirt with it. A sound of horror leaves my mouth as I reach for the necklace now dangling from his fingertips. My father, the monster before me, holds it above my head, tempting me to fight back and claim what is mine.

Defeated, I stare into his dark green eyes that I swore once showed love and affection but now emanate hate and disgust.

"This . . ." His eyebrows furrow, inspecting the necklace. A hint of sadness echoes across his face but then disappears, his face etched into a deep scowl. "This should no longer be your concern." His mouth tightens as he throws the necklace into the never-ending sea. Without another word, he walks back to direct the ship away from the coming storm.

My stomach drops, feeling emptiness as if a part of me has left with my necklace. I want to scream and unleash the anger that builds in my chest. Even the cold wind blowing against me can't control the fire burning beneath my skin. Instead, my eyes start to water as I peer out at the thrashing waves. I refuse to cry in front of my father or the crew's lingering eyes. Raindrops help disguise the tears that I can no longer control.

My small cabin and soft sheets call my name as I yearn for solitude. Only a few more steps to my door and I can unleash all the pain and sadness into my pillow. When I arrive, the door is half open. My brother sits on the bed, his palms hiding his face while his brown hair hangs freely across his shoulders in a fray leaving only a few strands still tied behind him.

"What do you want?" I ask. My brother stands suddenly. I close the door and lean on it, folding my arms.

"Why didn't you tell me you were searching for her?" Gus whispers as if my room can tell secrets.

I look at the floor, not wanting to see the sadness in Gus's eyes but also not wanting him to see mine. "Why would I tell you? So you could run your mouth to the captain?"

Gus takes a step toward me. "He asked me to keep a close watch on you."

Fire boils in the pit of my stomach. "You were a part of this!" I say, trying to control my tears, clenching my fists.

"He wouldn't tell me why! You know I just follow his orders!"

I bang my fist against the door, welcoming the pain in my hand riveting up my arm. "Damnit Gus! I hope someday you grow some balls! I was so close to finding our mother and that man was my answer!"

He steps closer, a mixture of sadness and hate swirling in his hazel eyes. "We don't have a mother. She left us. We are better without her!" Gus says in a low but angry tone.

"Because we are so loved here, right? He threatened to hurt you if I screwed up again."

"He wouldn't. He is only bluffing to keep you in line. You know that."

"Look me in the eyes and say that again." I step toward him, so we are face to face.

Gus focuses behind me, moving his jaw back and forth.

I decide to push him a bit more, hoping to see a glint of remorse. "But is it okay for him to hit me?"

His eyes are back on me, darkening. He opens his mouth to say something but stops. I wait, hoping he tells me that he will never let our father touch me again and that he will be the big brother I always wanted. But there's only silence in return.

I shake my head. "Sometimes I feel like I barely know you."

"I know I'm a screw up and have daddy issues, but you need to let her go. He's right about that."

"So, I just need to be an obedient woman and do whatever he tells me? You know he isn't telling us everything about what happened that day with our mother. There must be more to it! She didn't even say goodbye, just left without a trace."

"Let's not fight over this again. It's his ship, his rules. If you don't like it, let's leave. You and me. We can start our own adventure."

This isn't the first time we've had this conversation and I'm sure it isn't going to be the last. My brother always surprises me when he suggests leaving. He seems to want to leave and never come back but, without fail, he fights to impress our father. He is so indecisive.

"And just give up, no longer be pirates?" I ask, flailing my arms out.

"It's not giving up. Don't you ever wonder what else is out there? We could be anything we want. You have nothing to prove here," he pauses and clears out his throat. "You're too good for all this."

"I'm too good for this or I'm not good enough due to being a woman?" I grasp for my necklace, but only my clammy skin welcomes me, a reminder that it now lays on the ocean floor. "I know nothing else, Gus. The sea is my home," I whisper.

Gus lets out a big breath of air, hunching his shoulders. "That's not true."

A hard knock at the door interrupts us. I open the door to Gyn, the captain's slimy sidekick, standing against the wall.

"The captain wants ya to call your little merfriend. He wants a heavy ship to attack soon. And it better be worth it."

I roll my eyes and slam the door in his face, hoping it injured his already crooked nose.

CHAPTER 4

AXEL

Sweat drips into my eyes from the past hour of sparring but every ounce of my body demands to continue like smoldering ashes. The last three months have not been easy and no matter what I do, I can't seem to release this anger inside of me. A rise of sorrow strikes through me like a bolt of lightning. Biting it back, I lower my sword and resume my fighting stance.

My instructor, Theodore, raises his sword, matching me, the sunlight glaring against it. His breaths are heavy, and his shoulders lack the strength they had earlier this morning. He is not one to end a match until his opponent withdraws, but his furrowed brows and scowl make me believe I'll soon win this match.

"Haven't had enough," he states, his voice gruff, a strand of sweat trickling down his cheek. It's not a question but only an observation while his eyebrow with a long scar rises. He grabs his sword's hilt with intent, his arm muscles more pronounced as he steps toward me, ready for my move. Even with our age gap, Theodore still moves and fights like a lion.

A clearing of a throat announces someone is close, but I keep my eyes on Theo. Then there is another. Theo halts and looks behind me.

"Sir, you have been called to the council," one of my father's helpers announces.

If only my father and his council understood that my lessons are to be my uninterrupted time. For a few hours, I can forget all my responsibilities. Soon I will have the whole island of Glendora on my shoulders. Being the one to make all the decisions. Decisions that are not always easy to make.

This is part of my training so I can keep them safe, but it won't do any good if I'm always interrupted. Even waking hours before the rest of the trainees doesn't allow me to have a second for myself.

"Not now, Fedrick," I say firmly, hoping it will deter him.

"Your father insists this cannot wait," he yawns, clearly awakened just to deliver a message. My horse's reins are in his hands, ready for me to take.

Theo's sword slides back into his sheath, making me want to demand that this isn't over. That my father and the council can give me one more hour. For they are the ones that hired Theo, a highly prestigious soldier from afar, to teach me how to protect myself and the island.

"Axel, you should run it off at the beach later," he suggests, holding his hand out for my weapon.

I breathe out from my nose and roll my neck, handing him my sword. "Very well. Thank you, Theo," I say before turning and following Fedrick back toward the town on horseback. *This better be good.*

A rooster crows in the distance, welcoming the sun's appearance. The town is barely awake and light peaks between the brick buildings and markets down to the port where a part of *The Blazing Star's* sails blows in the wind.

"Would you like me to take your horse, Sire?" Fedrick asks once we arrive at the council building.

"Please. And you might as well take Clarence back to the barn. I'm sure I'll need a long walk after this."

"Very well," he says, looking me up and down at my black uniform that's more fit for training than meeting with the council. "Are you sure you don't want to change before entering?"

"No need, they are the ones adamant about me being here so quickly," I state. *The ones on my toes about being more trained in combat. So, they might as well smell one.* I smirk to myself, picturing the old men in disdain.

Fedrick gives me a sleepy nod and leaves with the horses.

I swipe my hands through my dark chestnut hair, sweat still on my forehead as I open the wooden front door with engravings of the blazing stars, a very popular purple flower that grows throughout the island. All eyes gravitate toward me as I enter the room, and I try not to fidget with my sparring uniform that is now sticking uncomfortably to my skin.

As the doors thud closed behind me, I flex my hands at my side to keep them still. Several of the councilmen wrinkle their noses, gazes judging in a manner that makes sweat prickle along my brow worse than sparring did.

"You made it," my uncle Orson says, obviously unhappy for the wait.

I reluctantly sit in my chair across from my father, my back aching while my leg muscles protest as I bend them. "Good morning, uncle. Council. Father," I say, trying to keep any annoyance hidden in my voice.

The three older men watch me intensely as my father doesn't even raise his head in acknowledgement. He is fixed on reading the papers in front of him. The councilmen watch my every move.

Sitting taller in my seat, I don't let them see my uneasiness as I put on my charming smile. "So, what is the reason for this rushed meeting?"

My father finally focuses on me. A glint of silver runs through his once dark hair. His weary blue eyes look older than they have in a long time. "I know it hasn't been easy the past months but it's time for you to devote yourself to Glendora."

For my father to even imply that I haven't devoted enough of myself to Glendora makes me clench my hands tight underneath the table, wondering where this conversation is even going.

"I know you have lost someone special—"

"Don't act as if she wasn't important to you" I say, barely containing the desire to shout. "Just because she wasn't blood doesn't mean she wasn't still family."

Father closes his eyes for a split second and stands. "I never said she wasn't. But as the ruler of this island, I cannot take time to grieve like others can due to a death. You need to understand I have been lenient on you for only this reason. But once you take over, you will not have the privilege to do what others can, for we cannot allow our emotions to take precedence over our people."

I bite my tongue, thinking about when my mother had died when I was younger. Never once did I see my father's grief. He only continued working, his days away from home becoming longer.

"For one choice can ruin everything," he says slowly, walking around the table and bringing the papers with him.

"Which is why I have you here this morning. To discuss not only your future, but Glendora's." He stops behind my uncle Orson and places the papers in front of him. "We were all aware when we made the decision to share our produce and medicine from the very soil of our ground that Glendora would become known to other islands. For centuries, we have been fortunate to keep this place hidden and never have to buy from others. This very land takes care of all our needs. But as we continue to sell, more will want to know about this island and why it's so special. We will need to protect our people, and for that I will need help from others. Others that are not from here."

He hasn't said it yet, but it's at the tip of his tongue. I can tell it's not something I'll want to hear.

"Axel, you have done well traveling to other islands and negotiating a price to sell our products. I have received many letters regarding how agreeable and fair you are to work with, so much so they desire an alliance with Glendora."

My shoulders stiffen for a second before reminding myself to keep calm, waiting for my father to finish instead of interrupting him like I did before. "What kind of alliance?"

Each step my father takes back to his seat seems more agonizingly

25

slower than the last. It is not until he resumes his seat and shifts his coat tails behind him that he clears his throat. Even then, he does not look at me. His focus remains on where his overlapped hands rest on the table. "Your uncle has been corresponding with Osteria, Nurehmia, and Florencia about providing an army to protect our borders, and our ships, from intruders. All this in exchange for a marriage alliance with you, my son."

And there it is. If someone was to ask me what I thought this meeting was going to be about, a marriage alliance would have been at the bottom of my list. Past rulers of Glendora have always married someone from the island and not for any gain other than finding a wife. For love. But now it looks as if I do not have a choice. I can't deny that we do need more protection.

Our people are not aware how lucky they truly are. Since I have sailed to different lands, I have seen the greed and hate of others. To where people will kill another for a small gain. But also, how the rich will separate themselves from the poor instead of giving a helping hand.

Theodore, my trainer, has spoken of wars caused by the smallest conflict. Though he will not even speak of the battles he has fought nor what he has seen, the hidden pain in his gray eyes tells me enough. I cannot allow anything to happen to Glendora. And if a marriage alliance will be part of keeping it safe, I will do it. But I won't let my father know this just yet, for this is a time to negotiate.

I swallow, helping my throat from being dry. "I have a condition. Given the atrocities I've witnessed in my travels, I request that prices are cut in half indefinitely," I say firmly.

The councilmen raise their eyebrows in confusion while my father smirks with amusement. Orson scrambles with the papers in front of him and stands, his eyes wide. "Absolutely not. We can't control what others do with the price once it's out of our hands. This is a business, not a charity."

I grind my teeth, letting the anger that's building inside of me lessen before replying. "When we first agreed to start sharing this medicine outside of Glendora it was because we had concluded that it has been selfish of us to keep this hidden for so long. We did this not to make a giant profit but to help others. Or is this just about the money?"

My father's bright blue eyes—that I inherited—stay locked on my own, ignoring his brother's outburst. "I'm proud of you, son. I approve."

The councilmen nod their heads in agreement.

Orson inhales loudly, his cheeks now a cherry red. "But Gerald, we can't just change our prices so drastically! It will make others question our decisiveness or even consider it a weakness."

My father raises his hand for him to be silent. "Sit, Orson. I have made my decision, and it is final."

Orson grunts and takes a seat, his jaw tight as he looks down at the table.

"But with this decision, Axel," my father says calmly. *Ah, yes, there is always a 'but.'* "The council and I have agreed it will be best if your uncle takes over the shipments while you stay here by my side. More than ever, we need to show you are here for our people. Many are looking up to us and others wavering on our decision to share Glendora with others. Not all agree with this change . . ."

Muscles in my jaw tick at the idea of Orson overseeing the shipments. I care for my uncle, but I can't ignore the shine of a coin in his eyes whenever we speak of profiting more from our land.

"Very well," I state. "Before this is final, I want to finish my voyage and meet with Toradian. They would be the last kingdom I have not visited, and I believe it's wise to be familiar with all lands, creating a relationship with them before I stay more confined to Glendora. They would also be the first with the changed price of medication and I want to be the one to discuss it." I say, eyeing my uncle and the council before looking back at my father.

Father nods and the council follows. "Very well," he states, the lines on his forehead looking more relaxed than I have seen them in a long time.

I stand, ready to leave this congested room and process everything that has transpired in the last twenty minutes. Mainly, I wonder how Nile, my adopted brother, will take me leaving while he's still grieving his mother's death.

"Axel," my uncle says, his voice a bit more forceful than I like. He shuffles the papers in front of him. "Before you go, we have some suggestions on who would be the best prospect as your future wife."

"You really think you know who would be best for me?" I ask, thinking my uncle couldn't get any lower than this objectifying list. He walks around the table, handing me the list that I plan to burn later.

Burgess, one of the councilmen, clears his throat, his long neck moving up and down. "Yes. We found which one has the best education and well-known prosperity."

I scan the ridiculous list of the three names I'd be choosing from.

"Sally Emberlem from Osteria?" I pause. "Did we not have an Osterian ship make port late last night?"

The older men exchange glances, their eyebrows rising, as my father's eyes darken. They clearly didn't think I kept tabs on who arrives and disembarks from Glendora.

"It takes close to three weeks to sail from here to Osteria," I say flatly and pocket the paper with the women's names. "So, she has known about this longer than I? That I could have been aware of this a month ago or even longer? Did you know of this, Father?"

"I am aware of the list, but not of any invitations," he says, his voice tight. "Looks as if your uncle forgot this important detail."

"I didn't think it would be an issue. You put Glendora's protection in my hands, so that's what I have done to my best ability. With the Glendoran ball only months away, I thought it would be the best time to have them visit." Orson pats my back. "My boy, I was only doing this so you could focus on your responsibilities while I dealt with this."

I breathe deep, smoothing my facial expression into a calm facade that hides the boiling anger. To believe he thinks he can just

28

deal with finding me a wife, like it's a chore. Like it's not important who I spend the rest of my life with. I'm aware they believe my time at home lately has been causing me to lose focus on other things. But I have someone whom I dearly care for who has lost the only family he has, and now I'm all he has left. Either way, keeping this from me for so long has gone too far.

"I'm not going to repeat this because this has been going on for too long. Soon my father will be passing Glendora to me. This is my home, and I love it just as you all do. We do not agree on everything but in the end, this will be mine to take care of. I will do what is best for my people. I will not have any more hidden secrets or be disrespected." As I speak, I make a point to look at each councilman in their eyes before focusing on Orson.

Orson tries to interrupt but I raise my hand to silence him, same as my father did moments ago. "I will find a wife," I say with conviction. My chest tightens with those five words. "I will consider your *list*. But I believe there is more to any woman than education and how much money they have in their pocket."

The room is silent. A glimpse of admiration appears on my father's face; one I never thought I'd see. Father bows toward me and the rest follow, including Orson.

I give them a slight nod and turn toward the door to exit. Right as I leave, I release the hardness that's been building in my chest. I want this day to be over.

Orson clears out his throat, following me close to my heels. "Is there something else?" I ask, keeping my stride away from town back to my home that's farthest from the sea, now wishing I had Clarence to gallop away.

He grabs a hold of my shoulder, pulling me so I face him. "Forgive me, Axel."

His words make me stop in my tracks. Orson looks around, avoiding eye contact. "I was wrong," he says, taking a breath and straightening his back.

Clearly, stating he made a mistake is hard for him to confess. He's trying, I'll give him that.

"I should have told you about this . . . situation."

My hands squeeze tight at my sides, I want to tell him this is more than a situation, this is my life. But I hold my tongue.

"You know I never had a son. And I only want the best for the Ardanian line."

Orson has always been one not to hold his tongue when a concern arises. He has a side of him where he's stern and straightforward, not leaving an ounce of sympathy in his voice when it comes to the better good of Glendora. It sometimes can be a bit abrasive and strong, but I know it comes from someone who was also raised to possibly rule Glendora, same as my father.

Another side of him is nothing like my father. Making a point to talk to me. To see how my day is. Making me feel like a human instead of some working monster that has no life to live but be the governor of Glendora.

"So, you see, Axel. This marriage is very important. I only thought of creating a list for you—"

"Can you stop calling it a list?" I ask harshly.

He fidgets with his mustache. "Then what do you want me to call it?"

"Anything but that. It already doesn't feel right to have written these women's names on a piece of paper as if they are cattle to be viewed and auctioned off."

"Fine. These prospects took a lot of work, and I thought if I could have them available for you to meet sooner than later, it would be a lot less hassle in the long run. It will give you insight before even meeting them."

I run my hand through my hair, wishing to be anywhere other than here. He acts as if it is easy, a simple task to finish. Packing the bulk of medication to be shipped to other lands and making negotiations, on top of taking care of Nile's needs, has been my priority. Not marriage.

"As I said, I will consider your options. I will also need to speak to Nile about this. This marriage will affect him just as much as it will me," I say, resuming my walk back home. "Good day, Uncle.

"One other thing, my boy. I may have also promised Sally Emberlem from Osteria that you will be joining us for dinner this evening," he says hesitantly.

I take a deep breath through my nose and slowly let it out. This is what I was talking about in the council room. Decisions should not be made without consulting with me first, but this has already been said and planned. So, I'll wear my charming smile and present myself as the poised son who will soon rule Glendora. "I will see you this evening," I say as I walk away.

A run on the beach couldn't come soon enough.

CHAPTER 5

ELLE

My eyes are sluggish, and the weight of my worries keeps me from getting out of bed. I lift my head, groaning as my body protests in pain. Holding pressure to my head, I hope it will help ease the stabbing sensation going up my neck.

Slowly, I force my legs to move out of the sheets, my feet touching the cold, unwelcoming floor. I stand in front of a small slab of a mirror, barely recognizing myself. My blonde hair is tangled with random strands sticking out where they are not supposed to. There are dark circles underneath my now pale green eyes that look like all life has left them.

I glide my finger over my red cheek. It's warm to the touch and swollen with a bruise in the shape of my father's hand. Surprisingly, his one slap hurt less than previous beatings, but his warning makes anxiety tug like a weighted anchor on my soul. He always uses my brother as leverage against me, but the fierce look in his eyes told me the truth. If I continue searching for my mother, I'll lose my brother.

Gus is convinced our father would never kill us. Just thinking it makes my mouth dry, but I know. We're no longer his children; we're crew members that can be easily replaced. Gus is wrong and I'm not going to be the one who proves that to him.

As I gather my clothes for the day, a sharp pain penetrates my chest when reality sinks in that I'll never get my answers. I've been sloppy and should have known my father is always watching. Knowing my brother was a part of it hurt worse, but he didn't mean it. I know he loves me, even though he stood there while I could have had my throat slit.

I don't blame him. The captain has never lost a fight and Gus isn't a fighter. No matter how bad my brother wants it, being a pirate isn't in his blood.

Gus likes to hide his softness. When it's just him and me, the brother before our mother left comes back. Our mother was strict about us both learning how to read and write. That there was more to just living on this ship.

Sometimes I'd find him secretly reading books about animal health or doctoring seagulls' wings at night when the crew made it a game to see how many they can hit with rocks. Behind his rough appearance and our father's manipulation, he is good. He is some-one worth fighting for.

I can never leave. All my hopes of finding my mother will now be hidden deep inside and stay there. My heartache is worth the pain if it means keeping my brother safe.

Back out at sea, the wind blows against the sails, causing the ship to travel slower than normal. Last night's storm caused no damage other than wetting the deck. I keep my head low while doing my chores, making sure the ropes, sails, and pulleys are secure. The time will soon come when I'll call for Illira, but not until the crew are back in their bunks. I'm the only one who knows how to contact her, and the only one she trusts. I question daily if that's the only reason why the captain keeps me around.

As I watch the sun start to set, I smile, thinking back to when I first met my friend.

It was a few days after my mother had disappeared. I sat at the back of the deck, hiding so I could cry in peace without any judgment. My father had just lost his leg and was lying in bed recovering, my brother not leaving his side. He's never spoken of how his leg needed a wood replacement, but I had an idea it was due to fighting to keep his position as captain.

The evening stars were brighter than usual, and the glow of the moon allowed me to see my reflection from the sea. My tears landed in the waves as I dangled my feet, the ship itself swaying back and forth with the current. My thoughts were not where they should have been that night. Thinking how it would feel to sink deep into the dark blue sea and lose myself. Maybe my last breath should be in the ocean.

I gazed back at my reflection from the water and another face close to my age appeared. At first, I thought I was seeing things and rubbed my eyes. As she came closer her eyes seemed to glow in the dark. I should have been afraid, but instead a calming sensation went through me. She slowly brought her head out of the water, and I was in complete awe. Her eyes were no longer glowing but matched the color of the dark sky. Her skin was pale, shining like the moon as her seaweed-colored hair wrapped around her arm like an octopus.

"He-hello," I whispered.

She veered back hesitantly, never taking her eyes off me. We both stared wide-eyed, mimicking each other's movements.

"Can you understand me?" I asked, not knowing if she could respond.

"I heard you crying," she said lightly, looking around me to see if anyone else was nearby.

"You could hear me? From all the way down there?" I asked. She nodded. "Oh, I didn't think anyone could hear me," I said shyly.

"I hear many things," she said, turning her head so I could see her ears. They looked different from mine. Bigger and pointed upwards as gills spread below her neck and joined with purple scales

down her shoulders.

"You really are a mermaid!" I said, covering my mouth in shock.

She lowered back into the waters, like the volume of my voice scared her. "A what?"

"A mermaid. You know half human with fins and scales," I said, making my voice calmer.

"You mean these?" She raised her bright purple tail, slapping it against the water hard enough that droplets landed on my face. We both giggled. "What's your name?"

"People call me Elle. What's yours?"

"Illira," she said, her voice sounding more like a song.

Mermaids are rare due to their scales being of high value, so most have been hunted and killed by pirates and poachers. In the past, my father was one of them. She's still shy toward others, which I don't blame her for. It's dangerous enough to visit me, but she always seems to show up on the hardest of days. The only reason she hasn't been touched by the captain is because she finds treasure for us. Either still afloat or below waters. We are a team, the two of us. She tells me where ships are sailing to attack and, as thanks, I give her something in return.

The biggest gift she has given me is the voice of the mermaids. We both enjoy singing and once she trusted me enough, she taught me how to call her. I've never heard anything so beautiful and enchanting, but it can also change into something more alluring, like a call that can turn deadly if you want it to be. I've secretly wondered if Illira's voice is more than just a mermaid.

It always gives me goosebumps as I sing the tune of the sea. It is not words but more humming, tasting sweet like honey coming from my lips causing the water to glisten and come alive. Even whales and dolphins join the melody, their distant reverberations dancing in and out of the ocean.

Most of the crew are now asleep and in their bunks. Only the sound of the waves hitting the ship can be heard. I call for Illira. It

35

usually takes close to an hour for her to show, but this time I barely finish before I see her glowing eyes in the deep. Her head appears out of the water, her eyes turning back to normal. She has small coral-colored seashells wrapped across her forehead, bringing out the green hue of her hair. An earring that I gifted her dangles from her right ear in the shape of a star.

"Hello, friend," Illira's dimples appear, reflected by the moonlight dancing along the ocean's surface.

I crawl down the edge of the ship where there used to be a statue of a siren, leaving a small space for me to sit. Pain radiates up my cheek when I offer her a small smile and a quiet, "Hi, Illira."

She swims closer, her eyes turn to a warning green glow that gives me the chills. "*He* hurt you again," she says, her voice going down an octave when she says he.

I can't ignore the change of the waves. They become more alive, rocking the ship with increasing vigor while Illira appears to be in a trance. I grab a hold of the platform I'm sitting on, grabbing hold of the railing so I don't fall. "Illira, it's okay. I'm okay, I promise," I say, trying to keep my voice calm.

She shakes her head. Her eyes go from black to a dark blue, and water splashes against her cheeks as she dips her chin. "I'm sorry. I didn't mean to do that," she says quietly.

I shrug. "It's nothing to worry about. Not everyone is powerful like you are."

Illira takes a deep breath and looks back at me. "I don't understand why you stay here. There are better places than this. I've seen it."

I groan, rolling my neck. "You sound just like Gus. There is nothing better than being at sea. Can we please change the subject?"

Illira's lips lift, becoming almost a small grin. Every time I've mentioned Gus in the past month, I swear Illira's demeanor changes, but it always disappears before I catch it. "Well, he is right," she says. "Sooner or later, it's going to be worse."

I don't want to discuss this. I half want to stand up and crawl back onto the top deck but instead a question hidden deep inside escapes my lips. "Do you ever wish you were someone else?"

Right when I ask, I'm about to tell her to forget it, but she whispers, "Yes. You?"

My eyebrows narrow. I tug my long sleeve down to cover my pirate brand on my wrist trying to decide if I should pretend I didn't hear her and just go on with why I called her here in the first place.

The sound of her moving away makes me look back to her. She looks as uncomfortable as I do, playing with her hair like there's a small fish in it.

I try to think of a time when either of us has really spoken about our past life before we met but nothing comes to mind. It's as if we have tried to keep the darkness, we have crawling inside of us hidden and create this false pretense that we are always strong.

But at this moment, I don't want to hide it. I just want to speak freely to my friend and ignore the urge to hide behind a tough exterior. So, I let the brace from my shoulders loosen and reply with a firm "yes."

Illira keeps her distance, opening and closing her mouth before taking a deep breath. "I could use my voice to kill if I wanted to. But I don't want to be a siren like my mother," she says, looking toward the east with a watery gaze. "The other half of my heart is of a mermaid, like my father," she says, looking back toward the west, toward the sea of Orlosha. "With being both, and after my parents were killed for being together, I'm not part of the mermaid or siren clan. So sometimes," her voice quivers. "Sometimes I wish I could be human like you. To not be feared or poached but be able to go on adventures with you. Or to have the chance to fall in love without these fins being in the way."

I freeze. My heart aches hearing that Illira's parents have been killed and left their daughter with no place to call her home. Why have we never spoken of this? Why does she feel the need to fall in love with someone?

Love.

I snicker to myself, knowing how pathetic and cursed the word alone could be. Illira knows how I feel about it. I can't fathom why anyone would want to go through such a thing.

The Turbulence seems to have attracted a crew full of heart-broken and lost souls; men that have nothing left to give but to the sea. The sea became their lover, selfishly consuming them. She's direct and never hesitates to let you know when she's angry.

I shake my head, noticing Illira is keeping her distance, like I may fear her now knowing she is part siren. "It doesn't matter if you are part fish, siren, or part human. You will always be my friend, Illira, and I know you would never hurt me with your voice," I say, never taking my eyes off her. "And I'm sorry about your parents, that should have never happened, but you will always have a home with me."

I'm unsure what to say about her wishing to be human. Wanting to keep the word love out of my vocabulary as long as I can, I take my dagger and cut my palm. I bring my hand out toward her squeezing it tight, letting a few drops of blood splash into the salt water. "I promise I will always be a part of the sea."

Illira takes one of her seashells, cuts her palm, and smacks her hand on to the ship, leaving a blood mark behind. "And I promise I will always be a part of your world," she says, a glint of wetness glimmering in her eyes.

I sheath my blade, wondering if I should go ahead and say why I also said yes to wishing I was someone else, but her one eyebrow raises, and she makes a humming noise. "Are you in need of a ship?" she asks.

"Yes," I say quickly, happy she changed the subject. "It needs to be a ship that will please the captain."

"Many ships have sunk due to the recent storms, but I've heard whispers of newer ships with many shiny things treading along these waters. I will find one for you."

"What is it you would like in return?" I ask.

"I don't need anything in return," she says. "But before I forget—" she throws something toward me and I catch it, a necklace dangling from my hands. The necklace my father threw overboard.

My mouth gapes.

"I smelled human blood yesterday near your ship and found your necklace not far from it."

I shake my head. Illira knows better than to come close to shore. It can be a death sentence for her. But all I say is, "thank you," before her tail flaps against the surface and she disappears into the water.

CHAPTER 6

ELLE

As I wait patiently for Illira to arrive with the ship's location, I try to keep busier than usual. Multiple thoughts race through my mind, causing my palms to sweat.

I need to be smarter and hide the necklace my father thinks he discarded. Now that I have the necklace back, it is a nagging annoyance of my failure. My only focus should be sailing the sea and enjoying what I love. I have my brother and Illira. That's all I need.

But I'm worried about the next ship we will attack. What if it isn't good enough? Since we lost almost everything from the last storm, the captain has been more unpredictable. If I fail him this time, what will happen next? Will he feed me to the sharks? Will he maroon me on some island? Could I find another crew to join? Being a woman will not help my cards, and the chances are very slim.

I let out a huge sigh and continue tightening and refastening rigging to help capture fish later. My hands ache and a few blisters pop open, causing them to burn. Unlike a lady's delicate soft hands, mine are callused and rough, stained from dirt and my fingernails are chipped.

Obviously, I'm not anywhere close to being called a lady but sometimes it would be nice to have prettier hands. Spreading out my fingers, I wonder what it would be like to have them smooth and clean. *Why does it even matter?* My father always says that if our hands have calluses and sores it proves we are true warriors of the sea.

"Want to duel, bad luck?" Gus asks, interrupting my thoughts. Embarrassed, I hide my hands behind my back. He gives me a questionable look but ignores my uneasiness. "Come on!" He taps my leg with his boot.

I stand, happy to no longer be sitting in one spot working on the nets. This would be a perfect distraction from all my thoughts. "Only if you're ready to lose."

"You wish." He chuckles, nudging me with his shoulder to follow him to the middle of the ship. He throws me a practice sword, drawing the crew's attention. "Alright, gents, who's ready to watch some fun one on one sparring?" Gus yells for all to hear, giving me a wink. "We all know who will win, but let's give this little gal a chance, shall we?"

I roll my eyes, pushing my sleeves past my elbows so they won't get in the way.

"Be prepared to be amazed by this so-called *little* gal who shows no mercy!" I shout back.

The crew surround us and make bets. Several laugh and I feel eyes judging every bit of me. That's fine. They can. This is all fun and games for my brother, but this isn't a fight I am going to lose.

Brushing my sweaty palms on my pants, I grip the sword with anticipation and ignore the pain of my popped blisters. I have been dueling against my brother since the time I could walk and am well versed in his movements. Making the first move will be a hindrance for me, so I wait for Gus. No doubt he knows what I'm doing, but he isn't the patient type.

I curtsy, begging him to make the first move.

A familiar over the top grin plasters on Gus's face. I laugh at the sight and relax my shoulders and arms. Gus thrusts his sword forward with a quick step. I skip back and block his blade. It is his classic first move which used to bruise my torso. But I have no

41

intention of receiving any type of bruise today.

"Are you afraid to hurt me? Have you forgotten how to fight?" Gus says, waving his sword back and forth, taunting me.

The ship rocks with the waves and I widen my stance for better balance. Sword held with both hands, I ask, "Who says I've forgotten anything?"

My brows rise mischievously to distract Gus. I'm already in motion, sweeping my leg low to the ground and hitting his feet.

"What the—" Gus falls on his back with a large thud. Before my sword can rest on his chest and ask him to yield, he rolls away, just missing my blade. His eyes are wide as he tries to catch his breath. I still have a few tricks up my sleeve, and I'm prepared to show him another.

Before he's on his feet, I strike at his shoulder. When my sword meets his, I duck and pivot, aiming for his hip. I keep my breathing steady as he pushes against me, holding his blade against my own. My ears ring from the sliding of the swords. Gus doesn't falter, keeping his weight steady with my own. I allow him to step into my space, thinking he has the advantage. Grabbing the end of his dull blade, I pull his sword toward the ground. He hisses and I smirk, adding pressure to his twisted wrist. His sword thuds to the deck.

Gus pauses as he watches the sword slide away while the boat rocks, stopping at the crew's feet. Only the sound of the waves surrounding us and our heavy breathing can be heard. I wait for cheers or some type of acknowledgment of my win but instead eyes are turned elsewhere.

Figures. I ignore the mumbling that starts among the crew. "Better luck next time, brother," I say, picking up his sword and handing it back to him.

He rubs his wrist. "You know you wouldn't have made that move if the blades were sharp. You would have cut your hand wide open."

"And what's your point?" I ask, "Sometimes you have to get hurt first to win."

He gives me an absurd look.

What my brother doesn't understand is if it was a real sword fight, I'd injure myself just to get the upper hand. Sometimes taking risks isn't always pretty.

"Now who's next?" I ask, bouncing back and forth from the adrenaline rush. I'm ready to pounce on anyone that comes into my path, feeling more alive than I have for weeks. Gyn steps from the crowd as if he rules the roost, spitting on the deck before me.

"Why don't we roll around and see who ends up standing?" he says with his crooked nose high in the air.

My giant overexaggerated grin gives the affirmation I'm in, but secretly my heart is racing with eagerness. I finally have a fighting chance with this idiot. I'll show him who should really be the first mate. He smooches his lips at me, making kissing noises. My cheeks burn at his insolence, but I widen my stance and readjust my grip on my sword. I'm smaller and quicker. Smug confidence coats his leathery skin, bringing out the fine wrinkles around his dark eyes a red bandana snug too tight across his shaven head.

Gyn charges.

His first mistake is using all his strength to strike. A quick side-step and I block him, grinning as I hear his feet trip over one another. Taking the chance to give him a taste of what a woman can do I spin and kick his behind. He skids on the deck, landing face first while his sword goes in the opposite direction. The sight of Gyn sprawled on the deck makes several crewmen burst with laughter while others stand with crossed arms, shaking their heads.

Gyn stands slowly, his back facing me. He turns, glaring as blood drips down his nose. Before I can step away, he lunges, grabs my shirt, and shoves me against the back railing. The impact forces a burst of air out of me and my stomach cramps with pain. He brings me around, my back hard against him, pulling back my braid as his other arm wraps around my chest. His heavy breath burns against my face with rage. My eyes widen when I feel a sharp point pushing against my chin. Warm liquid drips down my neck; Gyn must have pulled his dagger from his waist.

"Alright, Gyn, that's enough!" Gus shouts.

"If she wants to play dirty, we can play dirty!" Gyn growls against my ear and his spit flies against the side of my face. Pain screams from strands of my hair being yanked out as he pulls my head back more.

This isn't how this fight is going to end. I bring my left leg up and slide all my weight down his shin, greeting his toe with scorching pain. Gyn leans forward against me, screeching. I take his thumb holding the blade and pull it back while knocking my head backward against his.

Gyn falls back against the railing, flailing his arms as his weight carries him over into the sea.

"Man overboard!!" yells one of the crew members. Many run frantically, grabbing a heavy rope and throwing it over the ship's railing to get to Gyn. I cover my mouth in shock. I didn't really mean for him to go overboard, but he was so determined to humiliate me. Or did I?

I wipe a small amount of blood from the nick on my neck. Maybe it'd be better if Gyn did get carried off by the current. I shrug and forget my devilish thoughts as I hear a loud snort behind me. Gus stands there, his face red, trying to hide his amused grin.

I shake my head and lower my voice. "You better keep quiet or Gyn is going to hear you, and then I'm going to have to save you."

He holds up a finger, signaling me to give him a few seconds. His face slowly resumes his natural color and he wipes a few tears of joy from his eyes. "He deserved it. You sure showed him, Bad Luck. You're getting quick on your feet."

"And you're becoming an old man."

"Hey, I almost had you," Gus replied.

"Not even close." I shake my head, trying to hold back a smile.

Gyn climbs over the railing, soaking wet and cursing loudly. He stares at the deck, his shoulders slumping as he catches his breath. His eyes dart to me and, without warning, he rushes toward me like a bull. "You stupid little—"

"Don't even." My brother already has a knife pointed at Gyn's neck.

"You better watch it, boy. Captain wouldn't be happy with you threatening his first mate," Gyn snarls.

"The captain wouldn't be happy knowing his first mate was bested by a girl." Gus nods at me and waits for me to step farther away from Gyn before slowly lowering his knife.

Gyn squints as he looks me up and down, curling his fists on the verge of springing toward me again. I swear I can see smoke coming out of his nostrils, as if he's on fire inside. "You're on thin ice, little girl. Better watch your step. If this next ship isn't good. . ." He shakes his head, dragging a finger across his neck to mime slitting it. "I'd be happy being the one to end you." He returns to the cabins below without a second glance.

"Just ignore him," Gus says, tugging on my arm and leading me away from the rest of the crew.

"I think he's right, though. This must be good, or I may no longer be here soon," I say, pushing his arm away.

". . . and if that ever happens, I'll be there with you."

It's odd how my brother can be this one man that shows he cares for me and at other times he switches to what our father wants him to be. A father that I wonder will ever consider me good enough.

"Stop thinking it, I know that face," Gus says, nudging my head with his hand.

I look down, trying to hide the thoughts that I know are written all over my face. "Stop thinking what?"

"That you're not good enough. You know your way around a sword better than anyone here, can navigate open waters, and easily keep up with everyone here. Every soul on this ship knows it, they just will never say it."

"Well, I won't stop thinking about it until I hear it coming out of each of their own mouths! Until then . . ." I shrug.

"You are only fighting against the wind," Gus says with a monotone voice.

"Then I'll keep fighting until the wind backs down!"

He takes a heavy sigh, scratching his head. "Whatever you say, Bad Luck."

What does he know, I think. He has no idea what I go through daily. He doesn't have to always be on his toes. Having to prove he's good at what he does, time and time again.

Across the ship I feel eyes on me. The captain stands on the highest deck. Even with a wooden leg, his six-foot frame is a force to be reckoned with. He's focused on a deep conversation with the youngest of our crew, a redhead named Sam, and it's obvious he doesn't want anyone to overhear them.

The captain gives me a crooked smile, a smile that is haunting. It's a threat. A challenge. The hair on my arms stands, but I hold his stare. One thing I've learned is to never back down from a glare. The captain says something back to Sam while keeping his attention on me. *Crap*, I just found myself in a standoff with the captain. He is obviously already in a foul mood and egging it on isn't helping.

"Watch yourself," murmurs my brother, his lips barely moving.

With a slight jerk of the captain's head, he demands I go to him. It allows me an excuse to look where I'm going and not at him. I pull my shoulders back and walk confidently toward him, hiding the tremor that bolts up and down my body.

When I'm a few steps away, Velis swipes something red coming from his lips. His mouth is slightly pinched, as if he's contemplating. His beard is longer than normal, tied with a black band while his light brown hair tries to escape his black tricorn hat from all sides. His silence only makes my heartbeat quicken.

"You really should watch that face of yours. I won't tolerate it," he says flatly but again I hear a wheezing, gurgling noise, like someone is drowning in his throat.

I unfurrow my brow and lift my chin, breathing through my nose. "Yes, Captain."

Silence again.

I can't decipher if the sweat on my back is from the morning sun or the heat beaming off the captain. I walk away, thinking he is done with his threat, but a tight grip tugs on my arm.

Pretending the hold isn't causing me pain, I force myself to face him. His nostrils flare and his head tilts toward me. "Any news?" he asks, squeezing my arm one last time before letting go.

"Yes, Captain. I spoke with her last night. I should get an answer soon," I reply. My arm burns but I refuse to look at it. I don't need a reminder that my father hates me.

"My patience is wearing thin." He sways to the side catching himself on the railing. I nod and turn around, walking away as quickly as possible before anything stupid comes out of my mouth.

"Boy, meet me in my cabin!" he yells to Gus.

Gus's posture goes rigid for a second, but he gives me a slight grin and steadily walks into the pit of anguish. The captain joins him and slams the door behind them.

I'm not even going to dwell on what the captain is talking about with Gus. I have an inkling it's about me. I should have never gone that far with Gyn. It's not my fault I can fight better than him, or anyone else on this bloody ship. Well, besides the captain.

If anything, the captain should be proud of how well I've excelled in my sword skills. Should he not be proud of his own daughter? I huff out a laugh, thinking how ridiculous I'm being.

I showed everyone that I'm worth being here, so why do I feel like I have signed my death sentence?

CHAPTER 7

AXEL

Leaving Glendora was not easy, more specifically leaving Nile. When I said goodbye and promised him I'd be back soon, he tried to keep his red eyes hidden by focusing on his feet. I couldn't get him to look at me even as I sailed away. It felt wrong to leave him so early after his mother's death, but I knew he would be well taken care of. I kept his small stance in sight, Theodore standing close to him, his hand resting on Nile's shoulder.

Keeping the image of Nile close, I remind myself of the promise I gave to his mother to keep him safe. Theo is the safest man to be with and, unexpectedly, whenever he is with Nile, the hard soldier demeanor wavers into something softer.

At twenty years old, I already have the stress of taking care of an island but now being responsible for a child has almost been too overwhelming. Regret seeps through me, hating the feeling of relief for being away for a while.

It's now been weeks since I have seen land, the waves of the sea threatening for attention almost daily. Rain blows hard against the glass window, blueish gray clouds barely keeping enough light in my cabin. I'd burn a candle but I'm too worried it will start a fire.

My seat rocks to the side as another ripple of waves crash against the sails, and I barely catch my writing utensil before it rolls off the table.

Carmen stands in front of my desk, balancing herself with the movement of the ship like its second nature. "You would think with how many storms we have been through since we left Glendora, we would have taken the warning and turned back," she states while picking at her nails, a childhood quirk she can't give up. It gives away that she has something weighing on her mind.

"I would agree with you, but Toradian's leader has been relentless, sending letter after letter wanting this visit. Sounds as if many come down with a sickness on his land," I say, trying to seem as relaxed as she is but I'll never be close.

Carmen is a true sailor. Since I gave her the job of transporting goods to different islands, *The Blazing Star* has become her second home. There are days I envy her ability to leave time and time again while I can't. But whenever we journey out at sea together, it brings back the time we would pretend to fight pirates or battle against a giant sea urchin below, wishing those days didn't pass so fast.

"I heard he has a daughter," she says, still messing with her nails.

I unbutton the collar of my shirt and tug it away from my neck. "I've heard," I say, my voice deepening.

She shifts and places her hands on her hips, her short red hair standing out from the row of old books behind her. "Well, what if he also brings up a marriage proposal? These fathers are throwing their daughters out there for you to choose but what if none of them are compatible? Do you not think this is absurd?"

A groan leaves my throat; I do not want to discuss this. "Of course I do, but this isn't an offer I can easily decline. We need protection and this is the best option for our people. You and I cannot deny that we need an army. We should have prepared one years ago, but we have never had to deal with violence before, only very minor problems. So here I am, doing what's right."

"So doing what you think is right could leave you, in the end, unhappy and miserable. I don't want to see my best friend making the worst mistake of his life."

A warning bell rings above the deck and a knock on the door follows.

"Come in," I say, thankful for the interruption, ignoring Carmen's glare of disapproval.

Dibs, one of the newest sailors I hired, pops her head out from behind the door. "Land has been sighted. We should be arriving in Toradian soon, sir."

"Very well, Dibs," I say. My stomach turns into knots, wondering if Carmen is right. Maybe this isn't so much about the medicine, but a meet and greet with his daughter. She wasn't written on the laughable list Orson gave me but I'm starting to wonder if this is another set up.

Dibs nods and acknowledges Carmen, greeting her as captain. Before she shuts the door, I remind her to call me Axel, not sir, even though this has been the third time requesting her to do so. Even her twin sister refuses to call me by my first name.

Dibs's cheeks redden. "Yes, sir-Axel," she says, and leaves swiftly.

Carmen's brown eyes sparkle, eyeing me with one eyebrow raised.

"What is it now?" I ask, standing and gathering all I need to bring with me off ship.

She shakes her head, her hair following suit. "You have no idea how many women swoon over you, do you?"

"Ok, that's enough, go back to your captain ways and leave me so I can get ready."

"Yes, sir. I mean Axel," Carmen teases. Her laugh echoes out the door.

By the time we arrive closer to land, it's lightly sprinkling amid patches of the sun appearing through the occasional cloud, making the air feel a bit humid and sticky against my skin.

Toradian is an island I've never seen before. It boasts tall cliffs like Glendora, but these are at a grander scale that wrap around the whole land. Waves crash against the rocky surface as black and white birds fly above us, searching for food and nesting on the cliffside.

The only entrance is between two rocky bluffs that border a waterway which takes you inland. It's the perfect place for protection but, as we sail closer, it seems as if this ruler has no interest in taking care of his people.

At first glance, the lodgings are more like small wooden shacks that are barely kept upright by either leaning against trees or steadied with cement blocks. My chest feels heavy as a familiar fence which I have seen elsewhere cuts across the land, separating these homes from the well-maintained ones on higher ground. There's a gray stone castle beyond the fence. Even the ground nearer the shore lacks the dark green grass that carries its way up toward the richer homes.

Once again, I'm meeting with another ruler who has separated his people. Carmen doesn't hold her distaste as we sail closer to port and turns away from the growing crowd that is in awe of our immaculate ship. Many of them are thin and the children lack properly fitting clothing. They look as if they bathed in dirt.

"How can anyone be okay with this? I feel wrong being the one that has clean clothes and food in my belly while these people lack them," she says softly, tears swelling in her eyes.

I agree, but what can I do? I'm only one man. But an idea already circulates in my head. In my gut, this visit won't go as I'd like and I'm positive I'll have to make a choice I didn't want to do but will. I step toward the end of the ship, giving the small children a wave and a smile while keeping my sadness at bay even though a rage boils in my chest.

"If you would rather stay here on the ship than join me, you can. I'd understand."

Carmen shakes her head, rubbing her eyes with her arm before turning back toward the crowd. "No. I wouldn't want you to do this alone. If this man thinks you'd be interested in a marriage alliance, he has something coming."

We don't know if that is the aim of my visit, but I hope Carmen is wrong. His letters clearly stated he wanted to purchase medicine. Seeing his lack of care for his people, I doubt it's true.

Carmen follows as I disembark, leaving Dibs and her sister, Doolah, in charge of the rest of the crew.

An older woman in a pale dress and short silver hair greets us, followed closely by three soldiers dressed, oddly, in the dark purple and gold colors of Glendora's flag.

Her knees shake as she bows. "It is a pleasure to have you here in Toradian. Our King has been patiently waiting for your arrival. Please follow me," she says, sounding out of breath.

"It's nice to meet you. What is your name?" I ask, noticing she hasn't introduced herself and seems to be in a hurry.

Her head quirks to the side, like she's trying to read something she can't understand.

"Quanita. King Beris is my son."

I wonder why he has sent his own frail mother to greet us in his place but give her a slight bow. "It's a pleasure."

Her eyes widen before a slow rise of a smile appears. "Yes, very well. We don't want to keep him waiting," she says, turning for us to follow.

The smell of urine and sour milk is distinct as we follow. Crowds of people line the streets; sadness mingles with longing for better haunts their gazes. I swallow, holding back from wanting to cover my nose or gag. Instead, I give them small nods as I pass, wishing I had coin or food to offer.

We reach two tall red gates built into the pristine fence. More soldiers, these in full black uniforms, stand guard. After the gate are stone steps which route through homes that are better built and clean. The smell of pastries flows through a bakery window, blessedly coating the stale stench of urine from the homes now below us.

Quanita is breathing loud as we continue to follow the road

that joins multiple steps toward the entrance into the castle. Carmen nudges my shoulder. Quanita is moving more slowly, her back arching.

Without another thought, I put my arm around hers, holding her upright. She flinches like I may have hurt her but then leans her weight onto my side as we take each step.

"You're too kind, sir, but there is no need," she says slowly, though she does not let go of my arm.

"What kind of man would I be if I did not help King Beris's own mother?" I state plainly, thinking how odd it is that we are walking up all these stairs when surely we could have used a horse or carriage instead of putting his mother under such stress. Even the three soldiers with us show no remorse or concern for her.

She stops and looks up at me, eyebrows furrowed. "You are not quite like other men I know, though you look like them," she states, her chest moving up and down with exhaustion.

I squeeze her hand, unsure how I should reply, and guide her up the remaining stairs until we arrive at the grand entrance doors.

As they open, more anger builds in my chest with how lavish it is. High ceilings are adorned with hanging chandeliers and brightly burning candles. Dark maroon cloth drapes across stained glass windows that are tall enough for a red glimmer of sunlight to shine onto a golden throne where King Beris, I presume, is sitting.

Quanita stops in front of her son's raised throne. His eyes lower upon her and she keeps her chin down while introducing us. He must be close to his late thirties. His straight black hair frames his oval-shaped face and stops at his chin. He reminds me of the deer that run wild in Glendora.

Beris walks down the few steps with an irritating slowness. A crown glistens with the flickering candlelight, pronouncing himself as someone important. Unlike many other islands, Glendora rulers do not wear any type of crown for we believe it only separates us from our people by creating division and establishes us as more important. Once we believe we are better than others, we lose unity. And without unity, we are nothing.

Beris stretches his arms to each side, his wide long sleeves of red and gold moving with them. "Welcome to my home. It's been a long wait," he says. His sharp clap makes me flinch. "Quanita, find my daughter and let her know we have company."

I already don't like this man. When I shake his hand, his grip is harder than necessary. I've barely stepped into his home and he's already bringing up his daughter. My jaw tightens, hating how he speaks to his mother like a servant. If my mother was still alive, I'd be cherishing every moment with her.

"Come, come. You must be hungry." He eyes Carmen, who stands beside me, with interest. The heat coming off her makes me question if her red hair will soon turn to fire. "And who is this beautiful creature with you?"

The way he licks his bottom lip while looking at her as though she is a plate of food instead of a human being makes me regret bringing her with me. "This is Carmen, Captain of *The Blazing Star*."

He holds his hand out expectantly. Her nostrils flare but she holds her chin high as he kisses her hand. As he turns for us to follow into the dining room, I catch a glimpse of her hand sliding down her pant leg with disgust.

Beris turns his head slightly as he walks. "A woman as captain? I have never heard of the sort."

Carmen inhales to respond, but I interrupt her and say, "Yes, she's the one of the best. I wouldn't trust anyone else to take care of my crew or the cargo."

"I see," Beris says, his voice tighter and lower than before. He takes us to an overly large table full of food that would feed more than three people. Food which could be eaten by his people. He gestures for us to sit across from him.

"Do you like my soldiers? Did you notice anything particular?" he asks, indicating the three soldiers that have been following me since we made port. They stand around the room, looking ahead like they can't hear us.

"Their uniforms match *The Blazing Star's* flag on our ship."

"Yes!" He says joyfully and gulps from a flask, red wine dripping down his chin. "I wanted to give you an idea what your soldiers would look like if we became united. Your uncle was inviting in his letters, agreeing this would be a grand surprise. I'm sure none of the other islands you have visited have gone out of their way as I have," he says with poise.

I'm unsure what to say. My uncle Orson and I are going to have a very tense conversation when I get back. Carmen is right. This isn't just about medicine, which should be this man's first concern for his people. When we arrived this morning, I promised myself I'd be optimistic, but I'm clearly naive.

"It is a surprise," I say, trying to keep my voice steady.

Beris's eyes narrow. "You must not understand. The waters around these parts are infested with pirates and words of your grand ships are getting around. These soldiers are now yours, a gift for you to keep on your ship."

Before I can say anything, Quanita enters, and a young woman follows behind her.

"Ah, yes. My daughter, Natia!" Beris says, his smile meets his eyes.

She has long black hair that reaches her waist. I stand and, as I do, she moves her hips provocatively while walking toward me, ignoring any others watching her. I swallow, focusing only on her face. She stops too close for my liking and her hand brushes against my arm for me to take.

Grabbing it lightly, I kiss her knuckles. "It's nice to meet you."

She giggles, leaning forward like I've said something hilarious. "The pleasure is mine. No one told me how handsome you are. This is my lucky day."

I drop her hand, forcing a smile before sitting back into my seat as she takes the seat next to me. Her shoulder brushes mine. Carmen clears her throat, keeping her eyes on her food.

My appetite is gone, and my main focus is to finish this meeting so we can leave and never come back. "I'd love to discuss the medication you have requested with you. They are all on the ship

55

and ready, but I'm happy to share that our price has been lowered."

Beris drops his spoon onto his plate. "Do you take me as a poor ruler? I can pay the prices you required beforehand."

I think of all the hopeless faces I passed to get to his castle but block them away. "That is not what I'm implying. This has been a recent decision Glendora made to make it more hospitable and available for those who truly need the medication. But we can keep the price at what it was previously if that is more agreeable."

He grunts. "My people have no need for medication. They have no infection or disease." He eyes me, challenging me to say anything different.

This is going nowhere. "Then as a gift from Glendora to Toradian, we would like to give you a supply of our medication. For your hospitality and graciousness."

"Very well," he says flatly. "Quanita, come here," he says.

While they speak, Carmen leans close, and I whisper softly so only she can hear me. "Return to the ship, hide as many vials as you can and give them to the people. Be discreet."

Carmen doesn't flinch but whispers, "What are you doing?"

"What needs to be done. I'll keep them occupied."

"Carmen, please prepare the medication," I say for all to hear.

She stands and nods. "Yes, sir," she says, and calmly walks out of the room.

Beris watches her until she leaves the room. "Pity," he says. "She is very enjoyable to look at, but let's get down to what I really want to speak to you about."

I brace for what he is about to say and take a swig of my drink.

"I won't take no for an answer. I want you to take the soldiers for protection. I'm sure they will be agreeable to you, and they will show that Toradian is the best to protect your Glendora. They are highly trained. But I also want you to consider an alliance with us by marrying my daughter, Natia."

Blood coats my mouth as I hold my tongue tight between my teeth. There will never be a day I'd ever agree to unite Toradian with Glendora. Even his daughter seems just as ignorant as her father.

Her hand finds my knee and glides up to my hip. I grab a hold of it and firmly put it back onto her lap, reminding myself that I can't leave and that I need to give Carmen ample time.

"Thank you for the soldiers. I'm sure they will do their part and keep us safe back home. I am willing to discuss an alliance, but you need to know there are others asking for the same, so the decision will not be made hastily."

Beris rests his forearms on the table. "I can promise you; my daughter is the most beautiful and most talented compared to the others. Besides, once we are united, you are welcome to any part of my land, as I hope it will be with yours. I am very interested to know how you have produced this medicine that has been known to cure almost anything while others can't. Your island sounds very special, and I would hate for it to not have the army it needs to remain protected."

I clasp my hands tight underneath the table. Beris of Toradian is no ally of mine and another reminder that I need an army sooner than later.

CHAPTER 8

ELLE

It's been two days since I spoke to Illira. Each night, I've been standing at the back of the ship, waiting for her to appear, but she hasn't shown. This is taking too long. Something is wrong. I bite my nails and tap my foot against the wooden deck. Before I can call for her, staggering footsteps sound behind me. I pull out my dagger and turn toward the sound.

Gus appears from the shadows. "It's just me."

I roll my eyes and sheathe my dagger, looking over the railing for any movement or sound of a fin at sea. "Where is Illira? Do you think something happened to her?"

"When has she ever let you down?" Gus slurs, putting his hands on my shoulders. The scent of alcohol is strong from his breath. "It's pitch-black tonight, you can't see a thing out there."

I turn and make a point to look at his face. I've barely seen him since he spoke with the captain but now, I'm worried.

A lantern sways behind him, casting shadows on his face, but I can discern the shallowness of his cheeks. His dark brown hair is messy, and his shirt is shorter on one side than the other due to missing a button. When was the last time he changed or even cleaned himself? "Are you okay?" I whisper. "You look like you need to be drinking water not . . ."

He leans forward, almost losing his balance, and shakes a bottle in front of my face. "This is water," he says, eyeing me like I'm an idiot.

I grab the drink out of his hand. "What the bloody hell, Gus. I don't have time for this. Go get some sleep."

"We need to talk," he says quietly. Too quiet. His eyes search the deck.

"Hi, Gus." We both jump and find Illira beside the ship below. She has a wide smile, and her moonlit eyes fix on my brother.

I smack my hand over my heart. "Sea monsters! Illira, you scared me!"

"Wouldn't be the first time," she giggles, barely gazing in my direction.

"Hello, beautiful," Gus clears his throat, rubbing his brow. "I can't read to you tonight, there is something I need to do . . ." Gus slowly walks away, struggling to stand up right.

"Gus, wait!" Both Illira and I say in unison. Read? Does he read to Illira when I'm not around? How long has this been going on?

"Did I do something wrong?" Illira asks with concern in her eyes and something else that I can't quite distinguish.

I shrug. "I honestly have no idea, but I think it has something to do with the captain." *I can only focus on one problem at a time.* "Please tell me you found a ship."

"I did. It's bigger than I thought. The ship's called The *Blazing Star*. Your fa- . . . captain will be proud."

What a silly name for a ship. "Perfect. I needed to hear that." Soon we will have a ship, and my doubts can finally dwindle.

Illira and I discuss the location of the ship and confirm we will be able to attack within the next day. She will distract them so we can come from behind before they can get away. Since our ship is smaller and faster than theirs, we have the advantage. Soon, we will be swimming in luxury.

Instead of waiting until morning to tell the captain, I rush to his cabin. Before knocking, I hear raised voices. "This isn't right! She's better than anyone here and you know it!" someone yells. No, not just someone. Gus.

The next thing I know, I hear a smack as something bangs against the door, rattling the hinges and probably leaving a dent. I quickly tiptoe to the side and hide in a dark corner.

"I know what's best for this ship," the captain yells. "And boy, you will get a lashing if you bring it up again. Now get out!"

Gus barges out the door, rubbing his jaw, spitting blood across the deck. The smell of whiskey trails behind him. I flatten my back against the wall, hoping he doesn't see me as he passes by.

"That boy of yours is getting weak," Gyn says in a slithering tone.

I roll my eyes but hold my ground, hoping one of them will shut the door so I won't be seen. I'm already in hot water and if the captain finds out I'm eavesdropping, it will be my hind.

"He's getting soft," the captain grumbles. "You know what to look for once we get to the ship?"

"Aye. I'll be looking for small glass bottles, the color of sapphire. I've heard just one bottle of medicine can be worth fifty golden coins!"

The door slams shut before I can hear anything else, making me jump. I wait a few minutes and knock before I lose the courage. Gyn opens the door, scowling. "This better be good."

"I *do* have good news." I raise my voice so the captain can hear. "Illira found a ship and it's not far. I . . ." The door swings farther open, revealing the captain holding himself up with his cane. He doesn't have his wooden leg on. He barely allows anyone to see him without it. The sight reminds me he is still human.

The captain growls but then expels air from his lungs with a sudden sharp sound, leaning lower onto his cane. Specks of blood splatter on the ground as he hacks.

Gyn steps in front of the captain, hiding him while he continues. "What are you staring at, girl? Wake up the crew and start guiding the ship!"

I step away and force myself not to look back. The captain is sick. Is this why he wants another ship so soon? Is he searching for medicine more than for coins? What if what he searches for isn't on this ship?

My head hurts running through question after question. I take a deep breath, thinking back to a few days ago when I had one of those bottles in my hands. One that I should have kept. One that had the same emblem as my necklace. But I nudge the thought away. If the captain is sick, I can be the one who finds what he needs. I hate myself for wanting any approval from him but a small flicker of hope slithers into my veins.

The dark blue sky is clear. A multitude of stars guide me through the waters. Being behind the helm of the ship has always felt right. The crew are all awake and preparing for the attack, seeming more alive than I've seen them in a long time.

One of the cabin boys with shaggy red hair, Sam, starts playing his violin for us all to hear. Music always helps us stay awake and keep course. The rhythm of the song matches the sway of the ship, the main sail flapping in the wind like a dance. A cool breeze blows through my hair, and I close my eyes, enjoying the wind's soft touch. An old memory surfaces in my head.

My mother and father are on the top deck, dancing together hand in hand, laughing. Gus is playing with his stick sword around them, fighting against his imaginary friends. My father wears the biggest smile I have ever seen. His leg, still intact, guides my mother in a twirl, beaming with joy. She giggles and gives him a soft kiss on his cheek. Gus makes a grossed-out face, turning away with embarrassment.

61

"Oh, child. Someday you will want all the kisses you can get,"
my mother says, pinching his cheek playfully. "Gross, mom!" Gus
says, pushing her hands away. I look back at my father and he is
looking at me with a pure smile. He waves, encouraging me to join
the dance, grabbing a hold of my hand.

But then everything stops. Like a change of the wind, his smile
slowly dims. Turning into the color of the dark sea at night, he
looks behind me. My mother tenses and I follow her gaze, the crew
of men watching us. Judging us for having laughter in our life. A
slice they maybe once had but now despised.

My father lets go of my hand and walks toward them, barking
orders and never turning back. A coolness fills the air; my arms
covered with goosebumps. I didn't understand at that moment, but
something was changing.

If only I could see that smile again from the father I once had.
Maybe I could bring it back, but I shake my head, wanting the
ludicrous thought to never come back. No more hoping; it's time
to grow up.

The music ends and I open my eyes as a single tear falls down
my cheek. It is quieter and most of the crew have finished their
duties and returned to their hammocks to get some rest. I swipe
the tear away and decide it would be best to do the same. It is still
dark out but soon the sun will show us the way to our prize. My
stomach twists and for the first time I'm more than just nervous.
I'm frightened for what is to come.

When I open the door to my room, I find my brother sprawled
limp across my bed.

"I swear, if you have puked in my bed, you're dead," I say,
pushing him to wake up, but he isn't asleep. He groans with his
face in the pillow and turns over. His face is pale with blood shot
eyes. One cheek is darker than the other. No doubt an earlier gift
from the captain.

"Elle, I am so sorry." He stutters as if he is a kid again.

I push him over so I can sit beside him. "Gus, what are you sorry about?"

He sits up and stares at the closed door. "For allowing our father to hurt you. I hate myself for never standing up for you. I'm a coward."

I nudge his chin and make him face me, shaking my head. "Stop. You're no coward. You're not the one that forced his hand. Tell me what's going on. This isn't like you."

He stagers to his feet and starts taking my clothes out of my one drawer, throwing them into a bag. "It doesn't matter. We're leaving. I'm getting you off this ship even if I must drag you. I'm not letting another day pass without protecting you."

I catch his cold hands and make him stop.

"That's enough. You know I won't leave. Just tell me what's going on." My grip is tight on his hands, and I search his face, trying to understand what's gotten into him. How many times do I have to get through his head that I'm not going anywhere. No one can get rid of me that easily, but I've never seen my brother so vulnerable and uneasy. Usually, he's always trying to be tough, or a constant show off.

"Ship ahead!" Gyn bellows from above. My shoulders sag as I groan, wishing to get a few hours of sleep. But we're going to be attacking a ship sooner than I thought.

"Look, Gus, we gotta get ready. The captain wouldn't be happy seeing you in this state. Go clean up and we can talk about this after we're done."

He stares at me, head shaking enough that a few stray tendrils of his light brown hang around his face. His fists clench. "After this ship, we're done. I won't be able to protect you much longer if we continue doing this."

"Gus, I can stand on my own. You seem to have forgotten I recently threw a man overboard. Now, get ready. We have treasure to steal!" I give him a wink and look at him one last time before going back to the deck as a sense of uneasiness crawls up my back with each step.

CHAPTER 9

ELLE

Everything is chaotic on deck. Six cannons are ready in case *The Blazing Star* refuses to surrender. Others gear up with swords or daggers and roll up their sleeves to show their tattoo marking them as the pirates of the sea. Rigging is being prepared so we can catch their ship if they try to escape. *The Turbulence* is known for its speed and agility.

All seems to be in order, but my stomach feels like a jar of marbles is rolling around inside. This is it. This ship is going to be worth all the headaches and pain from the last couple of weeks. Illira has searched for many shipwrecks and learned well what types of ships carry the most possessions and wealth. Things will soon return to normal and searching for my mother will be completely in the past.

"Listen here!" croaks the captain. All movement on deck ceases. "I know we have barely been making it since the storm but this . . ." He points in the far distance where a ship is becoming visible amid the sun slowly greeting the horizon. "This will remind you why I am your captain! I never steer you wrong and this is proof!"

The crew shouts, nodding their heads and raising their weapons. I squeeze my fist, controlling my eye roll while the captain gets all the praise.

"We all know what to do. Let's get 'em boys. Hoist the flag!"

A slight morning fog creates coverage for our approach. My lips part as I catch a glimpse of the ship with its dark purple flag blowing in the wind. A giant yellow flower that seems like its glowing marks the middle, reminding me of a star. I've never seen such a magnificent ship in these waters, though I'd heard stories and tales when I was younger. This ship is spectacular with its rich dark colored railings and engraved stars on the side. I can only imagine how much food, money, tobacco, weapons, and hopefully medicine is upon *The Blazing Star*.

Forcing myself to stay focused, I run toward the side of our ship in search of Illira. I see a tail flap in the distance, getting my attention. I wave to let her know we are ready, and she disappears back in the water toward the giant foe. "Everyone, be ready!" yells the captain as I see him pull out his sword, staring at his prize with awe.

I sprint up to the higher deck as my brother does the same. He nods that he's ready, though his hazel eyes tell me a different story. I nod back, pushing away an eerie feeling of what Gus earlier said about not being able to protect me after this.

I grab one of the ropes that will soon hoist us to our prey. My brother and I have always been a good team. This day won't be any different.

The wind favors us, quickening our approach. Illira's soft hum travels through the waters, mesmerizing *The Blazing Star's* crew with her beautiful melody. As we get closer, I can see the other ship's crew looking at the opposite side of the deck, away from our direction. Some are pointing, others are barely moving, while more are jumping with amazement at seeing a live mermaid.

But wait. There are not just men but women onboard. I pause. Women? What type of ship is this that has females as crew members? This must be a slave ship, selling women for profit. I lower my chin, my jaw tightening, ready to strike. Their captain isn't going to like me much. The nervousness in my belly turns into anticipation.

We glide alongside *The Blazing Star*. Given its size, I'm surprised I can only count eight people onboard. Even if a few are below deck, it won't add up to our crew. They're outnumbered.

It's time for Gus and me to swing to their ship. Illira keeps her voice steady and true. We have done this countless times without problems. I grip the rope as tight as I can, take a deep breath and push off, landing lightly behind a woman and man still enthralled by Illira. A few feet away, Gus lands and we draw our weapons in unison.

"She's beautiful, isn't she?" Gus says proudly, his words overshadowing the silence as Illira's song ends. Their crew turns around. Several in the same colors as the ships flag reach for weapons while others lift their hands in surrender. All look at one another, obviously silently trying to determine their orders. We point our swords at their necks, ready to strike. Behind us, our captain is standing on the railing while grappling hooks are being thrown to allow more of our crew to arrive on deck.

Even with the captain behind me, I can feel his haunting eyes warning anyone who dares to make a move. This is one of the reasons the captain has become so famous and feared. His swift, quiet approach of gaining on ships without notice before it's too late. Even with his wooden leg, he burns with intimidation.

The man and woman in front of me must be close to my age. Neither of them takes their eyes off me. The man holds his hands in the air but the woman with bright red hair keeps her arms near her side, a dagger around her hip close enough for her fingertips to reach.

I step closer, pointing my dagger at her. "I wouldn't do that if I were you. Now, tell me who's in charge here?"

"You're looking at her," she says casually.

"I'm in no mood for jokes, now I'll ask one last time. Who's in charge?" My dagger is steady while I look around and notice what I didn't before. The few women on the ship are dressed nothing like whores but more like me. Dressed to work on a ship alongside the men.

My palms begin to sweat, and I almost lose my grip on my

weapon. This can't be. I've never in all my life been on a ship that employed women. This day is already becoming too much for me.

"Enough of this! Get in line!" Gyn yells, who unexpectedly stands behind me. "Shouldn't allow a woman to do a man's work," he adds. I jump slightly but try to keep my wits about me.

The captured crew follow Gyn's orders and stand in line. I hear my brother raise his voice down the line punching one of the crewmen, forcing him to go on his knees. Gus grabs a shiny object off his shirt and puts it in his pocket without hesitation.

"What's going on over there?" barks the captain as he walks toward Gus, his wooden leg hitting loudly against the deck.

"Nothing, Captain. Just a straggler who doesn't know when to be quiet."

"Cut out his tongue next time," says the captain firmly.

The redhead steps out of the line and holds herself rigidly. "We mean no trouble. Please take what you need and go." She speaks calmly but casts a concerning look toward the brown-haired crewman Gus just hit.

The captain rushes toward her. He pushes me aside to stand nose to nose with the redhead and pulls her head back with her hair. "Did I ask for you to speak, you filthy female? Tie them up!" says the captain, spitting on her face and stepping back for his crew to follow his orders. "We will go when we please but for now. We shall celebrate!"

She stands tall, not allowing herself to waver even when the captain's spit hits her face. As he walks off, her shoulders slightly slump, and she wipes off his saliva.

I grab her before she gets in any more trouble and start binding her hands behind her back. "You would do best to keep your mouth shut," I whisper in her ear. She doesn't reply but keeps looking back at the man Gus is now tying up. Curiosity of this man takes hold of me, and I decide to see why he is so appealing. I finish tying her hands behind her back as well as the man next to her. "Get on your knees and stay put," I demand.

The man is still on his knees, head down as Gus finishes his knot, mumbling something I can't hear.

"Already found something worth taking?" I ask, eyeing Gus's pocket.

He grunts, "Wouldn't you like to know," he says before barging away. Gus clearly hasn't gotten over what I said earlier but I know soon it will just be in the past.

"You're the troublemaker, eh?" I say, nudging the man with my foot. He slowly looks up, allowing me to see the fullness of his face. His light blue eyes capture my focus. My spine straightens while my toes curl. Those clear blue eyes could make the sea jealous.

"It's a little tight," he murmurs, causing me to fall out of a trance. His chestnut hair brushes his forehead, drawing me back to those mischievous ocean blue eyes with a darker blue on his cheek from Gus's earlier handy work.

"Care to loosen them for me?" he asks, twisting his body for me to see his hands tied tight behind his back. *So, we have a smart one here. No wonder Gus reacted the way he did.* Even though his eyes are immaculate, he sure is irritating.

I lean down, making a point to show he has absolutely no effect on me. "Like I told your redheaded friend, you better keep your mouth shut. You wouldn't want anything bad to happen to her, would you?" His muscles tense and his jaw clenches.

"Good boy," I say, tapping his cheek.

A crash of glass and slamming of objects are heard below before a voice yells, "Soldiers!"

Gus barrels past me toward the lower deck, his sword shining from the now beaming sun. "Stop!" I shout. "Better to let them come up!"

But he ignores me.

I sprint after him, passing the rest of the crew who are reluctant to follow. After all, it could be a death trap.

The closer I get to the stairs, the more sword clatter and grunts I hear. Without hesitation, I barge down the wooden steps, dagger held in front of me and ready to strike.

A man in a dark purple and gold uniform slashes his sword

toward me but I block it right before it meets my chest, falling backwards onto something wet, saturating the back of my shirt.

The man charges me with his sword raised again, but slips and falls on my torso, my dagger going deep into his chest. He goes limp, his full weight laying on top of me. I try to push him off, but his dead weight is too much.

A loud gasp from Gus echoes through the whole lower deck, making my skin crawl. To my side, Gus and Gyn are fighting two other soldiers, while one of our older crew members lies on the ground next to their feet, his eyes wide open looking back at me with no speck of life in them. But what concerns me the most is the amount of blood running down Gus's arm, especially when I notice the large puddle of blood near his feet. His breathing intensifies, while the soldier gains on him.

"Get down here, you cowards!" I yell, my heart beating hard against my chest. Banging footsteps down the stairs gives me hope that Gus can make it. He just needs to hold on long enough for one of the crew to help him, but I'm let down as Sam, the youngest and least experienced, appears. His arms are already shaking as he unsteadily holds his sword in front of him while he watches Gyn shove a soldier into some wooden crates, blue liquid splattering onto the ground mixing with blood.

Good, Gyn can help. But he is only looking around him, breathing hard as he rummages through the broken crates. Sam makes eye contact with me then begins dragging the dead soldier off me.

"What are you doing!" I yell at Gyn as I'm finally free of the dead man's weight.

The silence which replaces the clashing of swords makes my heart sink. Gus curses and slumps against the wall, fighting to lift his sword with his wounded arm. The soldier presses closer to Gus and my stomach clenches into knots. Kneeling, I throw my dagger at the soldier towering over Gus, hitting my brother's opponent right between his shoulder blades. But as the man collapses, I watch his sword slowly slide out of Gus's chest.

Covering my mouth, I hold the scream burning inside of me,

wanting to escape. *This isn't real. This can't be real.* Gus puts his hand over the blood leaving his chest, his movement prompting me to stay focused. To stop the bleeding. To not allow my emotions and fear to creep in. *The sword missed his heart. He'll live. He can survive this.*

I scramble over two dead bodies, swallowing back my nausea before telling Gus it's going to be okay.

Ripping one of my long sleeves off, I tighten it around his injured arm and put my hand over his own. The only comfort I get is watching his chest still moving up and down, silently praying to every god that I think of for it to not be the last.

"Are you hurt?" he asks, his hazel eyes barely open.

My once white shirt is saturated in blood. I shake my head, amazed he is asking about me when he is groaning in pain. "No, but don't worry about me. I need to stop the bleeding and find you some . . . some . . . medicine." I flinch at the last word. If only I'd kept the bottle from that drunk at the tavern. I curse myself for ever letting it leave my hands.

A broken box is thrown across the cabin, barely missing our heads. Broken glass and shards of wood hit my back, and I hover protectively over Gus, so nothing worsens his current condition. A piece of leather slides down my arm, the same symbol as my necklace. The same symbol that was around the medicine bottle before I gave it away.

"It's all gone!!" yells Gyn. "Every last drop and all because of you! Always bad luck! The captain is not going to be happy about this," he says, the sound of boxes moving around once again.

His glare burns against my back and my pulse races. Frankly, I don't care what the captain will think or anyone else for that matter. They can blame the female again because without a doubt they are right about one thing, I am bad luck. But all I want is for Gus to live and I'll do anything to keep him breathing. There must be at least one crate that hasn't been destroyed. "Sam, stop standing there and help me," I say, trying to keep my voice steady.

He is still shaking but kneels next to me. Gus mumbles, his hair now damp from sweat, his skin pale. "Save your energy, Gus. I'll be right back," I say, putting Sam's hand over where mine is on Gus's chest, keeping pressure against the seeping bloody wound.

Gyn is still rummaging through the boxes, giving us no heed. When a few of the men finally come down with their swords out in front of them, I contemplate attacking them for being such cowards. They deserve to be in Gus's position, not him.

"Gus needs to be stitched up," Sam says, wiping his face, unknowingly leaving traces of blood on his forehead. "Hurry and help!"

The two idiots, named Irving and Mosqueda, take note that there is only us still alive and pick up Gus. He croaks loudly when they grab ahold of his injured arm, but they ignore it, carrying him up the deck while Sam holds pressure to Gus's chest.

"I'll be right behind you," I say, my throat nearly choking the words. This is a moment to stay strong. To not let every bad thought come crashing against me and instead focus on finding even a drop of the medicine that can save Gus.

Gyn stands before me, his breathing hard and fierce. "You have done it now. If this is what I think it is, your days are numbered." He nudges my shoulder hard with his own and follows the men up the stairs.

Only me and four dead men are left below. The once familiar creak of the ship rocking with the waves will now only bring back memories of blood and death. I force myself not to glance at the bodies near me and search for an intact medicine bottle. My heart races hard against my chest, as each second passes. Not knowing if he is still alive. "Stop, Elle. Focus."

He is going to get through this.

All around me are pieces of wooden crates that once held dozens of glass bottles. But now they are just shattered glass. All the medication that was inside of them is soaking into the ship floor. More and more I find the leather straps around a shard of glass, with the familiar haunting symbol. Like my mother is taunting me while I search for a cure to save my brother. That her and this medicine are linked together in some way.

My foot trips over the man I accidently killed, kicking his arm. I freeze watching an intact blue bottle roll towards the stairs from underneath his hand. Gyn didn't think to look underneath any of the lifeless bodies.

I scoop it up and run up the stairs, holding the bottle tight to my chest.

Heat hits my face, and I squint my eyes from the blaring sun in search of Gus but all I see are the prisoners on their knees while a few of the crew stand in front of them and others carrying barrels or anything else they found onto *The Turbulence*. None of them even glance up at me nor take note of my loud breathing that I'm trying so hard to keep contained nor notice my bloody clothes.

Typical. But at this moment I'm glad I'm no one's concern. With Gus not in sight, he must already be on our ship, taken to the kitchen for stitches. I follow drops of blood leaving a trail toward our ship that's tied to the one I'm on.

CHAPTER 10

AXEL

The tip of the pirate's sword presses against the skin of my neck, and I wince.

"What were the soldiers below protecting?" asks the man with a wooden leg. The death mark tattoo on his wrist shows in grand display, the dark ink glinting with the sunlight. He needs no introduction because I already know who he is.

Captain Velis, a pirate I have heard horror stories about. Countless times I have been warned about him, by someone that knew him too well. He is the only man that has crossed my mind to kill if I ever laid eyes on him. And now he stands in front of me, threatening me and my crew.

"Something that doesn't belong to you," I say firmly, wishing he would stop eyeing the rest of my crew like they are prey.

Carmen, who is close by, tries to stand but falls back onto her knees. "Axel," she warns, the fear in her eyes makes me look away from her, wishing she wouldn't act like I am of any importance to her.

A deep laugh echoes across the ship from Velis, him eyeing Carmen with malice. His sword nicks my throat and a drop of warm blood trickles down my neck. "I'll say what does or doesn't belong to me. Now answer or you won't like what happens next."

"Medicine. It's medicine," Carmen blurts, wriggling to try and break free from her restraints.

Velis growls, his patience wearing thin. "What kind?" His sword shifts and he applies more pressure, threatening to do more harm as he nicks another part of my neck.

"The kind that cures almost anything! Take it and leave," she yells. I squeeze my eyes shut, wanting Carmen to stop speaking and to stop paying any more attention to her. She doesn't know how cruel this man can be.

But I hear a loud smack against skin, her red hair flying in the air and she lands on her side. "The bottles have been destroyed, you stupid woman!" says another man they call Gyn with a nose that is pointing more to the left than center.

"Don't touch her!" I try to force myself up, but then I'm on my side, too. My jaw burns and aches from the punch, and blood pools in my mouth from where I must have bit my own cheek. Hazy black spots dance in my vision until the silhouette of a blonde woman in a blood-spattered white shirt appears. Her face is pale. She holds something tight against her chest, wincing when a boot meets my stomach.

"Look at me, boy!" Velis hisses. When I don't oblige, he kicks me again another groan slips from me, but I keep my eyes on the woman. If I am to die today, I can at least enjoy those green eyes that remind me of the lush grass that grows on the rolling hills of Glendora.

She grimaces and continues walking toward the other ship, keeping her head low.

"What's that in your hand?" The captain says, catching me off guard. The girl stops, her back now facing us.

"Face me!" The captain growls.

She turns slowly, her face a blank slate like she is only strolling the deck without care in the world. But the hand behind her back gives her away, taking a step back closer to *The Turbulence*.

The captain glances down at her bloody clothes and ripped sleeve but shows no concern other than a slight curl of his lip. "What are you hiding?"

Loose strands of hair drift across her face as she shakes her head. "Nothing. Just a bag full of beans, thought I'd cook some up to celebrate with the crew."

Though I don't know her, the pitch of her voice sounds too high. She's lying.

A spine-chilling laugh breaks free from Velis's mouth. "You have never been a good liar. Now, show me what's in your hand. I won't ask again."

"Please, Captain," she says weakly. "You must have seen Gus being carried away. You must know how threatening his wounds are." She gradually brings the bottle in front of her, the unique sapphire color bottle glinting against the sunlight. "Gus isn't going to make it if—"

"That's it, Captain! What we've been looking for! She stole it!" Gyn says, barging toward her, his hand out like she's going to just hand it over to the spineless fool. She stiffens and puts the bottle back behind her back and shuffles her feet, hitting the railing.

"Give it to him," the captain warns, his hands curling into fists.

"Gus is going to die!" she croaks, her eyes now a dark green of worry. "I can get more for you. I'll even—"

"I SAID GIVE IT TO HIM!" Velis roars, his uneven steps banging on the wooden deck, thumping louder and louder with each step. The closer he gets, the more yellow I note in his skin. He holds his sword against the blonde's chest, jerking his head with a snarled command.

Tears fill her eyes but then she squeezes them shut as Gyn takes the bottle from her. Within a second, he has the cork off, handing it to Velis. "Drink, Captain."

CHAPTER 11

ELLE

My breathing is hard to control as I lift my tense hand, slowly unraveling my fingers. I remind myself to never forget this moment. This feeling of hope being snatched from me. The feelings of despair and guilt for finding this ship when I should have listened to my brother years ago to leave. His death will be on my hands.

"It won't work," Axel says, returning my attention to him. The captain's mouth is already on the bottle. He licks the drop of sapphire healing liquid from his lips. "Why should I believe you, boy?"

Axel struggles against his bonds, still on his side from when the captain hit him. The blue-eyed man takes a long breath through his nose, sweat dripping down his forehead. "Because I'm the one who produces it and you're doing yourself no justice but wasting all my hard work," he says flatly. "No food nor drink should be in your system for at least a full day before it can take effect."

The captain licks his lips, like he's tasting his own rage before spitting it out for all to hear. "I have no time for your lies," he snarls. "Gyn, slit his throat." He leans his head back, ready to swallow it whole.

"And if you waste it now, there are no more ships traveling these waters with this medicine for the next month." Axel's eyes do not waver, staring at the captain.

Hearing that this man knows how to produce this medicine creates a stir in my stomach. Can he make more? But what makes me sick is not knowing if my brother can hold on for a full day. This doesn't seem like the best time to be slitting his throat, not when we can use him. My mind races, trying to think what to do.

Gyn's sword slithers out of his scabbard, the sound raising the hairs on my neck.

"Stop!" I yell. My pulse thumps hard. "I've heard the same, Captain. If you take it now, it won't work. You need to wait," I swallow hard from my lie, my mouth dry. "And if he says he is the one that produces this . . . this . . . whatever it is, why not use him to make more?" I take a small step toward him, lowering my voice so only the captain can hear. "Or find information about these ships that transport it. I can get Illira to find them, we could get more and sell it to the highest bidder."

He puts his hand up for Gyn to stop, tightening it into a fist and bringing it to his lips, but then a glint of excitement flashes across his face. His lips curl into a grin.

The strain of my chest relaxes as I watch him put the bottle into his pocket.

"Seems you shall live another day, boy. But if I wait and a drop of this doesn't work, your whole crew will be taken to the sea of Orlosha. I enjoy feeding the monsters a treat from time to time." He turns toward me, taking something else out of his pocket. For a moment, I think maybe he has changed his mind and is taking the medicine now, but it's the leather strip that was strapped around the bottle.

My hidden necklace feels blaring hot against my skin as he inspects the branded symbol.

"Where do you make this miracle water?" he asks, shooting a suspicious glare toward me, though his question is for Axel.

"At the healing islands," Axel says, clearing his throat. My focus remains on the captain. Hoping to pretend that I have no clue what he is looking at, I stand tall, but he knows. He knows the symbol just as I do and I'm afraid of what may come of it.

"Gyn. Go to the redhead." Gyn turns away from Axel and holds his sword tight as he approaches her. "Answer me, or she won't see another light of day. Where do you make this?" He growls, his voice a threat that shouldn't be ignored.

"Glendora," Axel says hesitantly. At his soft answer, the red-head woman shakes her head with disappointment.

"I see," says the captain, his fist squeezing around the band before letting it go like it's hot to the touch. His eyes shift from the green that matches mine to a new dark yearning that makes my skin crawl. "Seems like we have a lot to plan for tomorrow," he grumbles before raising his head high, and slamming his wooden leg onto the ship with a loud bang.

"But for now, let's celebrate our victory!" the captain yells, the crew joining him with triumph. All have seemed to forget we lost one crew mate and another is severely injured. I bite the inside of my bottom lip, wanting to scream. I need to check on Gus.

"Don't just stand there. Take inventory and get it to our storage hold," Gyn barks, already opening a bottle of whiskey, his sword back in his scabbard.

I roll my eyes and jump off the railing from *The Blazing Star* on to *The Turbulence*. Spots of blood trail toward the kitchen door. Gus lays flat on a wooden table, his shirt stripped off, bandages wrapping around his chest and arm. I stand still, waiting for his chest to move up and down and when it does, I release a breath.

Sam stands next to him, his freckled face pale as he dips his hands into a bowl of water, washing away Gus's blood. "I stitched his arm and chest. I don't think any of his vital organs have been injured but he has lost a lot of blood and if it gets infected, I'm not sure we have anything to fight it other than alcohol."

I barely know Sam. He is maybe in his early teens, but with his talents for playing the violin and knack for treating the sick, he has already become a favorite of the captain's. Usually Sam stays clear of me, like a poison or, one could say, *bad luck*.

"Thank you," I say softly.

He gives me a small nod that makes him look twice his age before walking out the cabin door. Within a few minutes, I hear his violin joining the crew's celebration.

I run my fingers through Gus's hair, moving the strands sticking to his skin. His forehead is warm to the touch. "I'm here, Gus," I whisper.

He whimpers with pain, his body shaking. "Cold," he says, reaching for an imaginary blanket.

I rummage through the cabinets and find a worn-out sheet to lay over him. "This should help but you need to get some rest. I'll come back soon and check on you," I say squeezing his clammy hand in mine. He says nothing as his breathing deepens.

I tell myself that Gus is going to be okay, that he doesn't need the medicine that remains hidden in the captain's pocket. That he is strong and will make it through but if he does get worse, I'll have to make choices that make my blood run cold.

It seems the crew is competing to see who can get piss drunk the fastest. Usually this is my time to start moving whatever goods or weaponry we find on the ship onto our own. We could claim *The Blazing Star*, but the captain has a liking for his ship and his alone.

I venture back to *The Blazing Star* where its crew is still bound but split between the two, half closer to the bow, the other half near the stern. They watch me as I take inventory of all the goods on their ship. This is going to take me hours to move, longer than I want to be away from Gus.

Occasionally, I find the captain or Gyn watching me, making sure I'm not slacking while the rest of the crew play cards and celebrates something I wouldn't call a victory. Hours pass, my legs sore from moving barrels and carrying equipment on my own onto our ship and deciding it's been long enough since I've seen Gus.

When I return to the kitchen, Gus sits up with slouched shoulders, like the effort to move is almost too much to bear. "You need to lie back down!" I rush toward him but the next words from him are not what I'm expecting.

"You're leaving," he grumbles, pulling a pendant out of his

pocket and shoving it into my hand.

My mouth is dry. "Where did you get that?" I ask, inspecting the pendant. It has three stars attached to a half-moon, a twin to my own necklace.

"I noticed it on that man's shirt. It's what I took of his before our father could see it."

I don't bring up that the symbol is engraved on the medicine bottles I found nor that the captain already knows, wishing Gus would lie back down. "Elle, this is your sign to leave." He swallows harshly. "Please," he whispers.

Obviously, my mother has been sharing her emblem with another, but why? Not just anyone but the irritating man with breathtaking eyes that we left tied up upstairs. Was it a gift? Did he steal it? Why are they engraved on the medicine bottles? So many questions with no answers. But none of these matters, only Gus. My hand aches from how hard I'm holding the pendant. I slowly lift my gaze back to my brother. He looks frailer by the minute.

"Listen," he says, and then pauses. I keep staring at his hazel eyes. They remind me so much of our mother.

"I know you're going to try and fight me on this, but you need to leave *The Turbulence*."

When I try to interrupt, he leans closer and squeezes my shoulder with his good hand.

With a piercing stare and stern face, he reiterates. "Leave."

My head shakes. Heat builds in my chest. "You need to rest, Gus." I say, wishing he would lie back down. This is too much for him and it's almost too much for me. "Besides, the captain would go ballistic if I tried to find her again and he found out."

"It doesn't matter. He doesn't want you anymore. He wants you gone for good," he says flatly as he finally lies down again.

"That's not true," I say, even though deep down I know. The captain, my own father, does not want me. Realizing that my own blood sees me as nothing but a tool to be used and then thrown away hurts more deeply than I want to acknowledge.

"You're not listening. He is going to get rid of you one way or another. In his mind, he no longer has any use for you. But I'm not going to allow it. This is your chance for a new beginning."

I feel like I've been punched in the gut. Simple words have never hurt so much. My fears are true. I have never been good enough for my father. No matter what I did. It is a fact that's hard for me to grasp. He used me and now wants to throw me out like a piece of trash. Is that what he did to my mother?

Gus groans, his body shaking again. "Just leave," he says before closing his eyes.

I press my hand against his forehead. It's warmer than before, meaning Gus's fever isn't getting any better. I look at the stitches on his arm, they look good but the ones on his chest aren't as clean, the skin there is swollen and red.

This isn't how Gus dies; I won't let our pitiful excuse for a father keep the medicine that can keep Gus alive. There is no way around it, I'm going to have to steal it. I lower my head to Gus and whisper into his ear, "If I go, you go."

When I rush through the door, my face meets Gyn's scrawny chest. "The captain wants you," he says, eyeing me suspiciously.

"Is that what you do all day? Fetch like a dog whenever the captain commands?" I ask, stomping down the desire to thump him into the ground.

"You'll regret speaking to me that way," he growls.

I ignore his warning and head toward the captain's quarters as Gyn follows a few steps behind.

CHAPTER 12

ELLE

"It's your last day on *The Turbulence*," the captain states plainly while leaning over his long wooden table, focusing on a scrolled-out map. Gyn stands next to him with his arms crossed, grinning at me with an oily smugness.

My heart plummets. *Come on, Elle. Don't act like this hurts you more than you want it to.* "I . . ."

The captain doesn't look at me. He grunts and twists his beard. "You're the cause of all the boxes being destroyed, I have the right to send you overboard, but you have given me an idea. I am releasing *The Blazing Star,* and you are going with it."

My muscles tense. "I don't understand, Captain."

His dagger slams into the table, straight through the map before he turns and stares at me. "What do you not understand? You will leave with the ship. I saw the way that man looked at you, and I want you to use your womanly talents to get close to him. You owe me those boxes, and this is how you're going to do it. Learn his secrets."

Was he speaking of blue-eyes? What I saw in Axel's gaze was certainly irritation, not desire.

I clear my throat. "He won't trust me, not after I killed some of his men."

"Then do whatever you need to do to get his trust back. Do what all females do and lie. Now leave. Figure out your plan and play your part. I don't care what you do to convince them you're on their side, but I want you gone by sundown."

I bite the inside of my cheek, gaining the courage to say what I'm about to suggest. "I want Gus to go with me. He isn't going to make it if he stays here."

The captain huffs a haunting laugh. "You've no choice in this. Gus stays." He returns to studying the map, scowling at the hole left by the dagger. My breath hitches when he levels his glare at me again. "Let him be a reminder of what you will lose if you fail me."

I've already failed him so many times. But what he doesn't know is that I'm going to fail him once more.

"Yes, Captain," I say, and leave his warning stare.

I'm done playing his games and this time he will be the one played.

I've waited until nightfall hoping that the crew, especially the captain, have gotten drunk enough to pass out and are all back in their own hammocks. A few are still gambling below deck, and I hope they stay there while I go forward with my plan.

Two younger mates that have the duty of staying guard are playing cards on *The Blazing Star*. They should be easy enough to fight without a sound.

Axel's hands are still tied behind his back, but he's now sitting against the railing in the middle of the ship, kept separate from the others. I take a deep breath, hoping this will work, that this isn't going to be a big mistake. His chin is down. My boot grazes his knee as I pass by while carrying a large bag of sugar, hoping that if he is asleep, I will wake him.

Without waiting to see what Axel does, I focus on the two guards in front of me. I hear a few grumbles that even though they now have barrels of alcohol to last them a lifetime they were hoping for some actual jewels. I snort, disgusted by how ungrateful they can be.

"You have something to say, bad luck?" one of the men growls.

"Are you already so drunk you forgot my name?" I ask, lifting my chin and holding the bag as if it weighs nothing. "And in fact, I do." I swing the load of sugar behind me and slug the man in the head, forcing him to collide with the other so they knock each other out. I grab the knife from my boot and kneel next to the captive.

His blue eyes are studying me. They seem to gleam with the moonlight. I swallow, hoping this isn't a path to my death.

"We don't have a lot of time, but I need your word that if I release you and the rest of your crew, you will take me and the man that was injured with you."

Axel's lips press tight, and his gaze searches mine. I'm getting antsy and about to figure something else out when he finally says, "Agreed."

I nod and grab hold of the ropes binding his wrists. "But you both will pay for your crimes one way or another," he adds.

I stop, biting my lip. Those accused of the crime of piracy are either flogged, sent to prison for the rest of their life, shipped to the Northern mines that most only survive for a few months, or even hanged. I'm unsure how his people treat pirates, but I have no other choice; I need this man's help.

"Deal, but only I will pay for them." I'd endure any punishment as long as Gus lives and frankly, with all the mistakes I've made lately, I deserve whatever comes my way.

He nods in agreement and shifts his body so it's easier for me to cut his bindings. Once he's cut lose, I reluctantly hand him the knife so he can help his crew. "When you're done, meet me here. I need help to carry him off the other ship." I don't let him answer as I turn toward ones who are tied farther down the ship, but he grabs my arm, stopping me.

"I'll go now, while you get the rest loose. We can't waste time," he says, his face stern. I want to roll my eyes, already annoyed with him telling me what to do while also knowing he's right.

"He's in the kitchen, the door to—"

"I saw where they took him," he interrupts, disappearing into the shadows and onto *The Turbulence*.

I want to follow him but stay persistent on the course. Like he said, we can't waste time. I pray to the sea gods that no one sees him. Once I have *The Blazing Star's* crew mostly untied, they follow my orders to prepare the ship to leave despite their wariness.

Gus's painful cry sounds behind me. Blue eyes has him over his shoulder, carrying him over the railing and off *The Turbulence*. We all stop and wait to see if anyone heard his cry and after only a few seconds, we are moving again.

Most of *The Blazing Star* is shrouded in darkness, but as the waves slowly rock it back and forth, the moon's rays dance across the shadows of two human forms leaning against the main mast.

It's the redhead and another tied behind her back facing the other way. I cut the bindings I placed on her earlier today, briefly explaining the plan, hoping she doesn't think I'm somehow tricking her.

"Behind you." Her eyes grow wide as she pushes me to the side and tackles one of the crew men that I'd hit with a bag of sugar earlier. One hard punch to the face and he's unconscious again.

I wrinkle my nose, shocked that she could have let me get hurt but didn't. "Good one, Red," I say, throwing her one of my other knives. "Hurry. Raise the anchor, we're leaving."

Her jaw tenses. "I'm not doing anything else until you tell me where he is."

"If you're speaking of Mr. Blue Eyes, he's already been released and getting the ship ready to leave."

She looks around the ship and mutters a whisper that sounds both endearing and aggravated. "Axel."

"Don't worry, your lover boy will soon be back in your arms, so stop wasting time," I say. She rolls her eyes and releases the crew member next to her.

I take light steps back onto *The Turbulence*. My heart beats loud enough for the whole ship to hear. But with shaking hands

I cut every sail and rigging. Even at night and the coolness of the wind, sweat drips down my neck. I'm betraying everything I know, and a pinch of sadness cascades against me as each sail is slit.

I return to my mission, the one part that I've been dreading. The one that makes me feel like vomiting every time thinking about going into the captain's quarters. I really don't want to do this but it's the only way to keep Gus breathing while we're on our journey. *Away from . . .*

Our only home.

The feel of human touch on my skin makes me jump. My dagger points toward Axel standing next to me, his body going rigid. "You have done enough. We need to go now," he says with a sharp tone.

"Not until I get the bottle," I say, returning his stern look. "Or do you have some more medicine stashed that I don't know about."

He searches my face with the same expression as he did earlier, making me feel like he can read everything I'm feeling right now. He swallows before looking around the ship and back to me. A drunk cheer is heard below the deck. His jaw tightens. "I won't wait long."

"I don't want you to wait," I say in a harsh whisper and step away from him. His form is too close to me, making an uncomfortable light spark in my core.

His eyebrows rise.

"The wind is in our favor so prep the ship to leave now. I'll make it back in time," I command and head toward the captain's quarters.

Back pressed against the cabin wall, hand on the knob, I take a deep breath, instinctively squeezing my necklace for some type of support before going in. *This is for Gus.*

No lantern or candle is lit, but moonlight shines through the one window, leaving shadows in each corner and upon the walls. Only the sound of creaking wood and heavy breathing from sleep are heard. The captain's bed is in the same spot that it's always been. The same bed he used to share with my mother. A place I'd go to when the blackness of the sea at night scared me and found the comfort of my mother's arms. A haven without the judgmental eyes because of my sex.

Now as I enter all that I remember seems to be a distant memory that barely feels true. Like it was only a dream I have made up in my head when the truth is I have always been living a nightmare from which I can never wake up.

I focus on the slow, even rise of my father's chest as I take each step toward him. His fake wooden leg leans on the nightstand, with his clay pipe next to it. The hint of tobacco hovers in the air.

The bottle is not on the nightstand, but it's never that easy. Slowly, I open the top drawer, thinking maybe he has it hidden. Instead, I find an old map of trading routes and islands that have been discovered within the last century. Glendora is written near one of the islands with a question mark next to it.

A rattle of a deep breath comes from my father, making me freeze. My shadow of a silhouette prevents me from seeing if his eyes are open but then his breathing steadies. I need to hurry; my luck isn't going to last long, and *The Blazing Star* will soon be sailing away.

Underneath the map is an object. When I shift the map to the side of the drawer, my hands graze a pendant with the same emblem as mine. I thought he had gotten rid of it, but it lies here. Hidden. Seems I am not the only one with a secret. My father may act like my mother is a tyrant, but he hasn't let her go like I thought he has.

Next to it lays a pouch that feels cool to the touch. A turquoise glow emanates from the bag. This is it. Without hesitation, I put it in my pocket.

A hand wraps tightly around my wrist, the pressure intensifies. "I knew you would come here," the captain growls. His breath smells of whiskey and disgust.

I try to yank out of his firm grip. My hip knocks his wooden leg on the floor. Pain surges up my arm as I keep trying to break free. "You can't have it," I say sharply. He isn't going to get the bottle back from me. Not this time. With all my force, I put all my weight on the back of my leg and thrust my other arm forward striking him straight in the jaw. He rolls to his side and off the bed, giving me the chance to flee.

I barge through his door, banging loudly against the cabin wall, every footstep bashing against the deck.

"She has it!" the captain yells, the warning bell ringing for all to hear. "Wake up, you fools!"

The Blazing Star glides past me, the end of the ship soon to be next. My legs burn as I sprint past one of the crew. Lazy and tired, he's unaware what's happening as I push him into some barrels.

I'm not going to make it. *The Blazing Star* is speeding up too fast.

"Swing up!" Axel hollers, pointing toward one of the cut ropes still hanging from a sail on the upper deck. The sound of multiple boots running increases not far behind me. This is insane, but I grab hold of the rope, sprint hard toward the end of the deck, and fling myself in the air toward *The Blazing Star*.

My feet miss the end of the ship, my flailing arms miss the railing, and I plummet toward the dark sea. Axel catches my arm, holding tight. I dangle in the air, and half of him is over the railing. "Don't let go," he grunts as he pulls me up, flinging my body onto his as we crash onto the solid deck.

We're both breathing hard, his chest hitting mine with each breath he takes, his arms still around me. I have only landed myself on another problem. Pushing aside my worry of my future punishment for piracy, I remind myself that the only important thing is getting the medicine safely to Gus.

I roll off Axel, forcing myself *not* to look at him. I check my pocket, and a rush of air leaves my nostrils. The bottle is safe. I have it. I *actually* have it. I didn't fail this time.

I stare back out to the sea and watch as *The Turbulence* slowly fades away. Dread takes over me. A dark one-legged shape stands at the forecastle deck. His presence there burns my skin, branding me.

It's a warning. A warning that this isn't over.

CHAPTER 13

ELLE

"We need to give the bottle to him now," a deep voice says behind me. I'm still staring out into the dark waters, waiting for *The Turbulence* to somehow show any minute. My mind keeps playing tricks on me, making me think I see some object far away but then a large wave washes it away.

Warmth wraps around my arm but inside I feel like an iceberg ready to crack. Another tug. "We can't wait any longer if you want this to work," Axel says, the heat in his words bringing me back.

I pull my arm away from his grasp and turn toward him. His words do not make sense. "I thought he can't have anything in his stomach for a full day before it takes effect?"

Axel shakes his head. "The sooner the better. Follow me," he says, walking toward the stairs below deck.

I stop, not wanting to go back down there, back to the same spot where I killed two men to save my brother. The dead bodies must still be down there. The crew of *The Turbulence* took their own, wordlessly throwing him out to sea. I haven't had the time, nor have I wanted to think about having taken another's life. It was my first time ever doing so and I hope it will be my last. But no one needs to know that.

With the tattoo on my wrist, I'm considered the heartless and ruthless one. For how can one be part of *The Turbulence's* crew without having blood on our hands? The memory of the dagger leaving the tip of my fingers and going straight through the soldier's back like butter makes me cringe. A heaviness settles on my shoulders that I'm unsure I can bear. Counting every breath that leaves my nose, I follow Axel.

Below there are no bodies in sight, but the smell of metallic and blood is still in the air. Two women are sweeping up the broken glass and putting it into a pile. As I pass, I can feel their piercing eyes watching me. I haven't even changed my shirt or pants yet; the blood of those soldiers is still on me. Thankfully, Axel opens the closest door, and my gaze focuses on Gus lying on a bed inside.

The room is larger than any room we have on the lower decks. It has a small window looking out to the sea with flower engravings wrapping around like vines on the window seal with shelves of books on each side of the walls.

The redhead has a bowl of water and pats Gus's forehead with a wet washcloth. "He has a high fever; he needs the medicine now."

The sight of Gus looking so frail and pale makes my knees go weak. I swallow back the fear that threatens to leave my stomach and take the vial out of my pocket and bring it to Gus's lips. "Drink this. You will be better soon," I say out loud, wanting to believe it myself. His eyes remain closed, but he opens his mouth and swallows the liquid. He takes a deep breath, like relief has washed over him, and falls asleep.

Sitting in the wooden chair beside Gus's bed, I ask, "Can I have some time with my brother before . . ." I pause, unsure what Axel has planned for me. Will I be tied up just as I did to them? Will he add more scars to my back for each man that was killed?

The redhead narrows her eyebrows with confusion, glancing between me and Axel. He says nothing, leaning against the door and focusing on the lantern beside the window, his jaw tight.

She stands. "Yes, of course. I'll be back in a little to see if you need anything."

I give her a perplexed look, unsure why she would care what I needed but only nod.

Axel opens the door for her and doesn't look my way before exiting with her, shutting the door behind him. I sigh, happy to be alone with my brother. At least they have given me this time with him. "I'm sorry for everything, Gus," I whisper, taking his hand into my own and leaning my head onto the bed.

A rumble of thunder wakes me, my eyes heavy from sleep. The flickering lantern brings out the paleness of Gus's face. I look at the stitches on his chest. They're still red and swelling. "Gus, wake up." It's selfish of me but I want to hear his voice, anything to let me know that he is okay.

His eyelids flutter. "It hurts," he groans, the words barely making sense.

The door opens and the red head enters carrying a clean bowl of water, fresh clothes resting on her shoulder.

"Why isn't he better? How long does it usually take for it to take effect?" I ask, my voice no longer calm.

She puts the bowl down and feels his head. "Sometimes, depending on the severity, another vial is needed."

"So, you're saying this so-called healing medicine may not save him? That it's not this all-powerful liquid, but a lie?"

"I'm saying that we need to keep him comfortable and get his fever down. Once we arrive in Glendora we can give him another dose. Sometimes it can take longer than others to heal but it's also not a miracle cure."

"How long will it be before we arrive?" I ask, standing. The room now feels way smaller than it is.

She swallows. "About seven days."

This is too much. Everything barges against my chest. I need air. I need to feel the wind. I race out the door, not caring who sees me, and find the darkest part of the ship. Only the shadow of the moon peeks out from the rumbling clouds.

My knees buckle underneath me, and I drop. I grab my stomach, trying to control the pain coursing through my veins. As I do, I'm reminded of the blood on my clothes. Of what has transpired within the last day. I have left the only home I have ever known. I killed two people and now my brother lies below deck, hanging on to life by a thread. My throat burns as I try to refrain from crying. It boils like hot water ready to go over the edge. I can't hold it in any longer. All my emotions surge inside my body, forcing me to release it with a high-pitched scream. I am past the point of caring who hears me.

I groan at the thought of my brother dying, laying my head on the floorboards, and hiding my face with my hair. Tears flow until my body goes limp.

The cold breeze and hard pellets of rain wake me from my fatigued state and I curl into a ball. I allow the sound of the waves to soothe me with their melody. Goosebumps cover my arms as cold air hits my skin. I'm about to get up to find warmth, but firm arms wrap around me and underneath my legs. A faint smell of peppermint and musk fill my nostrils, inviting me to lean more into the sea of warmth.

My eyes are too swollen and heavy to open as I hear a door creak. Gently, I'm laid on a soft bed and tucked underneath a multitude of blankets. I curl into them and sigh with relief, falling into a deep sleep. Wishing the last eight years was only a bad dream.

CHAPTER 14

ELLE

Sun rays beam through a window targeting my sleepy eyes. I groan, rolling over and smashing my face into the pillow that has been my only comfort. Throughout the night I'd wake, all my memories crashing back in and leaving me sobbing. I slowly extend my fingers in and out, releasing the aches from clenching the blankets.

The course of my life has never been easy. I've had to fight to be a part of the sea life, but for what? Just so I can become a traitor to my one home and lose my brother? He is all I have. If he leaves, I will officially be on my own.

I inhale a familiar scent of peppermint and musk. Grabbing the edge of the bed, I force my body to move out from under the soft covers. My legs are bare, my bloody pants and shirt I was wearing have been replaced with an unfamiliar dark brown tunic that reaches my knees.

My surroundings remind me I'm no longer on *The Turbulence*. Everything is different. The room is twice the size compared to my pathetic bedroom. The soft sheets are burgundy instead of dark blue and match the comfy rug under my feet. The door frame is made of dark oak with a crystal looking doorknob. The smell of eggs leads me to the cedar desk next to the bed.

Someone must have brought in the food while I was sleeping. I can't remember the last time I ate but the thought of eating has no appeal. Food alone won't cure my pain.

At the light knock, I grab for my dagger that is no longer on my hip and instead snatch the closest object to me, a butter knife.

"Good morning," says the redhead as she hesitantly walks into the bedroom.

I lower the butter knife and tap it against my thigh, hoping she gets the hint that she's not welcome.

The redhead chuckles, making me feel like an idiot for thinking a butter knife could really scare her. "You will have no need for that other than for your food," she says, nodding toward the meal.

"I'm not hungry," I say bluntly.

She scratches her cheek and looks at my feet. "I brought you some clothes you can change into," she says, setting them on the dresser. "You should eat. It's not much but since we were recently ransacked," she says, widening her eyes "We will have to be frugal, so no time to waste."

I bite my lip and tilt my head in silent reply. Two short steps and I'm back to sitting on the bed, waiting for her to leave the unfamiliar room. My mind is still trying to process everything that happened the night before. It's as if I can only take one thing at a time or my body will start to shake.

She doesn't leave and focuses on my shaky hands. I firmly grip the blankets, trying to get my hands to still. My appearance must make me look like a crazy sea urchin ready to lose her wits and destroy all in her path, but I don't care.

"Is my brother . . ." I'm too scared to finish the question, my heart pounding a thousand beats a second inside my chest.

She gives me a soft smile. "He is okay. He hasn't woken but his fever has lessened so that's a good sign."

I press my hands against my knees and take a deep breath, rocking back and forth while repeating in my head, *he's alive, he's alive.* What I need now is a good drink and time to skip ahead six more days.

"My name's Carmen by the way," she says before finally walking out.

My stomach grumbles but I ignore it and lay back, pulling the blankets tight around me. I squeeze my eyes shut, begging for the aching pain to subside as tears run down my face. *He's alive.*

The sway of the ship wakes me from my deep sleep, rolling me across the bed. I'm unsure if another day has passed but I haven't left the bed, only to relieve myself and drink some water. I eye the new food that's been left for me.

Though I've not touched it, someone brought me another plate. My eyes roll, wondering why this person even bothers leaving me food. Why do they care what happens to me now that they are safe and have their ship back? Why have I not been locked up yet?

The waves force me out of bed, as if telling me I need to go outside into the fresh air. "Alright, alright!" I groan at the sea. Always so demanding no matter where I am.

I'm unsure if I have been locked up in this room this whole time or not but might as well check. I braid my hair, pulling it to the side and putting on the clothes Carmen left. The long sleeve green shirt is a soft fabric I've never felt before. Rubbing it against my cheek, it floats across my skin like a feather. The brown pants fit perfectly across my waist. I have never had such clean and well-fitted clothes before. It's nice.

My sweaty palm grasps the doorknob. The wooden door has a giant design of a purple flower. It is beautiful, so elegant, but also nothing a pirate would have on a ship. I lean my head on it, pushing away the image of my father's silhouette disappearing into the dark. Feeling uneasy, I sway back and forth, count to three, and turn the knob.

The sun heats my face as my eyes adjust to my surroundings. I never really had the time to appreciate how immaculate this ship truly is. So perfect. So clean and well kept. The trim around the deck is smooth with a fresh coating of brown paint. The sails above are not old nor covered in patches but white as clouds, moving in perfect unison with the wind. As I step toward the center of the deck, I only hear my boots hitting the boards instead of creaks.

A couple of women dressed similarly to me are swabbing the deck working salt water into the wood to prevent rot and fungus growth. I forgot it rained last night. They both stop as I pass by. One gives me a welcoming smile while the other glares. A scar runs down her black skin from the tip of her left eyebrow down to the side of her lip. Her green eyes aim straight to the black ship tattoo on my wrist.

I almost wince from her blunt distaste but focus on the railing, on wanting to see out into the great blue. I need to see something that is familiar to me. Something that makes me feel like I'm still aboard *The Turbulence*. The smell of the saltwater and sea breeze hits me with a hard blow.

Haunting thoughts of my brother lying ill in bed follow. I clench my teeth and pain rivets through my jaw. I welcome the discomfort, knowing it is well deserved.

A shadow of a silhouette appears next to me. I roll my neck, hoping if I ignore them the person will go away and leave me be.

"It's nice to see you finally out of the cabin. I thought Axel was going to have to carry you out of his room," Carmen teases, leaning on the railing next to me.

I sigh heavily, keeping my gaze on the rolling waves.

"I missed the sun," I say, my tone lacking any strength but then I pause after realizing what she just said.

"I've been in his room?" I blurt out.

Carmen fiddles with her nails, trying to pry out dirt as if she has no worries in the world. "Yes, he thought you needed something more comfortable than the canopies."

"Why would he care if I'm comfortable or not? Am I not a prisoner here?" I grunt, my arms tense.

"We have never had to deal with pirates before nor had a use to put a cage on board."

She continues cleaning out her nails. "These dang things. No matter what I do, they crack and contain so much dirt I could build a mountain."

I understand her dilemma but her way of talking to me like we are friends only annoys me. "I can sleep on the top deck for all I care. I can take care of myself." I flick my braid to the side.

Carmen leans her hip against the railing and folds her arms. "I never said you can't. We like to be hospitable toward our guest compared to *The Turbulence*."

"I'm no guest. Have you not forgotten you wouldn't have been here if it weren't for me? We could have taken your cargo and sunk this precious ship of yours," I say as a whirlwind moves inside my chest.

She steps closer to me, narrowing her eyes. "You listen here—"

"Leave it be, Carmen," demands a rough voice behind me. She opens her mouth but closes it again before she blinks slowly, not moving. I tilt my head, mimicking her, slowly blinking back. Her hair barely grazes my face as she spins away from me.

"You sure know how to make friends," Axel says, rubbing his clean-shaven chin. His short chestnut hair grazes his eyebrows and he searches me intently, blue eyes flicking up and down.

"I don't need friends. And as I just told her, I can take care of myself."

"I highly doubt that. You haven't eaten or got out of bed. So, as I see it, you have no clue how to take care of yourself."

I cross my arms and look behind him, trying to ignore that he is right. That I have made myself look like a foolish girl just as I did on *The Turbulence*.

"You think your brother would like you acting this way?"

"Don't you dare talk about my brother! Like you know anything about my life!"

"You're right, I don't. But there is no need to act as if we are your enemy now," he murmurs.

I unfold my arms, uncertain what he means. An older man with a full white beard and a missing arm approaches us, concern in his eyes. "Everything okay, sir?" the man asks, taking slow steps closer.

"Everything's alright, Fred. But would you please ask Gail to leave a bucket of water and soap in my quarters."

"Aye, sir."

I can't help but wonder what has happened to this man's arm but also how much use he could be on the ship.

Axel clears his throat. "Look, we have awhile on this ship together. All I'm going to ask from you is to pull your own weight around here and not start any fights. Can you do that?"

"Shouldn't I be locked up right now?"

"You can try and swim away or if you'd prefer, I can tie you up. But we could use some help on the ship before we arrive to Glendora."

Sounds about right. I'm always used one way or another.

"You act as if this is some type of game."

"What game would you call this? All I want to do is keep the crew safe and make it back on land before your old friends show back up."

"You don't have to worry about that, I destroyed their rigging, it will take them days to get it fixed."

Axel shakes his head. "I'm not taking any chances, and we all know one of the reasons *The Turbulence* is so popular is for its speed. So, will you help or not?"

"With my eyes closed," I reply, doing just that.

Axel is so close I can feel the heat of his breath. I open my eyes, and his broad shoulders are towering over me with his blue eyes fixed on my own. My stomach twists in a knot. I push the feeling away, refusing to act as if being close creates some type of unfamiliar stir in my stomach. We both stand still. Challenging one another to see who will move away first. It's not going to be me.

My heart races as his gaze explores my face. I can feel a tug of war inside, losing the fight and pulling toward this aggravating, stupidly handsome blue-eyed, man.

Axel steps back. "Good. Once you have calmed down, find Carmen. She'll tell you what to do," he says before hastily walking away.

Calm down? I taste a tang of blood from biting my lip to keep from saying anything else in response. But he can't have the last word. "Can't take the heat, can you?" I blurt out.

He stops and stiffens. His shoulders lift and fall with a heavy sigh. His silence irritates me, but I keep waiting for a reaction. Axel tilts his head to the side, turning so I can see his taunting smile. "Nah, I can take the heat all day, just not the smell."

With that, he leaves me to my own stench.

CHAPTER 15

AXEL

"We seem to have our hands full," Carmen states as I sit at my desk, wanting to think of anything other than the two pirates we have onboard. "Who would think we would be taking care of pirates from *The Turbulence!*"

I slam the book I'm trying to read closed and lean my elbows on the table, running my hands through my hair. What in the world was I thinking? What will my father think when I bring pirates into Glendora? I've never had to punish anyone for their crimes, and I could see it plainly on the girl's face that I hadn't a clue what I was doing. But what else was I to do? We would all be dead if it wasn't for her.

"And a girl pirate. I'm surprised she was even allowed on that ship. She's a fierce one, she is," Carmen continues.

I take a deep breath and stand, keeping my eye on the book I was trying to read. "That she is," I state. I'm reminded with the short amount of time we were captured how cruelly she was treated by those men. How no one seemed to care to ask if she was hurt when blood was smeared all over her white shirt. Or how pained her eyes looked when she was called 'bad luck' instead of her real name. A stab of guilt hits, realizing I have no clue what her name even is. I shut the book my mother used to read to me about mermaids who once walked on land. She would say that Glendora was a magical place not just for humans. That our island was once used as a source of life for all. This book has always been a root of comfort for me but at this moment, it isn't. I put it back in its place with the other books.

"Do you think her brother will live?" I ask, knowing he is lying only a room away.

She shrugs, pinching her lips together in deep thought before answering. "I'm unsure. His fever seems to have gone down, but his wounds haven't improved. We need more medicine, or I don't think . . ."

"I see." Not wanting her to finish what she was about to say. Anyone would be blind not to see he's not doing well even after taking the vial. I don't want to think how unhinged his sister would become if he did die. I pace toward the window, gazing out at the sea, wanting a glimpse of the bright sun hitting against it before going back to my desk. "And what about our food and drink? Was it all taken before we escaped?"

"We are short of alcohol and water. We're thin on food and with two extra mouths to feed, we're going to need more."

A map of the kingdoms is sprawled across my desk. Since we've been heading south, our ship is already too far away from most of the islands and turning back would only be detrimental. I pause. There is a smaller island, Yurma Island, east of us. I know of it due to my uncle visiting instead of myself while I stayed home with Nile after his mother passed. It was one of the deciding factors that we needed more of an army and training after a few of our soldiers were killed while transporting our medicine onto land. I grit my teeth, not wanting to put any more of my crew in danger.

"Go ahead and spit it out," Carmen says, looking at the island I have my sight on.

"We're going to Yurma Island to resupply. If we start fishing and put out rain bucket to trap water, we should be able to make it."

Carmen shifts. "Yurma is not a place I'd trust for us to dock at without getting unwanted attention."

I nod. "You're right, so only I and another will go. You will stay with the ship and the crew while we take our small boat inland. We will act as fishermen needing a place to stop for some supplies." I pull out a small key from my pocket, one that I always leave hidden in my mother's book.

The key opens a small drawer underneath the table with coins hidden inside. "I should have enough to buy some food and alcohol when we arrive."

"What about the medicine? I've heard that other islands are just the same, that the King keeps it only for his higher subjects while the others eat dirt. You would have to get past their guard. How would they believe you are who you are?"

A glint of sunlight shines warmly through the window onto my shoulder as I walk back and forth moving with the ship as it sways. Carmen's right. How am I going to ask this man, this King Divian who I've never met, that I'm Axel, the soon to be ruler of Glendora. I will need to figure out what to offer him in exchange for some medicine.

I stop, swallowing before saying what I'm about to. I open the drawer and pull out a crumbled paper, flattening it out. "My uncle. He made a list."

Carmen steps forward, her eyebrows narrowing. "What list?" she asks, her voice simmering with annoyance.

My finger runs down the names of eligible woman from each island. I stop at King Divian and trace the name next to his: Blaire, daughter of Heath Divian. A black mark strikes through her name.

"Your uncle is sick," she blurts. "Why is her name scratched out?"

My neck tenses, wanting to scrap this whole idea immediately. "I'm told that after he visited Yurma, Orson didn't think they would be worth inviting to the Glendora ball. So, I will personally invite him to Glendora, and his daughter."

"That may work," she states, not even looking up at me as she walks toward the small window and folds her arms. "So, you're really going through with it." She stares out the window.

An unease settles at the pit of my stomach. not wanting to talk about what I promised my father and the council before I left. "It is what it is."

Carmen puts her hands on her hips, tilting her head up and laughing loudly before looking back at me like I'm a fool. "It is what it is," she repeats mockingly. "Gee, I wish picking a married mate was so simple."

I roll my neck. "Of course it's not simple."

"And what about Nile?" she asks, her eyebrows drawing together.

Knots build in my stomach.

"He is still having a hard time, since . . ." She pauses, her cheeks flushing. "Since he lost her," she says softly. "And when you get back all your attention will be focused on dining with random women while he still needs you. And will whoever you choose love Nile just as much as we do?"

Does Carmen not think I worry about this? That I may not find someone in such a short time that would be okay with a young boy that isn't her own living with us? If Carmen only knew how many sleepless nights I've had. But I will make it work. One way or another, Nile will always be one of my main focuses.

I breathe loudly out my nose. "I know it hasn't been easy for him. And if I could take all his pain away, I would. But I will always make time for him."

Carmen gives me a tilt of smile. "I know you will." She puts her hand on my shoulder and nudges me back and forth trying to change the serious atmosphere to something cheerier, making me laugh softly. I'm instantly reminded why I asked my best friend to join me on this voyage.

"I'm sorry, I shouldn't have brought it up," she says as her face goes neutral. "But you know, we could just go to Yurma for supplies, we wouldn't even have to think about speaking with King Divian. I'm not even sure it's worth getting this medication for two pirates we barely know."

I've asked myself that same question. But I look back at the bookcase, reminded of my mother's words, that Glendora's magic wasn't just for our people to share but for all and I wasn't going to be the one to keep it from anyone that needed it. Pirate or not.

"It's worth it," I say as a glint of the blonde girl above deck passes through my mind.

"Then it's settled. And who will be going with you to Yurma while I stay on deck?"

A smirk slowly lifts one corner of my lips. "A pirate."

CHAPTER 16

ELLE

When I arrive back in the room, a bucket of water and soap is waiting for me. I thought I was going to have to hunt for some clean water myself. This kind gesture brings a yearning I've secretly always wanted from my past crew. It's so foreign it's uncomfortable. I thought after my deal with Axel, I'd be tied up or locked in some room, but I've been given clean clothes, food, and water.

The weight on my shoulders slowly dissipates as I wash away the events of the previous days. With each stroke, I picture all my worries and anxieties shedding off me. But I know they will come back with vengeance. They always do.

After a much-needed wash, I force myself to go back out on deck. I'm not sure how my next interaction with Carmen will be, but I'm not looking forward to it.

The two girls I saw earlier are still mopping close by. They glance up in unison, one waving me over while the other gives me a blank stare. My mind still can't grasp that women are doing laboring work on the ship. Work that I thought I'd never seen done by the hands of a female other than myself. I'm somehow both intimidated and intrigued.

Secretly, I want to know each of their stories. How did they get here? Have they been working on a ship for long? Would they understand my struggles? Deep inside, I've always wanted someone to talk to that was aware of the daily battle I go through.

"Carmen wants you moppin'," says the girl to my left, handing me the mop. I grab a hold of it, nodding and trying to keep my face neutral while also trying not to focus on the long scar on her face.

"Oh, come on, Doolah," says the other girl, knocking her with her hip. "Sorry, sometimes my sis forgets her manners. I'm Dibs and this is Doolah."

Glancing between the sisters, I notice they are almost identical. Their skin is as dark as the night sky, which brings out their emerald eyes. Where Dibs has her hair pulled back in a long-braided ponytail, Doolah's is cut short on the sides, leaving length on the top with curls. They're as tall as I but appear to be a few years younger.

Dibs puts a hand on her hip, giving me a bright-eyed look. "Well, are you going to tell us your name or do you want us to guess?"

"Elle. It's Elle."

"You sure are skinny, you should eat somethin' or you're not going to last an hour," Doolah says as she returns to mopping.

Dibs rolls her eyes at her sister, shaking her head. "Don't mind her, she doesn't do well with strangers," she says, waving for me to follow her. "I'll show you where to start. It's going to be a busy day. So far, the weather seems calm but boy, it has been temperamental. You never know what it will do."

Dibs's voice echoes across the ship, keeping me from getting lost in my wandering thoughts. I'm thankful for it. She speaks about her love of dancing but then spontaneously changes the subject of how grateful she and Doolah are to have a job on *The Blazing Star* while Doolah keeps to herself, only listening.

As we work and the day becomes hotter, they both barely break a sweat while I have tons dripping off my forehead. They are strong while my body is weak and fatigued. The wind is nonexistent, which does not help.

I've never mopped such a huge ship before, but after a few hours my back muscles are screaming for me to stop as my arms become more and more sluggish. Occasionally, I spot Carmen in the distance, watching me. It only keeps me going. I don't want to be the one to ask for a break. Doolah is right, though. I'm feeling weaker by the minute. My body needs food to keep me from falling over. But I'm determined to only stop once the twins call it quits. I'm not going to fail at this simple task.

"Let's all take a break!" Carmen hollers from the quarter deck behind me.

I sigh with relief and follow Doolah and Dibbs to where the rest of the crew is sitting in a circle around a barrel of water with slices of bread and jam. All look at me with interest. Some greet me while hesitating, glancing at my tattoo on my wrist.

A middle-aged man named Perkins offers me his stool, but I stay standing. If I sit down, I'll never get back up.

"Please, sit. He speaks with an exotic accent and eyeing me with worry. I give in and sit down, wanting the attention off me. I sip the water, savoring it and wishing it was whiskey.

Everyone seems content with a long day's work in the heated sun, still chatting back and forth, laughing. Tired, but happy. Fred, the older man with the one arm, is sitting close to a dark-haired woman that prepared the bread. Whenever the ship tilts from the waves, the sun brings out her silver strands. She lovingly pats his upper lip with a napkin, her grin bringing wrinkles around her mouth. He kisses her cheek, whispering "my sweet Gail."

I note Axel is absent. The last time I saw him was from our little conversation earlier today, telling me I smelled. The thought of his last words irks me in so many ways that I can't even explain it to myself. It really shouldn't bug me, but it keeps creeping back into my mind.

"Bread?" Carmen asks, handing me a slice.

My mouth waters but I swallow it away, ignoring the pain in my stomach. "I thought you said we are short on food."

She lowers her hand, taking a deep sigh. "Yes, but we should have enough. A few of us have been fishing to accommodate everyone."

"I can eat later." I take another sip of water, hoping it's a clue for her to leave me alone.

"Fine, but you have done enough today. Tomorrow, I'd like you to help me inspect the storage barrels."

"I haven't finished yet though."

"Doolah and Dibs can finish up," she says, taking a few bites of the bread.

I stare at the sea, keeping the bread out of my sight. My stomach grumbles for me to give in. But why should I eat when I'm the one who took the food in the first place? It's not the first time I've gone without food for days. I'd catch my own food. "I'd like to finish the job that's been given to me. Should only be fair."

Carmen shrugs. "If you feel up to it."

A sharp pain shoots up my right side, demanding rest. "I do."

I gulp down another flask of water and return to the main deck while the rest of the crew finishes their meal. My back and feet protest as I swab the deck. I spot Gail casting out bait over the ship, Fred standing near her, his one arm around her waist. A wave of loneliness takes over as I feel the absence of Dibs and Doolah. Laughter echoes from the crew.

Loud footsteps precede Axel demanding, "You need to eat."

Carmen must have told him I refused the bread.

Too tired to look up, I murmur, "It doesn't matter."

Silence lingers so long I assume he's left, but then he says, "It does matter." He moves in front of me, so I must look at him. "If you don't eat while working, you will get sick."

The wind finally appears, bringing with it the scent of peppermint and musk. "Needn't worry." I continue to mop, wanting him and his inviting scent to leave.

"I have a responsibility for everyone on this ship. Including you." He holds the mop as I try to yank it from him with no prevail. "Besides, we have a few things to discuss."

I stop and finally look up into Axel's intense blue eyes. "Go on with it. I have a lot to do."

He swallows and runs his hand through his chestnut hair. "First, I never asked your name."

I blink. Just a while ago he was telling me I smelled and now he is asking for my name. A huff of a laugh leaves my throat.

"What's so funny?" he asks. His lips slowly form a grin.

"Nothing, it's just I . . ." I didn't want to tell him that no man really cared what my name was other than calling me 'Bad Luck.'

Axel tilts his head. "It's just what?"

I eye him, biting my lip, unsure why I'm making this such a big deal. He lets go of the mop and brings his hand out toward me. "Here." I step back, ready to reach for my dagger, but he gently grabs a hold of my hand, bowing slightly. Warmth gathers up my neck. "I'm Axel Ardanian, son to Gerald Ardanian."

Laughter bursts out of me, cheeks flushing. I pull my hand away.

He folds his arms. "You're laughing again. Is it something I said?"

Shaking my head, I chuckle softly. It feels good to laugh. "Yes. Is that always the way you introduce yourself? Like some king?"

His eyebrows rise, a dimple appearing on his right cheek alongside a smirk. "I'm glad I can humor you. Maybe you can do the same and tell me your name."

I stop, allowing myself to think how I should answer. Should I make fun of him more and answer with 'Pirate of the great Turbulence, daughter to the tyrant captain of the seas.' But my answer is completely off key. "My full name is Eleanor. Elle for short."

I breathe in sharply, surprised I gave him a name that hasn't been spoken since I was younger. It's not that I don't like it, but it didn't fit after my mother disappeared. It was too raw. Too elegant and feminine.

He repeats my name—"Eleanor"—like he is savoring it. Like I have told him a secret only between us two. Or did it only seem that way because I've been longing to hear it again from someone's lips? Without hatred or distaste. From Axel it was kind and gentle. The distance between us feels too small, like the sun's heat has intensified within the last few seconds.

A loud yell from Gail turns our head toward the edge of the ship. "I have one Fred, it's giant!" A splash of water with a bright pink tail is seen before it goes back into the sea.

"I've never seen such an exotic fish before! Pull it in, Gail!" Fred says, his smile reaching his eyes. His excitement brings the rest of the crew to see what type of fish Gail has caught but dread drops to the pit of my stomach. I have only seen one creature with a bright pink tail. One that is called a descerver for a reason. They are rare but smart enough to trick a person into believing they've caught a massive fish and then, before you know it, they pull you in with more strength than a whale.

I trail closer, hoping I'm wrong. "Does it have a yellow horn on its back?" I yell, hoping they can hear me before it's too late.

Gail turns, her body leaning against the railing while Fred tries to reel in the fish with his one arm. "Yes, it's magnificent! It should be enough food to last us the rest of the voyage!"

Rushing toward her, I pull my dagger out, ready to cut the line, when Gail disappears overboard. Her feet flail and I hear a loud bang against the ship followed by a splash.

Fred cries out her name, taking off his vest, ready to follow her but I shove him aside and dive off the ledge. As I brace myself for the cold water, I hear a faint shout of "Eleanor" before I meet the deep sea headfirst.

CHAPTER 17

ELLE

Needles claw at my skin as the waves thrash against me. Dagger in hand, I swim toward Gail. Hearing her wheezing and choking makes me move faster, my arms already burning with exhaustion. I can barely feel my legs as I kick hard knowing every moment counts. A yellow horn appears above the sea. Only an arm's length away, I reach for her. She screams "No!" as another wave plummets against her, further separating us.

My eyes sting but I catch another glimpse of the giant fish's bright pink tail shining against the sun before it dives toward her. I flap my hands against the water, kicking and screaming, hoping to get its attention.

"Try to stay still, they are blind and are attracted to movement!" I yell, but the only reply I get back is her screaming her lover's name.

"Fred, I love you!" she yells before her head disappears under another a swell of water. She's not going to make it. She will either drown or the descerver will mutilate her. So, I do what any logical person would do knowing the one other thing they are attracted to. Blood.

I slice my now numb arm deep enough for blood to spread throughout the water. The yellow horn appears again, now focused on me as fresh bait. I wait, pulling off one of my boots. As it opens its giant mouth, its sharp teeth stained with red, I throw my boot next to me and create enough movement that it dives toward it, giving me a short second to puncture it deep into its neck. Its green scales are tough and with my strength waning, I'm unable to pull out my dagger. The descerver drags me down with both of our blood trailing behind it.

This is too much. My body is failing me, my hands losing grip of my dagger as it pursues Gail. It's as if I'm only a feather on its back. But Gail has a rope in her hand that's been thrown to her and is pulling her back to the ship. She's going to make it . . . if I give her more time.

Using the last ounce of my strength, I twist my dagger out of the descerver's neck, grabbing hold of its yellow horn and stabbing right into the top of its head. Orange blood oozes out. It spins me off, its tail cutting my shirt to shreds as it swims away.

My vision clouds, my eyes stinging from the cold salt water. I only hope I have killed it or have scared it away. When I think it's gone, a rush of water comes toward me, the yellow horn reappearing. This is it. At least I can die knowing I have saved someone that was worth saving.

A familiar hum echoes through the water and the descerver slows, turning right before it reaches me. Waves settle before I see her green hair.

Illira. Her arms wrap around me, holding my full weight and allowing me to go limp. "We need to get you out of the water. Your blood is going to attract others," she says in a voice as if she was speaking to a child. We move faster than I can swim toward the ship. Gail is safe and the rope has been thrown back for me. Before I can say anything, Illira tugs the rope over my head to wrap around my waist.

"Go, we can talk later." Her eyes are fierce with warning. "More are coming, I can hear them." I nod, and though my body is shivering uncontrollably, I force myself to give her a weak hug. "You're ship needs to move faster, he's coming," she says before yelling

"She's ready!"

He's coming.

Dread shivers along my skin as the rope tightens around my waist, pulling me up. Pain shoots up my arm as my body hits against the ship, making me moan as blood trickles down my arm. A crew I barely know looks down upon me with concern on their faces.

I'm ready to pull myself back up once I reach the railing, but Axel is already there grabbing underneath my arms, lifting me over the railing before gently setting me down.

"Fetch me a blanket and cloth for her wound!" he yells, chest heaving.

Beside me, Gail rests her head on Fred's chest, silently crying as he rubs her back. When we make eye contact, he mouths "thank you," and swipes at the tears in his weary eyes. I want to go to them both, but I'm aware my shirt is barely hanging on me, my bare back open to the crew.

I hear a few murmurs and stiffen, knowing what everyone has seen. Avoiding eye contact, I force my weak legs to support me and wrap my arms around my chest, questioning if I should dive back into the sea. Axel moves behind me, clearing his throat, hiding the view of my back. Hiding old scars I have always wanted to keep hidden. Scars I wish never existed. I search the waters for Illira, but she's nowhere in sight.

Her warning, echoing once more in my mind.

He's coming.

More blood trickles down my arm.

"Screw this," Axel says, taking off his own shirt and wrapping it around my wound.

Dibs runs up to us and throws a blanket over my shoulders. "Sorry, I would have been here faster, but I was trying to get the man downstairs to not come up."

My eyes widen and I turn toward the sound of staggering steps.

Gus is standing there, frantic, his eyes heavy and dark.

"You need to lie down." My teeth chatter against one another.

"I heard someone yell your name." He takes a deep breath. "And then heard that someone went overboard." Another breath. "I had to check." He sways back and forth, sweat trickling down his cheek.

It wasn't wise of him to leave his bed but knowing he was willing to, even though he's weak, makes my heart swell. Carmen approaches Gus, hesitating to touch him, to persuade him to go back below deck. I give him an encouraging smile. "I'm okay, I promise."

Axel steps forward. "I promise she is in safe hands."

They both look at each other. Axel nods like they are communicating without words. Gus swallows and leans into Carmen's shoulder as he slowly follows her.

"You can check on him in a bit," Dibs says, wrapping her arm around my waist and walking toward the cabin where I've been sleeping. I don't hesitate at her touch, appreciating her willingness to help. "But let's get you well first, and into some warmer clothes. I can't imagine how cold that water was this time of year."

Axel doesn't follow, but I can feel his eyes behind me. Like my back is still bare for him to see. "Everyone, please resume your duties. We need to arrive in Yurma as soon as we can and need to be fully prepared," I hear Axel say before Dibs closes the cabin's door.

My mind races. *Yurma.* It's the last place I'd want to return to. I haven't wanted to think too much of my father, but this brings back memories of him slitting the man's throat. Of the young child and mother desperately working in that shack of a tavern. Me giving away the one bottle of medicine that could have been given to Gus.

Dibs hands me a red blouse and brown pants. "That was very brave of you," she says.

My shoulders sag. The room seems to move more, forcing me to sit on the bed. Dibs pulls off my one wet boot before pulling out a needle and thread from her back pocket and grabs some alcohol on the dresser. "Let me see your arm. You have lost too much blood and the sooner I can stitch you up, the sooner you can change and rest."

The pain is nothing compared to what I have felt before. Watching Dibs stitch me with care makes me grin, wondering if this is what a friend is. "Thank you, Dibs," I say, lightly aware that my eyelids feel heavy.

"Think nothing of it. You are one of us now," she states, swinging her braids to one side of her shoulder as she stands. "You saved a beautiful soul. And you didn't have to do that." She snickers softly, "Who would have thought a pirate could be so kind?"

My loud laugh makes my head throb. "Don't spread that rumor around."

She gives me a small smile, pausing at the door. "You need to know." She hesitates before giving me a very sincere look. "Everyone on this ship has a past that's left us all with scars, but none of them judge each other for it. If you every want to talk, I'm here." She winks and leaves, allowing me to change out of my wet clothes, wondering what past everyone has that could be related to my physical scars.

Aware I haven't checked on Gus, I tell myself to get up but every time my feet hit the floor, my legs start to shake. A soft knock precedes Axel entering, shirtless. There's a small band of cloth surrounding his shoulder, all the way down to his elbow. I sit up. He opens one of the cabinet drawers and pulls out a shirt. I remember that this is his cabin, making me feel like I'm being a nuisance for taking over his space. His blue eyes narrow, studying the wound on my arm. "How are you feeling?"

My mouth goes dry. I watch his firm, muscular tan chest, his arms flexing as he puts on the shirt. No doubt he catches the attention of many.

"I'm . . . I'm fine, just need a bit of rest and I will be ready to finish my duties." He eyes me skeptically. "Do you really think I'd want you to go back to work after you have been hurt? After you risked your life to save Gail? Do you think I'm some kind of monster?"

I bite the inside of my lip, playing with the softness of the sheet I'm sitting on. It's hard for me to believe this man that stands before me could be different than the men I have known. It could be a trick but being on this ship and seeing how everyone is happy screams back at me that he is no monster but something else entirely. I want to answer him but somehow it feels too personal, so I change the subject.

"I hear we are heading to Yurma Island and not to Glendora. I don't think my brother can take a longer trip and the longer we are out at sea, the more risk we put on ourselves for the Cap—" I pause. I no longer have a captain. "For *The Turbulence* to find us."

He visibly swallows, "That's what I wanted to speak to you about before all this happened." Axel takes a deep breath, blinking several times, eyebrows narrowing. "We're running low on food, and this is the best place to stop before we head to Glendora. And—" He hesitates.

I rub my hand over my face, trying to lose the image of Gus up on the deck, so pale, so weak, and barely able to stand. "And my brother needs medicine now," I state flatly.

He nods solemnly. "He does." Axel leans against the wall, crossing his arms. "I want you to go to Yurma Island with me to retrieve it if you feel up to it. Have you been there before?"

"Once." I say, anxiety spiking at the mere thought of stepping back onto that island. That disgusting and pitiful place.

My stomach grumbles loudly.

"That reminds me," Axel says with a smug grin. "We won't be doing anything until you eat and rest." He pulls a napkin out of his pocket, unwrapping it to reveal a muffin. "Here." He holds it before me, and I inhale its sweet smell of cinnamon and honeysuckle. "It's everyone's favorite. I had an extra."

Taking it, I study the muffin like it's some foreign food I've never seen before.

Axel remains close, almost glowering at me now. "I'm not leaving until you take a bite."

The muffin is not warm but I'm already imagining the taste, the sweetness. Taking a bite confirms what it is. I debate to ask if this is a common way to make a muffin in Glendora, but I push away the thought, like my father is still here, demanding I forget about my mother. I gulp it down in two bites. It tastes like a lost memory eager to be set free.

"My mother used to make these for me," I say softly. I don't know if he replies. All of today tumbles on top of me, pushing harder and harder onto my chest. Gus . . . medicine . . . Gail . . . Illira . . . my scars . . . the captain . . . honeysuckle. My eyes feel heavy again and I curl in on myself, not remembering laying down. A blanket covers me, and I hear Axel whisper faintly, "Good night, Eleanor."

CHAPTER 18

ELLE

A reminder of Gus wakes me, the taste of honeysuckle still on my lips. Had I been dreaming, or was it true that we are sailing not toward Glendora but Yurma? I sit up and rub my eyes. Discomfort twinges down my arm and swelling surrounds the wound and stitches.

Still in the clothes Dibs gave me, I head out of bed to check on Gus. A cool fresh breeze whistles past me. The stars are still out, soon to disappear as sunlight makes a glimpse in the horizon. I hear movement on deck but don't see anyone as I follow the staircase below.

A lamp hangs next to Gus's door, swaying back and forth with the ship. I stop and look at the now empty area where the boxes of medicine and the dead men once lay. I swallow. A hint of pain surges in my stomach when I smell a whiff of lingering blood. Death will become of us all but being the cause of it puts a bad taste in my mouth. Taking another's life, I feel, has changed me into becoming more like my father. But I know I'd kill again if it meant saving my brother.

I jump as the door opens. Carmen stiffens in the doorway, her lips pressing together as she looks behind her. Axel is pacing back and forth, rubbing his neck with one hand, his focus is on Gus lying in the bed. I push past her.

My heartbeat rises. Gus's cheeks are hollower, as if he is withering away like a flower without any water.

Axel locks eyes with me, his jaw tightening. "He still has an infection causing a slight fever. We have been trying to keep him cool but without more rain, our barrels are running low."

I bite my lip, grabbing a hold of Gus's clammy hand. His eyelids flicker like he has no strength to open them. "He left me." His breathing quickens. "He left me to die," he croaks. A shiver runs down my arms, knowing who he is speaking about. I wish he didn't care about our father like he did.

My throat tightens. "Shhh, sleep Gus. I'm here." His hand squeezes mine weakly before he lets go and his breathing steadies.

"When will we dock at Yurma?" I ask, standing up and looking anywhere other than at Carmen or Axel. I can't bear to look at them right now, not with how close I am to tearing up.

"We're close. We should arrive by midday, giving us enough time to collect what we need and be back on this ship before daybreak as long as—" Carmen purses her lips, staring at Axel like she's contemplating what she should say.

I look back and forth between Axel and Carmen. They are clearly speaking to each other without words. "As long as what?" I ask, my voice pitching higher than normal.

"I have never met this King Divian, though my uncle has. I'm told it's dangerous even being at the docks. So, we plan to stay away from sight and take the quarter boat to the island instead, hoping it will draw less attention."

I didn't see what the big fuss was about. It's a good idea, keeping the others from stepping foot on the island, and not having to deal with the thievery that's common at the docks. Easier to keep our heads low. "Easy. And how will we get some medicine? I know you can only purchase it beyond their gates. We will have to find a way to get past them."

Axel shakes his head. "I will ask to speak to King Divian. They should let me through."

I walk out the door, not wanting to raise my voice and wake Gus. Carmen and Axel follow. "That's your plan. Do you have any idea how unreasonable that sounds? People lie everyday about who they really are. Yes, you're someone that makes the medicine from Glendora, but that's not going to get you through the gates."

Carmen crosses her arms. "Wait, do you not know who—"

"She's right," Axel says, casting a glance toward Carmen. "I can't just throw my name out like I'm someone of importance. They would see right through me. So, what would you suggest?"

"I know of someone that may be able to help. She may not be there any longer but she's a good place to start."

Dibs and Doolah come with us as we row the smaller boat toward Yurma's docks. Nervous energy hovers in the air. We stay quiet; only the sound of the paddles moving in and out of the water can be heard. I pull down the sleeve of my blouse, covering my tattoo.

Yurma Island appears different than I remember. The dirt roads have been cleared from trash while the buildings look like they have fresh paint. Even the stench in the air has disappeared. That's odd.

"What is it?" Axel asks, gazing around just as I am, his hand resting on his dagger at this waist.

"Nothing. I just remember it being a lot worse here," I state, looking toward the one dirt road I know leads to the Rusty Nail.

Doolah laughs faintly. "It was worse here before?"

"A lot worse, but that doesn't mean anything. I'd watch each other's back while you buy the supplies. What you need is only a few blocks down, you can't miss it. Just keep your heads down and no one should make a fuss." Doolah and Dibs shake their heads in unison, appearing more like the twins they are.

I head north, and Axel follows beside me, smiling and greeting the townsfolk we pass by. I roll my eyes, wondering what urges him to be so welcoming when he doesn't even know these people.

"You know when I told Dibs and Doolah to keep their heads down? I also meant that for us."

Axel smirks. "I don't think saying hello to a few people is going to cause trouble."

I stop, scrunching my forehead and wondering if he is from some fairytale land. "You have absolutely no clue what it's like around these types of places, do you? Like you can't just say hello to anyone or simply walk up to a gate and request the king's presence. Is this what all Glendorans are like? Naive?"

He quirks his head, his mouth tightens. "You're right, I may be naïve, but this is how I have been raised. To greet others, to make them feel noticed and appreciated even if I don't know them. Do you want me to act more like a pirate, like you?"

I give him another eye roll. "You wish," I scoff, and continue walking. My footsteps are loud against the dirt road. Clearly he has never been stabbed in the back before nor had to be cautious of everyone around him. Axel doesn't know anything.

The sign for the Rusty Nail hangs above the door. This door was supposed to open a new life for me. Entering, I'm ready for the wretched smell, but instead there's an aroma of saltwater and fresh pine. The wooden floor no longer has missing boards, and the chairs and seats are full of people laughing and enjoying each other's company.

A vaguely familiar woman greets us. Greta is a completely different woman than I had met weeks ago. Her silver hair is fuller, her gray eyes are bright with life, and her skin seems to glow. Her eyes widen as she sees me, giving me a bright smile. "You're back!" she says, putting down the mug she was drying and slamming me with a hug. My arms tighten to my sides, shocked at the idea of someone being so happy to see me. "Sorry," she says, stepping away. "I just never thought I'd see you again, to thank you."

Axel steps beside me, holding out his hand for her to shake. "I'm Axel. It's a pleasure to meet you."

I grind my teeth; his niceness is getting on my last nerve.

"Why . . . aren't you a kind and handsome one," she says.

Axel quirks his head like he does and gives me a smug look.

"Is this the man you were looking for when you were here last?" she asks, already filling up two glasses of gin for us.

Axel's eyebrows rise questioningly. I ignore him, shifting my weight.

"No. He wasn't." I lean forward, whispering, "I'd like to speak to you in private."

She hands us the glasses of gin. "On the house. Follow me." She walks around the bar, toward the corner with the door where I remember her daughter kept peeking out.

Greta leads us to the back room. It has a small bed and a dresser, nothing fancy but a decent enough place to live. A young girl sitting on a chair in the corner peeks her head up from the book she's reading. Her skin is still white as the clouds, making me question if the medicine helped her, but she stands up and runs to me, wrapping her arms tight around my legs. "Well, I see where you get your strength from," I joke, lightly patting her on the back. "I'm surprised you remember me."

"Mama and I talk about you all the time. The beautiful girl pirate who doesn't destroy but helps others."

I flinch knowing that I almost kept that medicine for myself.

Axel kneels next to her. "Tell me more about this beautiful pirate."

The girl giggles. "She saved us from the bad men and gave us medicine that made mommy and I all better but also gave us coins to fix our home. I no longer have a cough and can play again!"

Axel looks up at me, his blue eyes bright with admiration or something else I can't decipher. "That was very brave of her."

Heat rolls up my back at his piercing yet gentle stare.

I take the shot of gin and clear my throat. "Greta, we need your advice on how we can get past the gates. We are need of some medicine."

Greta places her hand on her chest, above her heart. "Why

dear, you must not know. The gates have been taken down. Heath Divian died not long after you left, and King Lucas is nothing like his father. There is a daily meeting at his court, allowing his people to speak of any concern or need. I know he has been very frugal with what medicine he has left since his father sold most of it. You must go now though. It ends at sunset and there's always a line of people waiting."

This may be easier than we thought. "Thank you for your help," I say, bowing slightly and smiling at the girl. She giggles and runs back to the chair, picking up her book. Its title, *Mermaids Who Once Lived on Land*, catches my attention.

A quick thought branches through my mind, thinking of Illira having legs. I huff through my nose, knowing it's foolish to wish for something that could never happen. I wave to the girl as Axel and I follow Greta back through the bar.

Greta grabs hold of my arm, pulling me toward her, her voice lower. "Keep your eyes out. Those men from last time are still around and like to stir up trouble."

CHAPTER 19

AXEL

We walk in silence from the Rusty Nail. Eleanor appears to be deep in thought, her eyebrows scrunched as she bites the side of her cheek. Her pace quickens.

"You seem to have a knack for saving people," I say, hoping to break the tension.

She stops. Her green eyes sparkle with hues of gold in the sunlight. "What did you say?"

"I said you seem to have a knack of saving people, like a good luck charm to have around."

Her gaze darkens as if I've insulted her. "Have you forgotten I still have a debt to pay for what I have done. I don't know why you are trying to speak to me like we are friends."

"And you don't know how to take a compliment." I reply, questioning how this woman can be so interesting and infuriating all at once. She continues walking, her long blonde braid whipping back and forth as she shakes her head.

She's right, though. We made an agreement that she will take punishment for *The Turbulence's* woes. But after she so recklessly risked her own life to save Gail, I question if she deserves any type of punishment. She barely knew who Gail was, but she jumped off the ship without a second thought. And those marks on her back.

It was no hidden secret she wasn't a favorite on *The Turbulence*.

What kind of monster would do that? I squeeze my fist, thinking of wringing my hands around the bastard's neck.

A building of tall gray stone and glass windows appears ahead of us. Guards in black uniform stand beside the dark wooden doors.

Eleanor approaches one of the guards. "Is this where we can speak with King Lucas?"

They both give a curt nod, opening the wide doors and allowing us entrance.

Inside the large open room are rows of dark brown chairs lining each side of the court. A red carpet leads toward the front where multiple people stand in line. I count a total of five golden chandeliers hanging above us, including multiple wall mounts highlighting the grand exterior with golden statues of men holding a sword across their torso, the tip resting above their heart. With how grand this place is, I start to question what kind of son this man could be. It's pointless to have such pristine elements while his people don't.

Our steps echo through the building as we wait our turn.

Eleanor taps her foot before turning to me. "I'm sorry," she says in a low voice, crossing her arms. "I'm just not used to everyone being so nice to me or anyone complimenting me. And when you told me I was like a good luck charm, that's the opposite of what I've always been told." She takes a deep breath, scrunching her nose like it's painful for her to even say it out loud.

"You don't need to explain anything to me and I'm sorry for calling you good luck. I'll be sure not to in the future."

She shakes her head, grimacing. "No, that is not what I meant. It just caught me off guard."

We stare at each other. Her green eyes seem to be asking for acceptance or maybe something deeper, but I can't quite decipher what it is. I swallow, wondering if she has always had light freckles across her nose and cheeks.

"Next in line, please," a man standing with a red robe hanging off his shoulders calls. The man who was in front of us brushes my shoulder with a huge smile and holding a giant golden staff. "Sell that wisely, Peck, and be sure to have a guard escort you to a seller."

"Thank you! Thank you!" Peck yells, in a joyous step and grinning at the guard who joins him.

Maybe this Lucas isn't so bad after all.

The man with the red robe laughs loudly, lowering his arm. "That was my father's favorite staff. He carried that atrocious thing everywhere. It gives me great joy knowing he must be rolling in his grave." Lucas claps his hands together. "Now, come. I don't mean to be a prude but it's time to eat and it's been a very long day," the new king of Yurma states, waving his hand toward him for us to approach.

He is younger than I thought he would be, maybe in his mid-twenties with sandy blond hair tied in a tight bun that helps enunciate his sharp jawline. He looks at me and then his lips curve slightly as he glances at Eleanor. "Please tell me why you have come. I don't believe I have met you two before."

My jaw clenches and I step forward, not liking the way he keeps glancing back to Eleanor. "My name is Axel Ardanian, son of Gerald Ardanian, ruler of Glendora," I add, bowing slightly.

King Lucas's eyes widen, and he straightens his posture while Eleanor adjusts her sleeves. "It's a great honor," Lucas says. "I never received a letter stating you would be visiting. Simon! Have the maids prepare a room for our guest."

"With gratitude, I shall decline for I have a very sick man aboard my ship and need to get back to him as soon as I can." I keep my voice steady and confident, something my father has taught me since I was young. "I'm here with a personal invitation to the Glendoran Ball, where I'll be announcing my engagement to unite with one of the kingdoms." I take a deep breath. "And with this invitation, I will grant you a full year of shipment of our medication for free. In return, I require one bottle of medicine for the man I have on my ship."

Lucas rubs his chin. "I see. I appreciate a man that gets directly to the point. You know, my father raged about this Glendoran Ball." The king fidgets with a button on his pristine coat. "He waited and waited for an invitation, knowing others had already received them. Father thought the oversight was due to my poor sister. He punished her by locking her in her room, telling her no man would ever want her now. That she disgraced our kingdom." His brown eyes flash with anger. "So, after he died, I've been trying to fix all he made her believe. And now, after all this time, she gets an invitation. I won't use her like my father wanted to so I must decline."

Eleanor clears her throat, her cheeks reddening.

"But that doesn't mean I won't attend. How can I decline an exchange of one bottle for a *year-long* supply for my people. I have heard many things about this island called Glendora, it piqued my interest." He looks back at Eleanor. "And who's this beauty? I'd very gladly have her as my own if she'd take me," he says with a grin that reaches his eyes. Elle smiles back, like she welcomes the idea. A smile I have never seen from her. One that compliments her beauty radiating like the morning sun. Something jolts inside me, wishing the gesture was toward me and not him. I grit my teeth and push the thought away.

"Will you be attending the ball?" King Lucas asks in a smooth voice.

Eleanor raises her chin and doesn't glance at me before stating, "Yes."

Lucas approaches her, his red robe gliding behind him. "Then I ask for one dance at the ball. One dance for one bottle of medicine." He takes her hand, gracing it with a swift kiss. Eleanor doesn't pull away, her cheeks turning a warmer hue.

I grind my teeth, squeezing my toes so I won't make a scene.

"Very well!" Lucas claps his hands together. "Simon, bring me a bottle of medicine for my friends." He walks toward the nearest guard, opening a grand door, the smell of potatoes and meat wafting through. "And I'll be seeing you two in a short time."

Simon returns quickly, setting down the box he was carrying, and opening it up like there are jewels inside. The familiar sapphire bottle lays on a red cushion. I grab a hold of it and slip it into my pocket.

"Thank you, sir." He says bowing toward me and closing the box.

There is no time to waste so Eleanor and I head back to the ship. The streets are dark, lit by only a few lanterns lining the dirt road between the town houses and shops. The smell of food and pastries make my mouth water as a few people walk by with baskets of bread.

"So," Eleanor says curtly, glancing warily at the shadowed streets. "When you told me you're the son of Gerald Ardanian, you couldn't have added the ruler of Glendora?"

"Would you have believed me?" I ask. "Your laughter when I introduced myself before says you wouldn't."

Before she can reply, a man hiding in the shadow's barrels toward Eleanor, knocking her onto her back. He pulls a knife from his back pocket. "Let's start where we last left off," he growls, spit flying as he speaks.

I clench my dagger and step between them, blocking the swing of his knife with my dagger and punching him with my other hand. He splashes into a water trough.

Eleanor is already up, blood trickling down her arm, her stitches have reopened from her previous wound. "We need to move," she says as two other men surround us, holding daggers of their own.

Placing my back against Eleanor's, I move with her as our attackers taunt us.

My mentor's lessons repeat in my mind: always let the opponent make the first move. That will quickly teach you how well the man knows how to fight. One of the attackers, who reminds me of a shaggy dog, makes the first move with his arm far in front of him, pointing it toward my feet. He's no notion of what he is doing as he sprints toward me. The other targets Eleanor.

We push off each other, causing the one shaggy man to trip over his own feet. I slash my dagger along his shoulder. When that doesn't stop him, I grapple with him until he lands headfirst into the dirt. Eleanor already has the other man on the ground. He holds a bloodied hand to his face and keeps groaning "my eye." A few heads pop out of the house windows, looking to see what the commotion is. "Guards! Guards!"

I grab Eleanor's hand and run, swerving between people.

"We demand for you to stop!" yells a guard, too close for my comfort. I look for a way out and find one.

"Do you trust me?" I ask. When I hear a faint "yes," I pull Eleanor into a dark alleyway, and push her up against the brick building. Leaning close to her ear, I act like I'm a lover telling her a secret. When I trace a finger along her jaw, she stiffens briefly but then loosens her shoulders and tilts her chin.

The guards rush past us. One of them yells, "They must have gone that way!" Their footsteps slowly dissipate in a cloud of dust.

We're both breathing loudly, the warmth of our breaths filling the space between us. Her breasts brush against my chest. My lips lightly touch her ear as I move to gaze at her, my other hand still on her cheek. She inhales from the caress but doesn't push me away.

"There never seems to be a dull moment with you." I say jokingly, wondering why those men were after her in the first place.

One of her arms lands around my shoulder, her hand travelling down to my waist, her lips close enough to reach with one movement.

I stiffen and grab a hold of the bottle that's in my back pocket and put it in her hand. I ignore the desire to lace my hand with hers. "Your brother is waiting," I say, stepping away, back toward the dock where Doolah and Dibs wait.

CHAPTER 20

ELLE

By the time we arrive back at the main ship, it's late and most of the crew are already asleep. Axel hasn't said a word to me since we left. He helps Dibs and Doolah carry barrels of food and water onto the ship, letting me go to Gus.

Once the bottle reaches Gus's lips, I feel like I'm able to breathe again, a surge of weight lifts off me.

"We did it, Gus," I whisper, stroking back his brown hair. "You're going to be okay now."

I lay in bed that night, recapping everything that happened in Yurma, especially learning that Axel is soon to be king of an island I barely know about. Not only that, but he will soon be engaged. Ignoring the slight pang of jealousy, I shut my eyes, hoping to sleep it away.

Someone knocks, and I sit up as Axel opens the door, reminding me that I'm in his bed. He smells like fresh peppermint soap and his chestnut hair is wet. "I don't mean to disturb you with it being so late, but I wanted to check on your stitches and also to see how Gus is? The medicine shouldn't take long to start working."

"Dibs redid my stitches and Gus's fever has already gone down," I say, tucking a strand of hair behind my ear, wondering If I should leave and find a cot. "I'm hoping that by tomorrow his wounds won't be as swollen."

"Very good. Then I will leave you to sleep." He turns toward the door but stops to look back at me. "Can I ask you a question?"

I nod my head with a whispered "yes."

Hands in his pockets, he steps closer to my bed. Being this close to him makes me feel a type of electricity through my veins. "Greta said you were waiting for someone at The Rusty Nail, but they never came. Who were you waiting for?"

I bite the inside of my cheek, unsure if I really want to answer. But there's sincerity in his blue eyes, so I decide to answer truthfully.

"I was waiting for a man to tell me where my mother may be," I say, taking a deep breath and waiting for the reprimand that always followed whenever I mentioned my mother. But none came. Somehow, it feels good to speak about her without being reprimanded.

"How long have you been looking for her?" Axel asks softly, hands still in his pockets.

"Too long. She disappeared eight years ago." My necklace—its design a match for the one on all the medicine bottles—still lays on my chest, demanding an explanation. Perhaps someone in Glendora will have answers for me.

Axel runs his hands through his hair, a habit I've learned he does when he's thinking. "I'm sorry you never found her."

"Now it's my turn to ask you a question."

Side dimples appear when he grins. "Very well."

"Who made you those cinnamon honeysuckle muffins you gave me?"

His grin broadens, the emotion reaching his eyes. "I did."

I scoot closer to the edge of the bed. "I can't picture you baking," I say with a laugh.

"Does it surprise you that I can cook?"

"Wait! You asked me two questions, so you still owe me another."

He blinks slowly, waiting.

"Who taught you to make those muffins?"

131

His smile fades, the light in his blue eyes dimmer. "A very close friend of mine."

"Oh," I say, hating to see how such a simple question made him sad. "I only asked because my mother used to make me the same muffins."

Both of his eyebrows rise. "I could show you how to make them when we get back to Glendora. It's quite easy." His smile returns.

I tense, thinking about what will happen when we arrive in Glendora. "But I'm under obligation to cover for *The Turbulence's* crimes when we dock."

He leans forward. "No, Eleanor. You have done enough, saving Gail was enough. When you arrive back to Glendora, you and Gus are welcome to leave, or stay."

Butterflies dance in my stomach when he says my full name.

Axel bids me goodnight, leaving me with more questions than before.

I take a drink of water, letting it soothe my dry throat. My stomach growls in protest. "Oh, hush up. You will get your food." I blurt, taking a short break solely because Dibs demanded I needed to take a break from almost a full day of mopping.

The door opens and a light breeze follows Carmen inside. The smell of beef and beans fill my nostrils. I lick my lips as my mouth salivates.

She stands in front of me, holding the tray barely out of reach. I stretch my neck to take a good look at what she brought. No bugs crawl on the food, nor is it covered in mold, something I became used to on *The Turbulence*. I feel like royalty enjoying a feast at sea. I reach for the tray, but Carmen takes a slow step back.

"I know we started off on the wrong foot, but I'd like for us to get along." Carmen clears her throat, shifting from foot to foot. "To become friends," she says, keeping the tray out of my reach.

My eyes widen. The word 'friends' brings my attention back to her. Carmen looks just as uncomfortable as I feel. I've never really had a friend other than Gus and Illira. Would Dibs and Doolah be considered ones as well? Carmen seems just as stubborn as I and probably won't let me have the food unless I agree.

Perhaps I could agree to two things today: Eat and try to be a friend. *However you do that.*

"Okay, if that's what you want," I say, holding my hands out and hoping Carmen will hand me the tray of food.

"See that wasn't so hard," she says, handing me the tray and sitting next to me, shoulder to shoulder like we are already close.

Apparently, Carmen has no concept of personal space, but I ignore it. I take a giant bite of the beef stew, savoring the flavor and tenderness against my tongue. Juices run down my face and a light moan escapes my mouth.

"Slow down, you're eating like a wild boar!" she says, handing me a napkin.

I give her the biggest eye roll, quickly wiping my chin and taking another bite.

A brush runs through my hair, pulling my head slightly to the side.

Dropping my fork, I swat at Carmen. "What are you doing!?"

"Your hair is a mess. Let me brush it out."

I shake my head so my hair leaves her grasp. "There is no need. I can do it myself later."

"This is what friends do, brush each other's hair."

"Don't you have anything better to do? Maybe you could brush your lover boy's hair instead." I say nonchalantly, even though a burning sensation builds in my chest thinking of them together.

"My lover boy?"

I swat at the brush in my hair again. "Yeah, Axel."

The bed shakes. Carmen's face turns almost as red as her hair and her head tilts back. She bursts into a high pitched full out laugh, thumping the brush against her leg. "Elle, you sure can be funny when you want to be."

I shrug my shoulders, taking another bite of my meal and put the tray on top of the dresser. "I'll clean my dish once I'm done."

"Changing the subject now, are we?"

I roll my neck from the tension building in the room. I really don't care either way but standing in front of Carmen, my emotions seem uncontrollable. Even though he is due to be engaged, it doesn't mean he can't have a fling with someone, and they seem to be close. I need to do something with my hands. As if she can read my thoughts, she holds out the hairbrush. I snatch it out of her hand.

She smiles and appraises me with wary eyes before turning around and swinging her hair behind her back. I bite the inside of my cheek; I've never brushed anyone else's hair.

"Well, if you must know, he is absolutely in no way my lover. He is more like a brother to me and has been in my life for as long as I can remember." Carmen pauses. "The bad and good."

I stay quiet, fighting a knot in her hair and wondering if it would be too pushy to ask more about their relationship.

"Well, he sure is a pain," I mumble.

Carmen scratches her cheek and focuses on her nails. I bite my lip, unsure If my comment offended her and ruined our little moment of conversation.

She sighs, slowly turning to face me. Carmen takes the brush from my hands and starts pulling out the loose hair as if she was the one now needing to keep her hands busy. "You are right about that, but you have no idea what he's done for me or the crew. For the whole island of Glendora for that matter."

My body stills. "What do you mean?"

She stops and huffs a huge breath. "I mean Axel has a lot of responsibilities."

"Yeah, I know. I finally found out he is the soon to be King of Glendora."

Carmen barks out a short laugh. "Yes, but . . ." She pauses. "Everyone on this ship has had their life changed because of him. They all have a story behind why they are here."

My thoughts immediately go to Doolah's long scar on her face, and Fred's missing arm.

I press my lips together, feeling guilty for being so hard on Axel in the beginning.

She smacks her leg, standing. "So how are you feeling? I know you have been through a lot the past few days."

I eye her with confusion, sensing she's hiding something. "I'm fine but it would be nice to finish the food you gave me."

Carmen grabs the bowl of food and sets it on my lap. "Good. You should probably finish that, then wash up and get ready. The music will be starting anytime now."

"Uh, get ready for what?" I say in between bites.

"The crew have decided we need to celebrate our new crew member."

She can't be talking about me. They barely know me, and I haven't been the friendliest. And Gus is still too weak to stand for a long period of time without needing to sit or lay down. "I think I'll pass."

Carmen takes the plate out of my hand. "That's what your brother said when I invited him to attend. Since he's still recovering, I'm going to let him get away with it. But for you, I'm sorry, that's not an option. You said you were feeling good. Besides, why do you think we were brushing each other's hair?"

I look at her with confusion. "Because you said that's what friends do!"

"Did I say that?" she says, putting her hands on her hips.

My eyes and mouth widen debating if Carmen has lost her mind.

"I mean, yes friends do brush each other's hair but really I was helping you get ready because we're celebrating you as the new crew member."

I stand, ready to tell her no, but Carmen is already a few steps out the door, hollering, "Don't fuss, just get ready. Captain's orders!"

The thought of having the whole crew celebrating me as part of the group makes my stomach tighten. I am unable to recall the last time I was included in something. My mind can't comprehend how I should act or feel. Are they not aware that once we make port in Glendora, Gus and I will no longer be a part of the crew?

CHAPTER 21

ELLE

Stomping feet create a steady rhythm for a fiddle's song, and the commotion reminds me I can't stay out of sight forever. Or maybe they won't notice if I never show up. A loud banging on the door quickly answers my doubts.

"Hurry up, Elle! You're missing all the fun!" Dibs hollers.

I frantically straighten my green corset and the white silk shirt underneath, tucking my necklace beneath the fabric. How women can wear corsets daily is a joke, but Carmen explained that it's something you wear for special occasions, like tonight. I brush my fingers through the unbraided waves of my hair that fall past my shoulders.

"Elle!!!" Dibs yells again, pounding non-stop on the door. The amount of eye rolls I have done today has to be a new record. I force myself to barge out the door and leave my fears in the room.

Dibs holds my arm tight, guiding me toward the center of the ship. "Well don't you look fancy."

Yes, I'm right. Today is officially a new record of eye rolls.

"You know if you keep doing that, your eyes are going to get stuck." Carmen says, grabbing a hold of my other arm. Both Carmen and Dibs giggle and warmness replaces the tight feeling in my stomach. Surprised by my emotion, I squeeze their arms in return.

The cool breeze blows through my hair, allowing my nerves to dwindle and my anxiety to subside. As I'm brought closer to the middle of the ship, the cheering gets louder. They're chanting my name. I squeeze tighter to Dibs and Carmen.

I search through the small crowd, nodding as I go by, smiling, secretly looking for Axel. His sky-blue eyes lock with mine and butterflies explode within my chest. My cheeks warm. He smiles, deepening his single dimple.

Standing outside of the circle with the sun setting behind him only emphasizes his strong features. His light brown long sleeve shirt wraps around his muscular arms while his dark blue vest that fits perfectly around his sculpted chest brings my focus to his eyes. His clothing doesn't fit a pirate, but a man with higher status and responsibility. A sick nudge rumbles deep inside me, hollering that no man has a place for my heart.

Carmen releases her hold and climbs on top of a barrel. She waves her arms grabbing everyone's attention and waits for them to quiet down. "Elle." She pauses, making sure my eyes are on her. "We all want to welcome you to *The Blazing Star*. Your determination to finish a task even when you barely eat shows how tough and resilient you truly are."

My cheeks redden as many nod with smirks and pure laughter from the truth of it.

"None of us would be here if it wasn't for you. No matter how long you shall stay on this ship, we consider you one of us."

My back stiffens. I'm on the verge of tears. Dibs bumps me lightly with her hip. The red sash around her head sways with her as it blows in the wind. I swallow, hoping to ease my tight throat and can only nod back to Carmen.

She slowly scans every member of the crew. "I am thankful for every one of you on this ship. Especially Axel, who saw light inside us all when we only saw darkness."

Axel shifts from foot to foot, nodding and smiling at each as if he's remembering each of their stories. Stories that, according to what Carmen told me, he helped create.

Doolah hands over a flask and Carmen raises it above her head. "Here's to another day as part of Glendora and this mighty crew!" Yells of "To Glendora!" follow as a tin whistle and fiddle begins to play.

Another squeeze on my arm and Dibs skips toward a few wooden chairs, plopping into one. "I thought you may want to sit for a bit. I know this kind of came out of the blue and you didn't get much time to rest," she says, bouncing her leg to the beat of the music, clapping.

The music picks up and I watch Carmen, Fred, and Gail join hands while moving in rhythm. The sun is slowly swallowed by the sea and the glow of the moon and the hanging lanterns cast shadows below their feet that portray two dances happening at once.

We only watch them for two songs before Dibs stands and grabs my hand. "Come on!"

Eyes wide, I shake my head as Dibs pulls harder. Doolah shows up and rolls her eyes before grabbing my other hand. I want to tell them that dancing is not my thing but can't due to how hard I am clenching my mouth.

She ignores my silent plea and says, "Let's go!"

My palms are already sweaty. The twins refuse to let go, holding tightly as we join the dance circle. I almost trip over my feet as the tempo increases, trying to follow the rhythm. Carmen bursts out laughing at my clumsiness. An unfamiliar joyous laughter bubbles from me, joining hers.

The joy upon everyone's faces creates a smile of my own that I can no longer contain. I can't remember the last time I smiled so big. The music speeds up as we skip back and forth, breathing faster. I swish my head, tugging away the strands of hair sticking to my face and lean my head back, letting all my hair fall behind me.

I don't want this moment to end. Never once have I ever felt so included.

Alive. Appreciated. Wanted.

We all part and join the circle, stomping and clapping to the music. Dibs jumps into the middle. Her bright green eyes shine and her long black hair flows back and forth as she effortlessly dances.

Doolah joins in, matching Dibs's movements. The beautiful elegance of their dance reminds me of Illira's singing. I picture her song matching the twins' dance, the perfection of how they place their arms, where they hold their legs, and how they flow from one position to the next.

Carmen places a hand over her heart, head tilting to one side. Her eyes swell with tears and tell a story of something I secretly want to know. A pang of guilt hits my gut. *Why haven't I taken more time to know them? To know anyone?*

Carmen said Axel found light when they only saw darkness. Unlike my father who takes advantage of others' grief and past pain, Axel takes them and gives them a reason to continue living. To be happy. To be shown they are worth something. Maybe I can be happy, too?

I'd hide behind others while watching *The Turbulence* crew enjoy themselves, drinking and dancing like there was no tomorrow. Being here makes me question why I ever allowed others to take so much from me. Why did I allow myself to tolerate so many things. I can already hear my brother telling me "I told you so."

The music slows, matching my change of mood. Everyone joins in applauding before either finding a seat to relax or a partner for the slower dance. That's my cue to sit down.

Before I make it to a chair, a hand grazes my arm. "Eleanor?"

The familiar voice and hearing my full name once more makes me go still. Aware of what he's going to ask, I close my eyes and take a slow calming breath. Butterflies build in my lower stomach and channel up to my fingertips. I turn slowly, failing to ignore the heat building in my cheeks. How can a man I barely know make me feel so different?

His bright grin is contagious and warm. I smile back, cheeks and neck now burning hot. His blue eyes focus intently on mine, and he takes my hand in his. Though a small inner voice says I should pull back, I don't.

"Would you like to dance?" Axel asks softly.

My hand instinctively tightens around his and my voice is no-where to be found. I nod. Axel's shoulders and jaw relax as if he was preparing for me to say no. A slight laugh spurts out of me from his uncertainty. Do I make him nervous? As if he heard my thoughts, Axel moves in closer, wrapping his arm around my torso.

The light breeze brings a familiar smell of peppermint and musk mixed with sea salt. A fragrance that always seems to be near since I've been here.

I follow his footsteps. My muscle memory kicks in, remem-bering the dance lessons my mother taught me so long ago. We glide back and forth, his steps matching mine. The tempo rises and he turns me into a slow spin. His eyes shine, matching the bright moon. I look down, afraid he can hear my heart banging against my chest.

If my brother could see me now . . . I wonder who he would be dancing with if he was here. I think of Illira, how if she had legs she would be gliding here with me.

"Looks like you were having fun," Axel says.

I shrug and say, "The musician has a talent with the violin, it's hard not to dance." I glance at the middle-aged violinist as we pass by. His eyes are closed, enjoying every string he plays. His black hair lays flat on his head, his skin more of a golden brown.

"Yes, Charlie is very talented. No one would know he's hard of hearing."

In my shock, I step on Axel's foot. "He's deaf?"

"Yes." Axel continues guiding the dance, seemingly oblivious to my foot atop his.

"But is it safe for him to be on a ship? Isn't it dangerous?" I say, lowering my voice to a whisper, looking around to make sure no one else hears me.

"You said it yourself. Charlie is talented and can do anything we can do." He pauses. "There are other ways to communicate than with just our voices."

"In what ways?"

The right side of Axel's mouth lifts and his hand tightens around my waist. He clears his throat. "Such as using gestures and signs with your hands. It's what I require for all to learn while they work onboard. If Charlie must learn how to communicate with us, why can't we do the same?"

I look back at the violist and see Fred and Gail swaying past him both speaking back to Charlie while making signs with their hands. Charlie nods and resumes the song.

"Can he also read lips?"

"He can. He's also an amazing navigator and has a good eye for incoming weather. He's usually in the crow's nest, probably why you haven't seen him much."

"You seem to have found a strong crew, no matter their circumstances. It's very kind of you," I say.

His eyebrows lift. "First compliment. I'll take it."

"Don't get used to it," I say lightly.

The music stops, changing to a fast song again. We keep hold of each other for too long before stepping apart.

"Would you like to go on a walk around the ship with me?" Axel asks, holding out his elbow for me to grab.

We walk slowly to the back of the ship. The night sky is lit with multiple stars and the glowing moon, but a few threatening clouds darken the horizon. The sea glistens like treasure, ready to be plucked.

"So, what are your plans when we arrive back to Glendora?" Axel asks. "As you know, you are now considered a part of this crew so if you decide to stay, you can. Gus, too, if he wants."

Since my main focus has been keeping my brother alive, I haven't had much time to think about what I want to do. We have nothing of our own, and I know my father is coming after us. I squeeze my eyes shut, blocking the image of my father's silhouette as I sailed away from *The Turbulence*. Illira's warning—*He is coming*—echoes in the wind.

"I appreciate all you have done here and can't thank you enough for getting medicine for Gus. But you don't know Captain Velis like we do. I'm sure he is hunting us down as we speak, and I can't put any of you at risk staying with *The Blazing Star*."

Axel takes a deep breath answering. "Not many know where Glendora is yet. Without an invitation from us giving them the coordinates, many get lost. Besides, we can keep you safe."

I shake my head and, out of habit, hold the pendant of my necklace. "You don't understand. He won't give up until he finds us."

Axel sighs and leans his back onto the railing, facing me. "Why were you the only girl on that ship? Were you forced to stay?"

I know what he's thinking. "No, I wasn't forced to stay. I was born on *The Turbulence*. It's been my home for eighteen years."

Axel fidgets, tapping his finger against the railing, his jaw tight. "What are you saying?"

Is he really going to make me say it? "Captain Velis is my father."

Axel shifts away from the railing and his eyes narrow. He looks as if he just tasted something unpleasant. He watches as I trace the necklace's emblem. "I'm told that many people started to make that emblem into necklaces and rings, believing that it alone will heal them. Is that why you wear it?"

I shake my head, blowing air out of my nose and thinking about how ridiculous that sounds. "No, this was a gift from my mother, given to me when I was a child."

He stills. "Your mother," he repeats. "The same mother that made you honeysuckle muffins and who disappeared eight years ago?"

"Yes," I say softly, wondering what is running through his mind as he leans forward, rubbing his neck.

I squeeze his arm, encouraging him to face me. "What is it? Do you think you know who she is?" My breath comes in shorter gasps, my heart rate spiking. All those years spent wondering and . . . has fate brought me to the answer I seek?

He shakes his head in disbelief. "I don't know why I didn't see it before. Of course you are her daughter, but she never told me she—"

"I swear to the sea gods, Axel, if you don't just tell me!"

"Your mother's name was Gabriella, yes?" he asks.

My heart feels like it's going to burst through my chest. "Yes," I say, my throat tight. Hope brings tears to my eyes. "When we get back to Glendora, could you take me to her? Will she be there?"

The ship rocks back and forth, warm air building around us. Thunder rolls in the distance and a flash of lightning brightens the sky, showing Axel's pained expression. His lips are tight, eyebrows drawn together, looking as if he is about to be sick.

Hope quickly dissolves, swallowed by the same despair I see when I look at Axel.

Axel's shoulders lower and he swallows. "I'm sorry but Gabby passed away."

An invisible wave pushes all the air out of my lungs. I stare at Axel's boots, trying to bring air back into my lungs. My eyes burn and my throat tightens. When I hear more thunder, I start to count, trying to breathe. One. Two. Three. Four. Five. Six. Another strike. The storm is only six miles away, building with rage, just as I am.

His hand gently rests on my shoulder, but all it creates is a burning fire that wants to escape. I flick his hand off, letting out an uncontrollable whimper.

"No!" I scream, trying to suppress the heat building in my chest but it only makes my body shake.

He tries to take another step toward me, but I take one away from him. "She has a son in Glendora. I can take you to him."

My hand responds to his words, slapping him across the face. He's lying.

Axel doesn't flinch. I want him to fight back. Be the type of man that my mother had left me to be around for over half of my life. Instead, he doesn't move, not taking his frustrating blue eyes off me. He opens his mouth but closes it, swallowing his words. Rain hits us like a tidal wave, soaking us both. I hear faint shouts around us and a bell rings from the crow's nest.

Carmen is beside me; her breathing matches mine, but for a different reason. "A storm is coming. We don't have much time before it's on us," she says to Axel, giving me a side glance.

Before I hear another word come from Axel's mouth, I make my way back to the sails.

This storm can try to kill me, but I have an entirely different storm to fight and this isn't it.

CHAPTER 22

ELLE

"**B**low out the lanterns, stow loose goods and the cannons!" Carmen shouts through the uproar of the waves trying to carry her voice away.

One by one the lanterns are snuffed, leaving only the wailing screams of the wind and the occasional sparks of lightning giving us a path to sail by.

I've only experienced the full fury of a storm a few times due to not having enough time to sail out of its unpredictable path. Tonight seems to be one of them. The thought of being ripped apart from the forces within keeps my hands steady as I raise the sails. We need to get ahead of the storm at all costs. I only hope we're not too late.

My clammy wet hands struggle to keep a hold of the sails. My grip falters, my fingers burning as the line slips through my weary hands. A hard chest presses against my cold drenched back, grabbing the rope.

"It's too late! We're in it now. They need to be taken down or were going to be pushed sideways!" Axel yells over the wind.

The thought of the last storm I had to endure creeps into my mind like a plague. So many lives lost. So many screams as men flew across the deck, terrified as the great unknown claimed them.

A man overboard in a storm is a man lost forever. I can't fathom losing one crew member of *The Blazing Star*. They are all too kind. Too thoughtful. Too good.

Worth more than I. If the sea demands one person, it should be me.

Concealing my fear of what may soon come, I help Axel lower the sail, hoping the others across the ship are able to do the same. My biceps are on fire now, my legs ready to slip underneath me at any moment. A rope is wrapped around my waist, cinched tight. Axel's head leans against mine to keep balance. He looks up at me, rain dripping down his nose, his hair flat against his head. He places his hand against my cheek, caressing it with his thumb. "I'm sorry," he says into my ear.

I'm unsure if his apology is for the storm that may soon take all our lives or for what just transpired. Maybe both. My hand instinctively grabs his and I squeeze, trying to keep the fear in my eyes hidden. He leans in and kisses my forehead before disappearing into the dark, a rope dragging behind him, connected to the main mast same as mine.

At this point all you can do is marvel at the forces of nature. We're no longer in control, but are we ever when out at sea? Once we think we are, she takes control and reminds us we are dust. A small speck of sand that can easily be blown away. I hold tight to the rope around my waist as the ship groans from the massive waves crashing against us. Hopefully with *The Blazing Star* being a heavier ship, she can keep upright.

Each strike of lightning illuminates the faces of my new crew. Dibs and Doolah are tying a rope around their waist, holding each other tight. Charlie is not far from them, shivering from the cold and holding to his violin and the mast of the ship. He tries to stay upright as the ship sways more vigorously. Where is his rope? He needs to tie himself to the ship. If he doesn't, he's as good as dead. His feet slip, but he pulls himself back up, his muscles straining to hold on.

I can make it to him. He's not going to let go of that violin. But he can't go this way. He just can't.

A giant burst of lightning urges me to go, lighting my path. I push hard as I can, my full focus on Charlie and refusing to allow the gust of wind to alter my path. The floorboards are slick from the rain, barely giving me enough traction to keep going. Charlie sees me coming and reaches toward me.

"Don't!" I yell, not wanting him to lose his grip. I know he can't hear me, but I hope he can see what I'm trying to say. He ignores me, keeping his hand out. The ship begins to tilt to the right. The weight of the rope around me keeps me from moving faster, my legs burning against the wind and rain. I use the last of my energy and jump toward Charlie's grasping hand. His grip, though wet, is strong as he groans out loud pulling me against him.

Frantically, I try to untie the rope around my waist. I can feel it. Something big building below our feet. *I need to get this off me!* My adrenaline and cold shaking hands only slow me. "Damnit!" I growl, unable to loosen the rope's knot.

Charlie shakes his head and tugs my arm, pointing toward something out at sea. I ignore him and finish off the knot. I wrap it around the mast and Charlie before he can protest. I'm too fearful to look at him, knowing what I'm doing is helping him but hurting myself. I pull the knot tight.

A thunder-like sound builds beneath us. Now I know what Charlie was trying to tell me. A giant wave is preparing to barrel into us. A crack and a moan burst above us as part of the sails crash against the deck. Debris shoots past Charlie and bangs into the side of my head. I have never felt so much pain at once. Warm blood mixed with rain drenches my face. My body begs to collapse, to give into the fear, and let go.

Charlie releases his violin and wraps his arms around me. Ears ringing, I groan, watching his beloved possession fall into the sea as a giant dark wave follows, plunging on top of us.

Charlie whimpers, trying to keep a hold of me. His arms wobble as the sea tries to rip us apart. The massive wave dissipates and we both gasp for air.

My mind is in a daze, vision going in and out, pain pounding in my head, eyes burning. Blood and salt coat my tongue, reminding me I'm still alive.

My feet go out from under me. Charlie no longer holds me, his screams fading farther and farther from me. I slide across the deck, trying to grasp something, anything. My fingers sting as splinters pierce through my skin. Intense sharp pain drills into my leg as I bang into the railing.

I'm so close to death I can smell it. Half of my body is swinging by a thread, ready to plummet into the sea. My hair sticks to my face. I can barely see what's around me, only trying to hold on to the last thing keeping me alive.

The sea is ready to swallow me whole.

"I hate you!" I scream at the violent sea. Ready for this to be over, my hold no longer on the railing, I close my eyes as my body lifts.

Fingernails dig into my skin.

"You're not leaving us that easily!" Carmen yells, holding my leg tight. A moan escapes my lips as I see Axel moving toward Carmen with Dibbs and Doolah behind him, all three still held to the ship by a rope. The corner of my lips lift, thankful to see them still alive before another wave slams into us, jarring both Carmen and I into the railing, creating a loud groan and a crack as it tumbles overboard. Nothing is now keeping me from joining the cold sea except Carmen's hard grasp.

Another burst of lightning lighting the horror on Carmen's face warns me this isn't over. Again, darkness comes, her grip loosening on my leg and moving down to my boot. Her hands shake, knowing at any moment her arms won't be able to hold my dangling body much longer.

"Elle, you must reach for me!" she screams, her red hair whipping back and forth against her face, barely able to keep her eyes open. "Please don't give up!"

My head is spinning, trying to tell myself to reach up for her but my own body denies it. It demands rest. To not keep fighting . . . to only let go.

CHAPTER 23

AXEL

Adrenaline kicks in and my stomach flips as I watch Eleanor dangle over the ship. Waves plow against her, trying to drag her in. She makes no sound as she bangs against the edge of the ship, limp and unmoving. My arm muscles cramp but I push through the fatigue, the rope around my waist pulling against me, restricting how much closer I can get to Carmen.

"She's slipping!" Carmen yells, her voice sounding miles away when she's only a few steps from my grasp.

I can come no closer. Dibs and Doolah are next to me on their toes, one reaching for any part of Carmen to grab while the other tries to pull her rope toward them.

"The weight, it's too much!" Doolah cries in frustration.

My heart beats hard against my chest, knowing what reckless decision I'm about to make. There is no hesitation as I reach down for the small dagger in my boot and begin cutting my rope loose.

A banging noise echoes around us, louder and louder as something barrels closer. But there is no time to worry about anything else, my boots skid against the wet deck, stopping next to Carmen. Holding on to the edge of my rope, I reach for Eleanor and grab a hold of her waist. A groan of relief escapes Carmen as she collapses against Dibs and Doolah, her whole body shaking as if she used

150

every ounce of her strength to keep a hold of Eleanor.

Once Eleanor is in my arms, I hold her tight, not letting go of her cold, wet frame as the wind and waves barrel into us one after another. The woman in my arms is Nile's sister. Gabby's daughter. How could I have not seen it before? Another frigid wave crashes against the ship. The rope burns my hand as it tries to wrench free of my hold. Salt stings my eyes.

Another banging noise echoes across the ship as a large object flaps in the wind. My boots slip and I lose my footing, stumbling to move away from what's about to plummet against us. The ship teeters back toward the sea, its mouth opening to swallow us whole. My hand flares like its being burned from a flame, the edge of the rope leaving my fingertips. I wrap around Eleanor refusing to let her go, as my back meets our watery grave.

Is that all the sea wanted? A life before it would calm its inner core; or did it just want a taste. To take something whole and play with it before spitting it back out.

To believe I'm alive is an understatement. I always thought I'd see the hands of death once I was older, almost welcoming it. Instead, I've embraced it sooner. This was my choice to fall into the thrashing waters. To not let go of Eleanor.

My hand grips on to the floating door that was once part of *The Blazing Star*. The same door that I'd catch myself standing next to late at night, knowing Eleanor was on the other side. An unexplainable tug drawing me to her. I know how meticulously the engravings of the flowers that bloom in Glendora has been engrained into the wood. Where the drawing of the stems will start and the stain of purple begins, becoming brighter and brighter, resembling when they bloom only in pure darkness.

Now Eleanor lays upon it, her frail body barely visible as the thundering clouds hang over us. Off and on the moon appears, allowing a shadow of her face to be seen, blood seeping down her cheek from her head. I move half of my body on top of her, trying to keep the door from tipping up as another wave spurs us up and back down. Placing one of my leathery hands on her head, I locate the cut and apply pressure, hoping to stop the bleeding.

My mind goes elsewhere. Anywhere from wondering what swims beneath my dangling legs in these dark waters. Back to Glendora. Picturing Nile playing swords with Theodore, or racing toward the closest pond to go fishing. But then unwelcome paralyzing thoughts enter. I have broken my promise to return. Realizing I've never had a real wholesome conversation with my father other than what appeases him.

My eyes sting. "No," I grumble out loud. One way or another we will make it back.

The distant rumble of thunder catches me off guard, making me jump from my stupor. My eyes are heavy. The dry half of my body slips back into the cold water, bringing me back to awareness. I try to pull myself back up, grabbing the end of the door close to Eleanor's head and the other over her waist, but as I do the opposite side teeters up, threatening to roll her onto me and into the sea. I grumble about wishing to get my full body out, but I take a deep breath, breathing in and out of my nose and slowly drag my chest up against Eleanor's side. This will have to be enough.

For a moment I search around us, hoping somehow the ship is near. That the ray of light shimming above the horizon will show me the way back. But all that greets me is pure isolation. I lay my chin on the door and watch as Eleanor's chest moves up and down. Her long blond hair is mostly dry and blood coats parts of her cheek. I have been able to stop her wound from bleeding, but I hope it doesn't attract any uninvited creatures to us.

A distant splash of a tail or fin shifts my attention to the opposite side of the door. I'm reminded once more that my legs are dangling freely in the dark water. I slowly reach for the dagger still strapped around Eleanor's waist, pulling it out and ready to strike what is swimming nearby.

The sound of bubbles vibrates around me as a pearl white hand with long nails moves out of the water, resting onto Eleanor's neck. I raise the dagger, hesitating as I take in the familiar wonder that follows.

"You will have to use something stronger than that to kill me," the mermaid says, her green hair swaying against the slow waves behind her. Aware that she is only checking for Eleanor's pulse, I lower the dagger, noticing a slight flinch of the mermaid's hand as I move it away.

"She's alive," I state firmly, trying to keep any hidden fear from my voice.

She keeps her eyes on me, lowering her mouth in the water with a hmmm sound. The sea seems to respond, making the door shift with a slow vibration, the water turning into variations of blue and then stillness. This was not the same sound that I heard her sing when I first saw her on *The Blazing Star*. It was more memorizing, like it could control your every footstep, begging you to join her like a . . . a Siren. But what Siren saves a human? I can sense her protectiveness over Eleanor as she uses her green hair to wipe away the dry blood.

"The ship you were on is a day or so away. Close to land." She pauses, her eyes darker and more potent. "You are lucky I found you; blood can be smelled for miles. I'm surprised it hasn't attracted anything else yet. But I should be able to keep them distracted before I get help. Keep her safe," she says in a low vibrato, one that carries a hint of fear.

"I will," I promise, feeling the need to stay still, that I was not one for her to fear.

She blinks and glances down at where Eleanor holds her necklace and her eyebrows narrow. "There is also another ship not far, but not the one you want any part of." She sighs. "When she wakes, tell her to call for me after sunrise."

Before I can say anything, her head disappears under water. A purple tail flaps in the distance.

CHAPTER 24

ELLE

Saltwater splashes against my face and up my nose, making it burn. I cough it out, recognizing the taste of blood mingling with the saltwater in my mouth. My eyes refuse to open, already feeling the touch of the bright sun against them. I moan, my throat burning as I rock to my side and reach for a solid surface, but it only meets water. Forcing my eyes to open, I see a dark deluge of water ready for me to fall into.

A strong hand grasps my arm before I fully engulf myself.

"Woah there, Eleanor," says Axel.

Another splash of water hits my face, waking me completely. Everything is hazy around me. Pain pulses in my neck and my head feels like it's about to explode at any moment. I squeeze my eyes shut and open them again, hoping my vision is playing tricks on me.

I find myself lying on what looks like a door while Axel lies next to me, though his legs are in the water below. He doesn't say anything but watches me look over him. His right eyebrow is completely swollen and his cheek is blue and purple with a small cut across it. Half of his shirt is torn, his vest dangling on by one loose button. I try to pull myself up, but pain throbs up my leg and into my thigh when I attempt to move it. A spark of horror runs through me as I finally realize where we are and what trouble we are in.

"Don't move. I've barely been able to keep you on this thing," he says, steadying his hand across me to get the door to stop rocking.

"But . . ." I'm frantically searching around me for anything that gives me hope of survival. Sun glitters on top of the water. It would be beautiful if we were not stranded in the middle of pure death. This isn't good.

"The ship?" I ask, trying to control my breathing but go frantic as his clear blue eyes darken, telling me everything I need to know.

He shakes his head, his hair in a fray across his forehead. "I haven't seen it since—" He pauses, licking his cracked lips.

My mind races, thinking of Dibs and Doolah. Carmen. Charlie. Gus. "Do you know if everyone was able to stay on the ship?" I ask, hoping my worst fear isn't true.

"As far as I know, they were strapped to the ship. There haven't been any signs its destroyed." He says firmly, like he wants to believe what he is saying.

If my memory serves me right, Axel was also tethered with a rope. "You were also. I remember."

Axel takes a deep breath, focusing on the engraving I lie upon before glancing back up to me, his lips parting. "I just couldn't."

Heat builds within my chest. My thoughts scramble to understand. "Couldn't what?" I ask, my voice rising and giving me an immediate headache.

He shakes his head, his blue eyes never leaving mine. "Leave you to the storm."

The insanity that leaves his mouth makes me want to laugh and scream. "Well, now you have signed your death warrant. I am of no importance to you. You should have let me die."

This time Axel meets my raised voice with a huff of a laugh. "That's not true. You are important." He shakes his head again, jaw clenching as his lips tighten, like he's trying to keep from saying more.

A rush of memories hit me at once. My mother. She's dead and

Axel knew her. I have another brother. All this time Axel has had a life with them. I consider berating him, to yell about the depth of hurt I'm experiencing. But my body tells me to conserve my energy. To rest. My head spins like it's been beaten by a rock while my leg throbs each time I tense my muscles. So I say nothing more and beg for sleep, closing my eyes.

When I wake again, it is to the soft touch of moonlight. A splash of cold water hits my arm. Axel is still next to me, his teeth chattering and he's pulled himself up more. Half of his body sways in the dark water, like bait. A groan leaves my throat as I look to see if there is any room I can give him without us both falling.

The only way it will work is if I lay partially on him. He rests his head on his arms and his body shivers, the door moving with him. I clench my jaw, knowing I can't leave him like this. Even if it may leave us in an uncomfortable position.

Slowly, I lift myself, trying to stay steady by grabbing hold of both sides of the door as it sways back and forth.

"Don't. You will flip over," Axel says in a soft, stern voice as he lifts his head.

I can see him enough to notice he can hardly keep his eyelids open. "You can't stay in the water, it's not safe."

He says nothing, not denying it as the sounds of water lightly lap against the door but doesn't move. "You're getting on here with me, there's enough room," I demand, grabbing a hold of his arm, coldness shooting up from his touch to my hand. I bite my lip when he doesn't follow through. "Please," I say softly.

I'm afraid he will continue to ignore me when he says, "We can try. But if it starts to tip over, just leave it."

"Fine," I say, keeping a hold of his arm. I scoot closer to the middle, balancing myself and bracing to help pull him up. "Ready?"

He shakes his head, teeth chattering as he counts, "One, two, three." I pull him toward me, trying to keep my weight on my side as the door creaks and moves down into the water from Axel's weight. His grip weakens for a short second. "Keep going!" I demand. My side lifts more but I lean away from Axel, letting my legs fall into the water as he finally pulls all the way up and quickly flips onto his back.

I grip tightly to the edge of the door, my butt barely staying on the wood. My legs scream for warmth. By the sea gods, how is Axel able to move? Now that he is on his back, he opens his closest arm toward me. "Okay, you can lay down now."

There is nowhere else to go but into his arms. I can either stay seated like this or commit.

"I promise I won't bite," he says playfully, making me forget for one second that we lay in the middle of the open sea. Challenge accepted.

"If you did, I'd bite right back," I reply before laying on my side, placing my head on his firm shoulder. Not missing his slow smirk; his one dimple appearing as I decide to keep my arms to my sides. Axel's arm wraps around my waist, steadying me as the platform sways. But even after it stops, his arm never leaves.

The brush of his stubble tickles against my forehead. "Your friend came by," he says plainly, as if we were talking about how bright the stars were now shining upon us. I glance up at him, body warming at how intimate this feels as we speak to one another. His lips are so close to mine.

"Illira? When?" I ask, wondering how she had the courage to come so close to another man.

His arm around my waist shifts and his thumb lazily caresses my side. "While you were asleep. She said you need to call for her at sunrise."

If it's not too late, I think to myself. Who knows what may be stalking us in these waters at this very moment, but I keep that to myself. One does not survive something like this. Even if she brought help, it would take days. Without thinking, as if my conscious demands comfort, my arm slides across his stomach, needing more contact.

My hand graces his opposite arm, feeling multiples scars and uneven skin beneath it. Axel stills. I slowly slide my hand down his arm, waiting for him to pull away but he doesn't. Remembering when I last saw him shirtless, he had fabric wrapped around this bicep.

He answers my silent question. "It's from a fire when I was younger," he says, letting me leave my hand resting upon his scars. "Don't worry, it doesn't hurt anymore."

"I'm not worried," I reply, hoping to break this moment that almost feels too personal. Too much like we want to speak about things we like to keep hidden. He breathes out his nose with a silent laugh, his thumb once more moving against my waist, like he's giving the okay to ask what I want. And there is one question, that's now burning inside of me. "Did she?" I pause, feeling like a lost child begging for breadcrumbs. "Did she ever speak about me?"

Axel takes a deep breath, pulling me in tighter. I move my head more onto his side, watching the stars as he speaks.

"She had her secrets. There was a time, when she was still pregnant with Nile, I'd find her late at night leaving the house. I was never sure why but one day I decided to follow her. I found her standing in the sand, staring out at sea like she was searching for something, holding tight to a similar necklace to yours. I finally had the courage to ask her, and she told me that she had done things in the past she regrets and had to make a choice no mother should have. But that's as much as she would say."

Silent tears fall from my eyes, wetting his shoulder.

Axel swallows and I focus on his chest moving up and down as he breathes. Focusing on his steady heartbeat, trying to calm my own. "Gabby is the one that asked if the symbol of the moon and stars could be put on all the medicine bottles that left Glendora. I never knew why it was so important until now. I wish she would have just told me."

I bite my lip, trying to control the tightness in my throat. A spark ignites inside, like a hidden flame in my chest that has been in darkness ready to be released. Knowing that she is the one that pressed for those symbols to be on the medicine gave me some comfort that she did care. That she in some way loved me. I release the tightness that's been inside of me for eight years in one long exhale.

It's silent for a few moments. A soft breeze moves past us. I don't move away from him, nor him from me, as we settle into each other's arms, knowing we are only using each other for some sort of comfort.

"Our ship, *The Blazing Star,* is named after a popular flower that grows in Glendora." He pauses as he takes a deep breath. I wonder why he's telling me this but continue to listen, enjoying his soothing voice. "They were your mother's favorite. I'll show you them someday."

I nod against his chest, knowing it will never happen but make a longing wish as a star shoots across the shimmering dark sky.

I wake from a slight nudge, sprinkles of light appearing above the water greeting me. Sunrise. My throat begs for moisture, for water but I know what I must do.

"Are you feeling up to calling your friend?" His voice cracks with the question and I hear his harsh swallow. We need drinkable water. My back aches as I lean up on to one arm, my shadow shading Axel. I lick my lips, my head throbbing with pain and begging for me to lay back down.

Swallowing to create more moisture in my mouth, I begin to sing the same song that Illira taught me so many years ago. I close my eyes, feeling Axel's intense gaze on me. I pour out what I can and let the song flow through me into the very sea. Hoping it's enough for her to know where we are and guide a ship back to us. I reopen my eyes. Axel appears to be in complete awe, his bright blue eyes wide, matching the clear morning sky.

"That was beautiful," he says in a low, admiring voice.

He looks at me as if I've done some miracle, his mouth slightly open before giving a small grin. The bruise on his cheek looks less purple but the swollen bump above his eye hasn't lessened. I want to ask if it hurts but think better of it and lay back on my side onto his shoulder. "It's nothing," I state, already feeling the morning heat against my skin.

He huffs a laugh and murmurs. "I wouldn't call that nothing."

"Don't," I say, moving my head closer to him to shade my face.

"Don't what?" He asks, moving his chin down to look at me. Knowing his warm blue eyes await mine, I lower my head more.

I clench my fists, wanting to suppress what's been whispering in the back of my mind. "Don't act like there is something fascinating about me. We wouldn't be in this mess if it wasn't for me. I'm bad luck and now you will die because of it."

His callous hand rests against my cheek, a soft request for me to glance up at him. So I do, even though I'm afraid to see pity looking back at me. Instead, it's his sunburned face and neck with cracked lips but his blue eyes radiate with affection.

"You are not bad luck," he says firmly. "You are the most magnificent and strong woman I have ever met. Gabby would be proud."

I swallow back my tears and nod before his fingers leave my cheek and he lays his head back down. We don't say much for the rest of the day, both going in and out of sleep. My stomach growls but I ignore the hunger pains. Sometime when I was asleep Axel managed to take off his vest and create a partial shade for us by laying it across his knee and covering our heads. It's given some relief, but it doesn't keep away the threat that will soon submerge us both.

CHAPTER 25

AXEL

Darkness once again. The moon and stars hide between frays of dark gray clouds. The only thing keeping me from losing hope of being found is having Eleanor's body next to mine, her arm once again around my chest. I have to believe that we will survive this, that we will be found.

A large splash catches my attention. Sprinkles of water land on us. Eleanor jolts from her sleep and grips my arm tightly for support as the door rocks from the wave the nearby creature made.

Multiple clicking sounds echo below us. Eleanor relaxes against me. "Whales," she whispers with relief. Goosebumps slide along the back of my neck as we both lay in awe, listening to their elaborate songs ranging from low moans to high-pitched whistles. I'm thankful to listen to the symphony of the sea, trying to not take notice of the spread of the ocean journeying as far as I can see and instead imagine Glendora's vibrant soil only a step away.

Eleanor flinches and I wonder if she has fallen back asleep. I move my chin to look down on her as the moon looms between the clouds, noting the freckles across her nose and cheeks. They remind me of the multitude of stars from last night. Regret creeps into my mind, wondering if any of the women I was supposed to meet would be anything like Eleanor. Doubt tugs at my mind.

"Can you tell me about Nile?" she asks in a soft whisper, her eyes still closed.

I take a deep breath, not liking how weak and hoarse her voice sounds, wishing for any type of moisture other than the expanse of saltwater surrounding us that we cannot drink.

"He is a lot like you. Brave, adventurous . . . opinionated," I add, hoping to get a chuckle from her but instead silence. I clear my throat, thinking about what all I could tell her about Nile. He is such an open book compared to Eleanor. "He doesn't seem to know the word fear. He loves to climb to the very top of trees just so he can see what the birds see." I hear a faint, amused huff from Eleanor. "I'm unsure where he gets all his energy. He is either chasing frogs, riding his horse, or catching fish but I'm happy he has so many things to enjoy, even after—"I pause. "After Gabby passed away."

I feel her distance herself from me even though she is tucked close to my side. "Who's been taking care of him since she left?" she asks, a crack in her voice.

"I have," I whisper. She doesn't say anything, so I continue. "He has freckles on his nose and cheeks, same as you. More seem to appear every summer since I can barely get him to come inside. Don't be surprised if he tries to drag you everywhere with him," I add hastily, thinking maybe it can be some type of purpose for her to hold on to.

But she stiffens, moving her arm that lays across my chest back against her side. The missing contact is too stark.

"Stop saying those things, like we are going to make it." For the first time she turns away from me, flipping around to her other side before the door can move into the water. "I need a minute." Her voice sounds tense, like she can't trust it.

My mouth opens and closes, wanting to give her some type of comfort but nothing comes out. Whales continue their songs until they even disappear into the vast ocean.

Before my eyes succumb to sleep, my mind plays tricks on me as a distant star appears. It dances on top of the water until it vanishes into the roaming clouds.

CHAPTER 26

ELLE

A shuffle of voices gathers above me with shouts of my name sounding so near and yet distant. I keep my eyes shut, believing I'm being haunted in a dream. Gus calls for me again and again.

"Stop," I rasp, feeling the door rock back and forth before it thuds against something that steadies it.

Water splashes against my face, spurring me to turn up toward the bright sky.

"Eleanor," Axel says faintly before I force my heavy eyelids open, not wanting to wake up to another day at sea. But as I do, a ship appears swaying next to me, a blur of faces peering over the railing. I lift to my elbows, wondering if I have officially lost my mind.

I place my hand onto the side of the ship, feeling solid roughness of its mass. "It's real," I say out loud, my throat hoarse.

"Hold on, Elle!" Gus yells as I look back up to the top of the ship. I squint, trying to see through the gray curtain that has become my vision. I focus on Gus's voice, knowing the tall familiar silhouette above is his.

The tight, stiff feeling of my lips restricts the faint smile I give him. But pain greets me again as it gathers up my neck and throbs against my skull, the gray curtain now turning to full black.

Warmth engulfs my entire body, relaxing my strained muscles. I take a slow deep breath through my nose as I snuggle into the warmth. I'm welcomed with a tight squeeze. The familiar smell of peppermint and musk awakens my senses. I stiffen. Thoughts swirl, trying to remember where I am. The last thing I remember is everything spinning around me and trying to focus on staying upright . . .

Axel.

I slowly force my eyes open, but no arms are around me. Did I dream of him lying with me?

"Elle." he whispers, but the voice isn't Axel's, it's Gus.

I scoot up on a bed, noting I'm in an unfamiliar cabin, my head pounding. I take a deep breath, thankful to be anywhere else than that uncomfortable door. Gus sits on a stool next to the bed, his eyelids heavy.

"I thought I lost you," he says, leaning back in his chair and staring at the ceiling thoughtfully.

I tug the blanket over my chest, noticing I'm only in my undergarments. My necklace is cold against my skin. Memories of what transpired before the storm rush in, making me dizzy. I wish his skin wasn't so pale, that his cheeks were fuller, and that his glint of mischief had already returned.

"You were right," I say, wondering how I'm going to tell him about our mother.

His eyebrows narrow. "About what?"

"Our mother," I say faintly. A roll of sickness grumbles in my stomach.

He rolls his neck and breathes out his nose. Gus scoots to the edge of his seat, hazel eyes more aware than I have seen since he was hurt. "I know, Elle. I know about Nile, too, but we can talk about that later. You're dehydrated and need to rest."

I bite the inside of my cheek, my jaw tense.

"Our father can never know," I groan as more pain surrounds my head pulsing where I feel a large bump.

My vision blurs, but I need to finish. "We have to keep him safe," I say before I hear a faint "Land!"

The slam of a carriage door briefly wakes me. Horses nicker. My arm is around Gus's shoulder as we walk toward a white house with long pillars. A young boy rushes toward Axel and jumps into his arms and I note the small freckles across his face. His sweet laughter fills my chest with joy before I am once more taken into darkness . . .

Peppermint. Honeysuckle. Musk. Salt.

I can smell it all.

Sunlight beams onto my eyelids but I don't want to open them. I don't want to wake up to what is no more. The light isn't real. I know once I open my eyes, more darkness will find me. It always does. It never leaves. Bad luck echoes in my mind repeatedly, drowning me.

But then a hint of something soft and soothing takes over. Something young and carefree. Something almost familiar. A small, warm hand wraps around mine.

"Do you think the medicine is helping?" a young boy's voice asks with concern.

Could it be? My heart tells me yes, but my brain tells me no.

I'm lying in a bed I've never been in. In an actual room, not a cabin on a ship. I'm on land. On solid ground. My eyes burn, trying to focus on the boy sitting next to me. *He looks so much like . . .*

"Gus?" I moan, barely able to get the words out. My bottom lip is more swollen than I remember.

"We will come back later, Nile. She needs rest," Axel says from my other side.

Frantic, I hold tight to the little hand. "Wait!" I croak. In no way is this young man going to leave my sight. The room is silent as I capture every detail of his face, noting how his familiar hazel eyes are doing the same. His light brown hair falls a tad past his small ears and, like me, a few freckles dot his nose and round cheeks. No doubt a favor from the sun. He looks to be taller than most eight-year-old boys that haven't quite grown into their body yet.

I smile, remembering how gangly Gus was before he sprouted into his more masculine form.

Nile nervously smiles back, his cheeks turning a light pink. A faint laugh escapes me. "What's so funny?" he says, bouncing closer to me.

"You look so much like your brother," I whisper, my eyesight blurry.

Nile wraps his arms around me. I close my eyes and take in the warmth of his hug, his hair smelling like daylight and cinnamon.

"Well, aren't you friendly," I say lightly as the muscles in my arms protest, hugging him back.

Nile pulls back, looking more concerned than any kid should be. "Mom always said hugs can fix sadness."

The word 'mom' stings with jealousy, knowing that he most likely was able to say goodbye before she . . . *Don't. Not right now.*

"She was right. You give very good hugs," I say, ignoring the nonstop pain in my head.

"Axel says soon my hugs are going to be stronger than his," Nile says, looking up at the man standing next to me.

Axel catches my eye and smiles slightly. Dark circles mar the skin below his eyes but the bump on his eyebrow is gone, only a slight discoloration on his cheek remains. He goes to his knees, meeting Nile's gaze. "You are absolutely right," he says, shagging Nile's hair. Nile giggles and grabs a hold of Axel's arm, pushing it back. Axel pretends he has no strength and falters, a carefree gleam momentarily shining through.

Axel clears his throat. "Nile, I need you to go find Carmen and tell her Eleanor awake."

"But I've barely gotten to talk to her!" Nile pouts, crossing his arms in defiance.

"And you will, but I need to speak to her alone for a moment," Axel says, standing.

Nile bites his lip as it starts to quiver.

"Heyyy . . . it's okay. We're going to have all the time in the world to spend together," I say, giving him a few scratches on the back.

Nile sighs, gives me one more hug, and slowly walks out the door.

My back muscles start to ache as I pull myself up to lean against the headboard. "He acts like I'm not a stranger," I say, still staring at the door Nile just left through.

Axel swallows. "He's friendly to a fault."

I bite my cheek, trying to contain the tears. Why did it have to take so long for this to happen? Why couldn't it have been in a happier scenario?

"How is your head feeling?"

"It's . . ." I touch my head and feel bandages wrapped around it. "Okay."

"You were hit by some debris. Thankfully you didn't break your neck." He sighs and moves the blankets above my thighs, his fingers brushing my skin. I shiver, feeling goosebumps tingle up my body.

"You also banged your leg up pretty badly." From my calf to my thigh is a giant dark purple and blue bruise that were hidden by my pants while we drifted at sea. There are even a few deep scratch marks, courtesy of Carmen's nails digging deep into me when she attempted to keep me from falling overboard. "We don't believe you broke it, but it may hurt to walk for a while."

I run my finger down the marks, remembering how easily I gave up before Carmen grabbed my leg.

"How long have I been here?" I hesitate to ask the next question, afraid of what he would say. "Is everyone alright?"

"You've been in and out for a couple of days." He stops, voice softening as his eyebrows narrow. "Sadly, we lost Perkins."

"Oh." I remember meeting Perkins a day after taking the ship, him offering me his seat. I only hope his death was quick. "And Charlie? Did he lose . . ." I shudder, thinking how lost he must feel losing something so precious to him. I still can hear the beautiful music he played. So flawless and enchanting.

Axel's shoulders stiffen and his jaw hardens. "Objects can be replaced but not people. You saved him. That's what matters."

I can tell he wants to say more but instead runs his fingers through his hair.

He's right. The violin can be replaced but I don't like the fact that Charlie lost something so special to him. Even if it was just a violin. I reach for my necklace and find it around my neck. Feeling guilty I still have my possession, I fiddle with it. Both Axel and I are quiet, only the sound of wind blowing through the trees through an open window can be heard.

My cheeks redden, feeling Axel's full focus on me. Days ago, he and I embraced each other out at sea. But now that we are here, I remind myself that we were forced to hold each other only for survival. None of it means anything more.

I look around the room, pretending to be interested in what I see. The bedroom is twice the size of the small cabin I lived in on *The Turbulence*. The floor is a brown oak with a cream-colored rug that matches the curtains. Purple flowers in multiple yellow vases painted with small butterflies are placed throughout the space, contrasted by wall painted to match the blue sky. It almost feels like I am lying outside in a garden.

Axel fidgets with his dark green vest. "Gabby decorated the room," he clears his throat.

How am I supposed to take that? My mother decorated a room while I was searching for her, fighting to survive. I bite my cheek.

Tension fills the space between us. Axel takes a seat, resting his elbows on his knees and leans forward, close enough I could touch him if I wanted to.

My body instantly warms, remembering this man's arms around me. The only arms that never made me feel threatened. There's nowhere else to look but into his entrancing eyes, or down at my blanket, so I choose the latter.

He nudges my chin, softly tilting my head up. It's a move of his that makes my lower stomach flutter. His icy blue eyes set on mine, his lips firm. "I know you're upset, but I promise that I'll do whatever in my power to help you and Gus to feel welcome here," he says in a deep voice.

Things will never be the same. My mother is gone and nothing can change that. And being known as pirate won't make it easier for others to adjust to my presence. *Will Glendora be just as open as Axel and the crew of The Blazing Star be?* Either way, I now have a younger brother who needs me. A brother I would have never known if not for Axel. A battle begins within myself, threatening to hold this pain and anger while a small part of me wants to just let it go. I can feel it ready to burst like a kernel ready to pop. In so many ways I want to give in to this pulling feeling that I have toward him.

Axel's breathing quickens and his cheeks slightly redden.

I don't want this . . .

I don't want this . . .

My hands clench the blankets, fighting against the urge to move forward.

When I take a deep breath, his scent fills my nostrils. So warm and safe. I bite my bottom lip, too scared to let my true feelings escape. How can this man be so business-like one moment and then look at me like he would burn the world for me the next? His intense expression changes to a wonder of exploration, looking from my lips to my eyes.

"Tell me what you need," he says softly, his voice like silk slowly running along my skin.

I could let myself break free into his plump, beautiful lips. I wonder what it would feel like.

Distant laughter comes from the other side of the closed door.

Axel tenses and leans back, moving away from me. I grab a hold of his arm as a few strands of hair fall into my face. "Can you take me to her?"

He tucks the stray hair behind my ear, his finger grazing my neck. "Yes. Just tell me when and I will."

I whisper "thank you" as the door bursts open. Axel resumes his business stature. Nile breathlessly scrambles on the bed while Carmen follows behind with a tray of hot tea.

"Well, looky here! Miss sleepy head finally decided to wake from the dead," Carmen says, pouring some tea. "Here, some chamomile. Should help with the headache."

I take a gulp and cherish the warmth flowing down my dry throat. "Thanks, I needed that," I say with a small smile.

"That's what friends are for," she says, giving my hand a tight squeeze. Her calling me her friend still feels awkward, but I try to embrace it. "Now, I actually have a bath ready for you, so the boys need to leave." She eyes Axel and Nile.

"That's not fair! I just got back here!" Nile says, folding his arms.

"I know but don't you want your sister to get all cleaned up so she can play with you later?" Carmen asks.

So, Axel must have already told him about me and Gus.

"Well . . . uh . . . yeah . . ." he says, though he appears bothered by the thought of leaving me again.

"I can't wait to play with you Nile, but Carmen's right. I probably should get cleaned up. You don't want a stinky sister, do you?" I say, nudging him and making a yucky face.

Axel walks around the bed and holds his hand out. "It's also time for your riding lesson. I think Drako would miss you if you didn't visit him today."

Nile takes his hand and hops off the bed. "Okay, I'll go to this one, but Elle and Gus need to ride with me next time."

My eyes widen. Riding a horse terrifies me more than a raging storm. I have never understood how others can fully trust an unpredictable animal that could kill them with one kick.

I scramble for a reply and look to Carmen, begging by widening my eyes in hopes for her to find a way out of this situation. *Anything but ride a horse.*

Carmen smiles mischievously. "What a good idea, Nile! I'm sure Elle would love it, too."

"Please!! I promise you will love it! Mother always rode with me," he says.

I look at Axel for help but he only nods, clenching his mouth. I have no clue how I'm going to ride a horse, but I guess I will if it makes Nile happy.

"Okay, I promise," I say, trying to look more enthused than I really am.

Nile yells, jumping up and down and yanking on Axel's arm.

"Now, shoo! Shoo! I could smell Elle all the way from the hallway."

"Gross," Nile says, plugging his nose and walking out with Axel.

Carmen watches the door shut and turns around, putting her hands on her hips and scrunching her eyebrows together. While her deep brown eyes almost seem to be glowing with fire, matching her bright red hair. "What was that about?!"

I move slowly out of bed, noticing that someone had put me in a cream-colored nightgown. "I agreed to riding a horse, what else should I have said? And what is this?" I ask, running my hands down the silky cloth.

Carmen grunts, clearly annoyed with my last question. "On the ship! You almost got yourself killed!"

"Oh, it . . ."

"It was stupid! That's what it was!" she says, giving me a death glare. "Do you not understand what it would have done to Gus? To Axel? To the crew?"

Carmen glares at me, waiting for my reply. I bite my cheek, looking up at the ceiling. What did she want me to say? *Maybe I'm tired of always fighting.*

I stare back at her, hoping she had calmed down, but she is still the fiery red head from a moment ago. My eyes roll and I fold my arms.

"I swear, Elle, if you roll your eyes one more time!"

"Ok!" I spat. "I'm sorry." I pause, my throat tightening. "And thank you for the claw marks. Maybe someday I can return the favor," I retort, feeling more like myself again.

Carmen leans forward. "Maybe every time you look at them, it will be a reminder that we don't give up. That you have people that care for you."

My mouth opens and closes, shaking my head. "You guys barely know me," I whisper.

Carmen sighs. "You don't have to know someone for a long time to care for them. And remember, we are your friends," she says, throwing a bar of soap into my lap, the scent of honeysuckle wafting from it.

I stare at the reddish pink soap, the fragrance bringing back memories from my past. "Thank you," I say, making a point to look as sincere as I can.

"You're welcome," she says, walking to the door. Hand on the knob, her shoulders slump and she turns around. "You should be thanking Axel."

I raise my eyebrows. "For what?"

"I may have given you those nail marks but when that wave hit us all, Axel didn't give a second thought as we all watched him hold you before plummeting into that ocean." She wrings her hands together.

My limbs feel heavy. I grip my arms and find bruises in the shape of hand marks. No wonder they feel so sore. Axel risked his own life to save me. They all did.

"I thought I had lost you both." Carmen looks outside the window. "He has barely left your side since," she said faintly. "And I'm not sure if Gus is a fan of it," she adds.

I run my hands over my face, not wanting to go over what

transpired on the ship. Thinking of Axel deciding to go overboard with me creates a rise in my stomach.

"I am aware of what he did, but he shouldn't have."

Her mouth opens in shock. "I'm going to be pretend I didn't hear that. He made a choice. A choice that many would be too scared to make. Just be easy on him, Elle. That's all I ask."

This isn't the first time Carmen has asked me to be easy on Axel. Once I offer an affirmative nod, Carmen walks out. I bend my knees to my chest, pain radiating up my right leg. Pain that will soon heal and be nothing but a memory. The pain I'm more concerned about is the one pumping through my veins into my heart. A heart that would have stopped if not for Axel.

CHAPTER 27

ELLE

The bathroom is like stepping into a rose garden. The wallpaper has white, red, and pink roses blooming in lush cascades. Candles are placed around a clawfoot white tub that is filled with bubbles and sunlight from a large window heats the room. A tall white mirror stand is in the corner, allowing me to look at myself fully. I barely recognize the girl.

My cheeks are more pronounced, clearly bringing out the weight that I have lost. My bottom lip is a dark red while my legs and arms have bruises and small cuts. I unwrap the bandage around my head, my blonde hair sticking to it. I have a small bluish bump on the right side with a few stitches. I run a brush through my hair, untangling it where the bandage was and making sure not to pull too hard around my injury.

The sweet warm fragrance embraces me as I immerse my body into the water, leaving my head out. I sigh, not remembering the last time I had an actual bath. I can already feel my muscles relaxing. The thought of staying in this room for the rest of my life is tempting as I slide farther down, putting my whole head under water. Holding my breath, I can hear my heartbeat echo as if the water itself was alive. Breathing.

Thump . . . Thump . . . Thump . . .

I'm still breathing but my mother is not. It isn't fair.

I squeeze my eyes, banishing my thoughts and holding my breath for as long as I can. I burst up, gasping for air and clenching the sides of the tub. In and out, my chest fills back with oxygen.

As if the water has instantly turned to ice, my naked body shivers. But that isn't it. It is still warm; the honeysuckle fragrance is still there. My inner self is turning against all that I am trying to hold back. Fighting to stay in control. *I'm stronger than this.*

The pain of loss is almost too hard to bear, ready to claw out of my skin. I wrap my arms around my knees and cry. I let go of the hope and thoughts of how things might have been. It is over and there is nothing I can do about it. I squeeze harder, trying to hold back the scream that is at the tip of my tongue. Instead, my sobs become louder, and I start hiccupping, trying to catch my breath as my chest tightens.

Rocking back and forth, the water splashes against my back and out of the tub. I glide my arms down my legs, feeling the deep scratches along my shins.

My body feels drained, like I'm trying to move through thick mud. I'm beyond tired. The energy I once had is gone and barely enough to get myself out of this tub. So, I lean back into the bath and let the remaining tears fall silently.

A couple of hard knocks wakes me.

"Eleanor?" Axel hollers from the other side of the door. The knob jostles loudly.

My lips and toes are numb. The candles next to the tub dwindle and barely any sunlight is coming through the window. I stay quiet, hoping he will just leave.

The knob shakes again with more urgency. "I'm giving you five seconds to open this door or I'm coming in." Silence. "Don't think I won't do it. I have a key!" he warns, banging onto the door once more.

Yeah, he's not changing his mind. I hustle, grabbing a nearby towel lying on a chair.

He comes in.

"That was not five seconds!" I yell, still standing in the tub and barely covered by the small blue towel that was apparently meant only for my hair.

"You didn't answer," he says, looking at my towel and then at anything but me, his cheeks turning a light pink.

"Well, I fell asleep, and you barely gave me any time to respond," I say, goosebumps crawling up my skin. He doesn't move. Water drips from my hair and back into the tub. His gaze lingers on my exposed thighs, slowly lifting to my neck, and stopping at my lips.

I bite the inside of my cheek, body heating alongside my awareness that only a small flimsy towel covers me.

He swallows and quickly turns around so his back faces me. "My apologies, you had just been in here for quite a while and when you didn't answer . . ." He puts his hands through his hair and takes a deep breath. "I panicked."

I rush out of the tub and wrap a larger towel around me. "You should find better things to do than worry about me."

"I can assure you I have many things I could be doing rather than worrying about you," he says, irritation creeping into his voice.

"All it seems like you've been doing lately is coddling me or trying to save my life, so..." I bite my lip, knowing I shouldn't have said that. I can't seem to get rid of this man. But inside me a light seems to glimmer a bit more when he is around. I shake my head from the silly thought.

He turns back, his stance more business-like, his eyes strictly on mine. "If you think I have nothing better to do then you're not as smart as I thought you were," he says, tugging on his vest that fits perfectly around his broad chest. "But Nile is expecting you for dinner. Carmen left your clothes on the bed. I'm sure you can find your way."

Axel leaves the door open.

Sometimes I wonder why no one has sewed my mouth shut yet. I'm sure if Carmen heard me now, she would give me a tongue lashing.

A long dark green dress with a brown belt lays on my bed. The fabric is soft and smells like fresh air on a spring day. I hold it against me, letting it swish back and forth. It is like nothing I've worn before, except for when I was very young. The remainder of my life has only included pants since they're more practical to wear while working on a ship. *But I'm now on land.*

It is more proper for women to wear dresses, not pants. But I am not just any woman. I toss the dress back onto the bed, upset with myself for even thinking I'd put it on. I frantically look around the room and inside the closest, finding nothing that will suit me. I stare back at the dress like it will eat me. I groan and pick it back up.

The full-length mirror in the corner of the room allows me to see my full figure in the sun dress. I can't help but let a slow smile emerge. It hugs my curves, and the belt strap perfectly accentuates my hips. As I ponder why I'm enjoying wearing a dress, I decide to put my hair back in a braid. If *The Turbulence* crew saw me now . . . I roll my eyes and walk away from the mirror, picturing myself being thrown overboard within a few seconds.

I never wanted to be a lady. I'm better than that. Strong willed. Tough. A skilled fighter and navigator. But this dress is . . . nice. I feel more feminine than I ever have before. I take a long deep breath, growling at the end and questioning what I even want anymore.

Just because I enjoy wearing a dress doesn't change who I am.

The door creaks as I survey the unfamiliar hallway. I have absolutely no clue how big this house is, but by the grand stairway a few steps away from my door, I can conclude it's not some ordinary house. Compared to my room, the walls are more muted with beige coloring and a dark wooden trim that matches the floor. A maroon rug runs down the hallway and the staircase.

On my left, the candle-lit chandelier offers a glimpse of each portrait's face. A small young face full of life depicts Nile with a charming childish smirk, holding a young dog that reminds me of a long corn cob. A slender woman stands next to Nile, her hand on his shoulder bringing me to a complete stop. Familiar hazel eyes stare back at me, the same that she shared with Gus and Nile.

My mother stands tall with her long wavy blonde hair flowing down her back. She's wearing a dark green dress, like the one I'm wearing. I look back at her hand gently placed on Nile's shoulder, full of protection and love. I bite the inside of my lip, feeling a giant hole in the pit of my stomach full of sadness, want, and anger all mixed into one. I hope Gus hasn't seen this.

"This whole time you were okay," I whisper to myself.

She had another child to love and cherish while I was slandered and challenged by my beast of a father. I can understand why she never went looking for us. She had this giant home to live in with probably no worries about money or her house being destroyed by the raging wind or wild storms. For dang sake, she had a painting of herself on the stupid rich looking wall with a completely different family. Maybe I never knew her. Maybe I only made up a story in my head that she truly loved Gus and me while trying to hide the real truth. That we were nothing to her but a long forgotten past.

Little footsteps rush up the stairs and my pulse races, afraid I'll be found in such an emotional state. I quickly descend the stairs, gripping the railing to keep myself in a strong stance while my bruised leg nags me at every downward step.

"Elle! Our dinner is getting cold!" Nile says, grabbing my hand and pulling me down the stairs two steps at a time. "Come on, I'm starving!"

I pinch my lips trying not to laugh at how out of breath he is by the time we're on the first floor. But with strong determination he keeps hold of my hand, bringing me into the dining room. A giant dark wooden table fills the center of the room, surrounded by at least ten chairs. Axel and an unfamiliar man rise from their seats as I walk in with Nile.

Multiple windows around the room catch a glimpse of the sun disappearing behind large trees and rolling hills. Landscape paintings hang along the burgundy walls, lit by another unique chandelier that hangs from the ceiling.

"I found her!" Nile says, pulling out a chair across from Axel.

When I meet Axel's gaze, he looks away and resumes his seat. Clearly, Axel is trying to hide his earlier irritation.

"Where's Gus?" I ask.

Nile looks at the empty seat next to him. "He said he needed to sleep but Axel said I can bring him food once I'm done with mine." He perks up like something else pops into his mind. "Do you like the dress? I picked it out just for you," Nile says, sitting next to me.

My heart sinks, remembering how loathe I was to even put it on. "Yes, it's very beautiful. You have good taste."

Nile gulps his water, wiping the rest from his mouth with his arm. "Good. Mother always loved the color green."

Axel looks at Nile, giving him the sweetest smile. I take a quick breath, knowing I need to say something to him. Anything for Axel to know that I was sorry for the way I recently acted. "Thank you, Axel, for the room. It's lovely," I say in a rush, hoping he will look up from his food.

He pats his mouth with his napkin before saying, "Think nothing of it." He glances up just long enough for me to smile back at him. He offers me a small grin, his blue eyes shining a bit brighter.

The man next to Axel clears out his throat with annoyance. "Where are your manners, boy? Are you not going to introduce me?"

Axel eyebrows rise. "My apologies. This is my uncle, Orson. Uncle, this is Gabby's daughter, Eleanor."

Orson blinks slowly and light glints off the top of his bald head when he offers me a slight nod. "It's nice to meet you. I hope you enjoy your visit. Your mother was very kind."

"She's not visiting, she's living here now," Nile interrupts, shoving a giant bite of mashed potatoes into his mouth. I hold my tongue, knowing this isn't the time to discuss living arrangements.

Orson fidgets in his chair. "I'm sorry, this is news to me. My nephew doesn't always keep me informed," he says, clapping Axel on the back.

"Eleanor is welcome to stay or leave as she pleases," Axel says nonchalantly, ignoring his uncle's hard pat.

Orson's jaw tightens before taking a swig of his alcohol. "Well, darling, I'm sure everyone will welcome you with open arms. Glendora is full of diverse characters, especially those who were on that ship with you."

The demeaning way he says 'darling' and 'characters' makes my core burn. And what did he mean by the ones on *that* ship with me? His shiny bald head is giving me a perfect target for my butter knife to land. "Everyone has been very welcoming. I'm looking forward to seeing Dibs and Doolah, especially Charlie."

"They have been asking about you. I'll take you to them when we go riding tomorrow," Nile says, almost finished with his food, his eyes appearing heavier by the minute.

Oh, sea monsters, I completely forgot I promised I'd ride tomorrow. My stomach tenses. For one thing, how am I going to ride in a dress? I don't even know where my clothes are that I was wearing on the ship.

"You will have some more clothes by tomorrow morning. I'll make sure they include a few riding slacks," Axel says, as if reading my mind. "Which reminds me, Nile, it's close to your bedtime. If you're wanting to bring Gus some food, you should do it soon. You're going to need to be up earlier than usual if you're going to finish your chores before riding."

Nile yawns, slouches out of his chair, and gives me a surprise kiss on my cheek. "To keep the sea monsters away. Good night, sis," he says lightly, walking back to the hallway carrying a plate of Gus's food with him.

The word sis makes my heart sore and already I can feel a powerful need to protect Nile. My father's face appears in my mind making me cringe.

"Is the food to your liking?" Axel asks with slight concern in his eyes as his gaze flickers down to where I'm absentmindedly playing with my food with the butter knife.

Orson huffs. "Of course, she does! This is probably the best food she has had in years, with living on that pirate ship and all. She could use a little meat on her bones."

Axel inclines his head toward his uncle, exhibiting a noticeable tension in his neck. "Uncle, I won't have you make any unseemly comments about Eleanor or where she has previously been."

"Yes, yes, I'm sorry. I believe I'm just a bit troubled from recent events," he says, patting his bald head with his napkin.

Axel tenses his shoulders. "What recent events?"

Orson looks back at me. "Darling, this is more man talk, but I'm sure you won't mind."

"Not at all," I say, restraining from kicking him under the table.

"Now that you are back from your quest . . ." He pauses and gives me a quick look before turning back to Axel. "I'd implore you to consider changing your workers' hours. Without their limitations, we could have had a shipment ready by now."

"As I have said before, Uncle, unlike my father, I want them to have time for their family and loved ones."

"I understand, but maybe if we hired some others, without—"

Axel drops his fork onto his plate with a sharp clatter. "Without what?" he asks, challenging him.

"If we hire a few others that don't have certain limitations that would do a better job, and faster, allowing us to create more profit. There is talk from others in town that are confused why you have hired different types of people."

"I'll stop you there. We are making enough, and these so-called limitations are causing no hindrances. They are all talented hard workers and have never been late on a shipment. If someone has a problem with it, they can speak directly to me."

I sip from my glass, hiding my smile. If only this man understood what he's saying. Orson reminds me a tad of my previous crew, thinking just because I am a woman, I have limitations. Axel only said what I have been wanting to say for years.

"Your father would never—"

"I am not my father and never will be. He is the one that

trusted me with this responsibility and him not showing up for dinner tells me he is not too concerned about this the same as you apparently are." Axel stops and takes a deep breath, running his fingers through his hair. "I plan to give everyone here a chance to make a fair wage, no matter their limitations," Axel says, gathering the dishes from the table even though his uncle still had plenty of food left on his plate. I wonder where Axel's father is at this moment. Why isn't he here discussing this instead of his uncle?

"I don't understand you, boy. You have help. Have them do it."

Ready to do anything other than just sitting and listening to Orson, I finish my plate by taking two giant bites of the mashed potatoes and help Axel with the dishes.

"Like I said, they deserve time with their families. I think I'm more than capable of cleaning dishes."

His uncle sighs and stands, pushing the chair back in. "Axel, you are like a son to me. I promise to help you keep the business running. But I must remind you there are still stipulations that need to be held for Glendora to be completely yours."

Axel puts the pile of dishes down and faces his uncle, standing tall, power and confidence radiating off him. "No need to remind me. I'm well aware of what needs to be done and by the end of Glendora's ball, it will be."

The sound of me clanging plates onto one another echoes in the now quiet room. I don't dare raise my head. I had completely forgotten about the ball, reminding myself that Axel will soon be engaged. Is that the stipulation his uncle is speaking of?

His uncle steps closer and puts his hand on Axel's shoulder. "You say you're not like your father, but at this very moment, I just saw him in you. I know you will do great things."

Axel's jaw tenses slightly, almost as if it was a figment of my imagination. "Good night, uncle."

"Good night, boy. And Elle, I'd love to take you around Glendora sometime and give you a grand tour."

I put the plates down, wishing I wouldn't have to say what I am about to. "I'd enjoy that," I say with a giant cheesy smile.

He bows and leaves the room. Once I hear the door close behind, I ask Axel about what limitations his uncle was talking about. Axel piles the silverware on a plate before answering me.

"Let's just say I have hired some people that others wouldn't due to things that are beyond their control and given them a chance to work and be treated as anyone should. Some judge too easily by the eye but something I learned from your mother is that hard work can be shown in many ways, even if they are different from others."

I pause, wondering why my mother said that. But I know why. She was once a pirate and had the same treatment from the men as I did. We were judged just for being female, even though we worked just as hard as them. We were treated as if we had some disability while Axel hired Charlie, who is deaf. While I was shocked, he would do such a thing, he only brought up what Charlie is good at and required the workers to learn sign language. I think of Fred, the elderly man who has a missing arm, and his wife, Gail.

"I think that's very commendable of you. You have given people a chance when others wouldn't have. I noticed on the ship how hard they work for you," I say. Our hands touch when we reach for the same plate. I don't move away, thinking he will but he doesn't. He moves closer.

Spontaneously, he takes hold of my hand. "Your hands are beautiful," he says, grazing knuckles with his thumb.

I can't contain myself and burst out laughing, hoping for the rush of butterflies to dissipate. "I've never had anyone call them that."

"You can learn a lot from someone's hands."

"And what are my hands telling you about me?"

He turns my hand over, and I watch as he runs his fingers over my calluses. Shivers run down my spine. "That you're a fighter." He traces a long scar from my pointer finger down to my wrist. I try to pull away, but he doesn't let go. "Someone who loves deeply but hides away in fear of losing it."

He looks up at me, his ocean blue eyes telling me a story. These are the eyes of a man I have never grown up knowing. A man that I can't deny is intriguing and desirable. I can sense he wants me to lean closer, asking but not taking. I take a deep breath, only to be further entranced by his smell of peppermint and musk. His lips are so close to mine, begging to be savored.

Plates crash to the floor next to me, falling from my hand where I'd forgotten I was holding them. Jumping away from him, I place them on the table.

"Don't worry about it, I'll clean it up. You should rest. Nile will be keeping you busy all day tomorrow," he says, sounding a bit out of breath.

I can barely say anything, knowing what we were about to do. That I was about to kiss Axel. This is not why I'm here, to start having feelings for a man. No, I'm only here for Nile and Gus. Them alone. I nod and rush back to my bedroom.

CHAPTER 28

ELLE

I lay in bed for hours, fighting the urge to find Axel. To have that one kiss I can't stop thinking about. How it would taste and feel. To get it out of my system so I will stop acting like a lovesick puppy.

Taking the giant pillow beneath my head, I smash it against the mattress a few times, releasing the tension building inside me. A few times turns into a few more but ends once feathers start flying around me. "I swear, Elle, you need to get your act together," I growl at myself.

After stuffing all the feathers back into the pillowcase, I make a mental note to ask Carmen for a needle and thread tomorrow.

There's a faint knock on the door. Still in a crouching position, I stare at the door, not believing my ears. No one should be awake at this time. But another soft knock follows.

I slowly tiptoe to the door and crack it open. A shirtless Axel is walking back to the door across the hall from mine.

"Axel?" I whisper, hoping maybe he won't hear me. Axel stops and turns, the moonlight shining through the hallway windows casting his shadow.

"I thought I heard something," he says in a light whisper, taking slow steps back to me, his bare chest becoming more visible.

By the sea gods, please stop coming closer. How can a man be built so . . . so . . .

I shake my head. "I tripped. I didn't mean to wake you," I say, closing the door a bit more and hoping he can't see my cheeks turning red hot. But it doesn't stop him and instead he reaches for my cheek, smirking.

"You have something in your hair." He pulls a feather from my messy hair, twirling it around with his fingers. I try to grab it from him, but he moves his arm out of reach. "Were you having a pillow fight without me?"

I reach for it again, leaning on my tiptoes, my cheeks growing hotter when my hands meet his muscular chest. "Just give it back," I say, knowing I need to focus on the feather and not Axel's half naked body so close to me.

"Not until you promise you will invite me for the next fight," he says, chuckling under his breath. There it is again, the playfulness that occasionally appears before he turns back to being so business-like.

I twist around him and jump, grabbing a hold of his right arm. Pulling it toward me, my hand stops as I feel multiple scars and uneven skin beneath it. Axel stills, his face darkens, matching the shadows around us. It's quiet, only the faint sound of the wind outside can be heard.

I slowly slide my hand down his arm, waiting for him to pull away, but he doesn't. Instead, he turns toward the moonlight, and I see his disfigured arm up to his shoulder, remembering he said it was from a fire.

"Was she there?" I ask, talking about my mother.

He sighs, grabbing a hold of my hand and gently setting the feather in my palm. "She was."

I nod, still circling my finger up his bare arm, hoping by my actions that he knows it doesn't bother me. In some ways, it makes him more appealing. Knowing he isn't all perfect but also has hidden scars, like I do.

His eyes are tender and warm. "You could say she saved my life."

"How so?" I ask, enjoying his soft touch only for it to swiftly be taken away as he walks toward the portraits on the wall.

I follow him and stop next to a portrait that I can only guess is his father standing next to his mother. Axel has the same strong chin and chestnut hair as the man, but Axel's eyes are gentler, like his mother's. I wonder if he is even going to answer my question.

"Living with my father after my mother passed wasn't easy. I barely saw him and when I did, it was only to teach me about the business and how I would continue to make Glendora prosper." His voice deepens. "I wasn't his priority, Glendora was. So, most of the time when he was gone, I had free time to do whatever I wanted and made a point to get in trouble enough to force my father to speak to me. Even if it was for a scolding, I didn't care."

He gazes toward the portrait of my mother and stands still again, going quiet. I take a step closer to him. *Axel and I have a lot more in common than I thought.*

"By the age of thirteen, your mother showed up for a cooking position, extremely pregnant with Nile." He laughs lightly. "I'll never forget the first time I met her. I had a bloody lip from getting into a fight with a stable boy and destroying some fence, letting all our horses out into the town. My father threatened to keep me locked in my room, but your mom was persistent that she could do more than cook, that she could also keep me out of trouble." He faces me, his eyes glistening.

"I'd never met such a determined woman. I was a handful, but she never gave up on me even while she had an infant to take care of." He pauses, swallowing something I wasn't sure he really wanted to speak about. "When our barn caught on fire, I rushed to save the horses, including my mother's favorite, leaving these burns on my arm." His jaw tightens as he looks at his scars. "The marking changed me, my arm was still functional, only maimed from the outside. Gabby helped me to not focus on the scars but on others. From there on, I promised myself I'd be the man she saw in me, scars and all. So, from there I found others that needed work but wouldn't be hired due to their . . . Well, you know, as we discussed downstairs."

So many emotions run back and forth within me. I want to scream due to the hardness and pain battling inside me whenever he talks about my mother. And I'm not sure that will ever go away. There are so many unanswered questions. But this man standing in front of me is not something I ever believed could exist. So real. So gentle.

I've only been on land for a few days and already I feel lighter. An urge to jump into his arms is strong, wanting to feel his warmth around me. So, without thinking, I hug him. He stays still for a moment and then wraps his arms around me, pulling me in tight and lifting me off my feet. His hold reminds me of when we laid together on that flimsy door, unsure if there would be a tomorrow.

Axel slowly puts me back on my feet. He clears his throat. "Goodnight Eleanor," he says turning toward his room in the dark.

"Axel," I say, knowing I need to say it before my courage fails.

"Yes?" he whispers, his voice full of want, sending shivers up my spine.

"I'm ready for you to take me to her," I say, barely able to control my voice.

"I will take you tomorrow after your ride with Nile." His door creaks open, a fray of candlelight shining out of his room.

"Good night, Axel," I say, closing the door and sliding my back down until I hit the cold floor. The candle in my room is barely lit but I watch it slowly flicker out until it's completely dark. This time I welcome the darkness because I know it will only last a short while before the light comes back shining a little bit brighter than the day before.

CHAPTER 29

ELLE

Nile barely contains a laugh as I try to jump onto the saddle of a giant pure white mare that I'm sure can breathe fire. Gus leans against a tree watching me, stating he never agreed to ride and would rather observe from the ground. His stance is on guard, and he wears his dagger close to his hip as if our father could appear at any moment.

My legs shake as I put my foot in the stirrup, silently praying to the horse gods that this won't be the way I die. I swear the mare can hear my heart beating a thousand times a minute. Her dark brown eyes pierce through my very soul.

"My lady, can I help you?" A stable boy, probably a few years older than Nile, asks, holding the horse named Bertha from fidgeting back and forth. "Grab ahold of the horn. It will help you pull yourself up into the saddle," he adds. *How in the world did this horse not terrify the others? She is so huge. So intimidating.*

I swear silently, knowing I'm signing my death warrant as I grab a hold of the horn, launch off the ground, and land in the slick saddle. "I got it and call me Elle," I spurt out, holding the horn as tight as I can with both of my hands.

"I'm sorry my la . . . Elle," he says with a small smile, handing me the reins.

What am I supposed to do with these? I wonder as I grab hold of them.

The stable boy takes a step back and purses his lips together as if he is trying to contain a laugh before saying, "Just relax your body. She can feel you tense up, and if you start squeezing your legs like that, she will think you will want to go forward . . . fast."

At this point I'd rather fight a giant Kraken than allow big Bertha to take me anywhere. How I let Nile convince me to do this is beyond me.

"It's okay, sis," Nile says, trotting up to me with his much smaller horse wishing I had that one instead. I try to control my notorious eye roll. "All you need to remember is if you want to stop, pull the reins like this," he says, bringing his reins toward him. His dark brown horse stops immediately.

"That's all, huh?" I say sarcastically, my heart is beating even faster.

Nile giggles. "Yes, and when you want to go forward or faster, just squeeze your calves. Bertha barely needs to be told to go fast, she likes it."

Oh, great. They just put me on a fire breathing dragon that would rather run away with me instead of taking a casual stroll. Just perfect.

"Come on, silly. There really isn't much to it. Just follow me. Watch!" Nile says, circling around me and then trotting around the tree where Gus stands. Before I can even ask Bertha to follow, she's already trotting behind him.

"Wait, Nile! That's too fast!" I yell, my butt bouncing up and down on the saddle like a ship hitting hard waves.

"You are not going to learn how to ride at a walk. Just follow me and learn how to move with the horse, and don't forget to breathe," he says, sounding more like a young adult than an eight-year-old boy.

I keep my eyes on Nile, watching how his horse follows whatever direction he moves his reins. I keep one of my hands on the horn, too scared to completely let go, while the other holds the reins and I try to mimic Nile. Gradually, my body relaxes, and I gain confidence in my actions, which permits me to observe my surroundings more attentively.

Rolling green hills are all around us, the smell of the sea not too far away. Purple flowers bloom all over, reminding me of the ones engraved on *The Blazing Star*, bees buzzing between them. Nile trots next to me, his smile brighter than the sun. I freely smile back, my worries beginning to drain from me.

"See? It's not bad, you just need to start riding with me every morning," Nile says, leaning forward to pet Bertha's neck. "She can be a handful at times, but Mother loved her. I can't remember a day when she didn't ride."

"This was Mother's horse?" I ask, side-eyeing Gus.

Nile nods, a hint of sadness in his gaze as he focuses on Bertha.

If I could take any hint of sorrow from Nile's life, I would. "I like your horse. Have you had him for a while?"

The sun brings out the green of his hazel eyes as he looks at me. "Not too long. Axel promised that if I helped at the stables every day and rode daily, he would buy me Drako."

"You didn't want Bertha?" I ask, noticing we are going toward the town when the roofs come into view. Faint chatter can be heard in the distance. I turn to find Gus following not far behind, looking around as if he is scrutinizing everything in his path.

Nile shifts in his seat as if he is uncomfortable. "No, Bertha isn't mine. She's yours now," he says softly.

"Mine?" I ask sharply, pulling back on the reins and hoping Bertha will stop like Nile said she would. She does, thank the sea gods.

"Do you not want her?" Nile glances between us each, bottom lip pouting slightly. "Are you both planning to leave?"

My mind races, trying to figure out how to answer his question. Everything is going so fast. What will Gus and I do now that we have Nile? I'm still drawn to the sea and am not sure if that will ever go away. And what about Illira? I haven't spoken to her since she saved me from the descerver. But also, will our father find out where we are?

"Nile, you are a part of me now. I don't plan to leave you, but there may come a time when I'll need to leave for a while. Would that be, okay?" I ask, hoping it doesn't displease him but also doesn't feel so much like a lie.

He shrugs. "I guess."

"Good. Now where are you taking us?" I say, hoping we can change the subject.

"Charlie wanted to see you. He's helping at *The Blue Flask* with Carmen while the ship is being repaired," Nile explains, already looking more upbeat.

I giggle, thinking of my eight-year-old brother taking me to a pub. I'm sure at this time it won't be as rowdy as it can be in the evenings. I think of the man I knocked around at the last tavern I visited. I really don't want Nile to see that side of me if I can prevent it.

People bustle about the streets and vibrant flowers adorn the buildings, their blooms reaching toward the sky. Many greet Nile and he greets them back. *A trait Axel must have passed down.* He proudly introduces me and Gus as his older sister and brother, which causes me to feel a strong bond between us three.

I receive a few nods as I pass by, but I can't ignore the few glances and snickers. They point at the dagger around my thigh. Surely other women here do the same. Gus hastens his pace slightly to walk beside me, like he wants to shield me from others.

As we ride along the street and approach *The Blue Flask*, two younger women close to my age glare at me. I stand taller in the saddle, keeping my head high. "Why would Axel allow such a woman to stay at his place? She probably has a disease from living out at sea. We shouldn't get too close," I overhear one say and the other laughs loudly.

How do these women know I'm staying at Axel's home? It's only been a few days since I've been here, and people already know about me? My whole body starts to burn, ready to turn around and give them something to truly talk about.

"Alright, I've had enough," Gus says, stepping toward them. I stop him by putting my hand on his shoulder.

"Don't," I say lightly as if talking about the weather. "Nile," I murmur warningly.

He shrugs my hand off, tilting his head to the side as if considering listening and then continues to follow along with us.

The girls' laughter echoes off the stone buildings as we pass them. Taking a few deep breaths, I focus on each of Bertha's steps until we are directly in front of the pub.

Nile leads us to a standing post for the horses where Gus helps him off his horse and then shows me how to tie Bertha. He stands close to me, fidgeting with his jacket as we can still hear the two young women giggling, giving me looks I'd gladly like to swipe off their faces. Gus steps in front of me so I can't see them, Nile grabbing his hand before saying, "Ignore them, they know the ball is coming up and are only jealous."

"Nile!" Carmen yells, rushing out of the pub, scooping him up, and twirling him around. She puts him down and embraces me, squeezing my entire frame. "Don't worry, Gus, I won't twirl you around. You're too heavy."

Still not used to getting hugs, I lightly hug her back and follow them into the pub. Almost all the tables are taken besides one that has four plates full of food. I lick my lips, ready to devour the awaiting biscuits. With each step, I can feel my legs tightening and my behind is numb. "I feel like I've been beaten. I say, massaging my hind.

Nile bursts out laughing. "You're just not used to it, but it gets better the more you ride," he explains, taking a bite of his sandwich. *Thank goodness*, I think before joining him, savoring every bite of the food. I glance at Gus who is looking around like he is ready to be attacked, tugging on his long sleeve to cover his infamous pirate tattoo. I remind myself that he never had the time to get to know some of these people, including Carmen.

Carmen brings us water and puts the fourth next to the open seat.

"Are you not joining us?" I ask around a mouthful of biscuit when Carmen doesn't sit.

"I wish, but as you can see, we have a full house. Axel should be here soon though," she says, winking before heading back.

I roll my eyes, taking another bite of my sandwich and ignoring the butterflies fluttering in my stomach. But then I stop, remembering what he promised he would help me with today. I turn to Gus, nervous to ask if he wants to go. I play with my napkin, keeping my voice low. "So, Axel is going to take me to our mother's grave today, do you—"

"No," Gus says sternly, taking another bite of his sandwich. I'm unsure how to reply knowing that later today I'm going to make him talk. One way or another.

He seems distant even though he's sitting right next to me. This is the first time we have had the chance to really speak to one another, to enjoy a meal together. "You look very stylish in your new shirt and pants, even your boots shine," I say, moving my eyebrows up and down, nudging him with my elbow.

He grimaces. "Nile begged me to wear this and remarked that I had an odor," he says with a subtle smile. "But he wasn't wrong," he added. "He also noted that my hair smells like daisies because I accidently used woman's soap."

I burst out laughing, leaning toward his hair that's nicely tied behind his head to take a big whiff and inhale a subtle light, sweet and musky scent. "Well, are you just fancy."

"Speaking of fancy, I heard you wore a dress," he says taking another bite of his sandwich, tilting his head with amusement as if he won a game, waiting for my reply.

My mouth opens wide. "Who told you!" I ask and before he can answer, Nile is giggling. I point my finger toward him playfully, "You!"

A pure light laughter follows next to me, Gus joining in with Nile. My heartbeat quickens, as I observe the two and savor this moment. A moment that is so pure and carefree, hoping there will be many more.

"The man of the hour!" an older man seated at a nearby table yells, raising his drink in the air alongside others. Axel stands at the entrance. His presence brightens the room. Standing tall and with purpose, his dark green vest and slacks fit perfectly against his body. He politely shakes hands with others, his face somewhat serious but also sincere while greeting them. His light blue eyes search the room and stop when he sees me watching him. A small dimple appears when he smiles at me. I quickly turn back around and focus on my meal, catching Gus giving me a sidelong glance.

"Did you both have a good morning ride?" Axel asks from behind Nile, shagging up my younger brother's hair before glancing my way again.

"We did! Elle likes Bertha and is going to ride with me every day," Nile says, still gobbling up his food.

I bite my tongue, still not sure if riding was for me or when I'd agreed to ride everyday but I nod anyway.

Axel sits next to me, his shoulder grazing mine. "Did you sleep well?"

Thinking about last night, my cheeks start to tingle. "I did. The bed is very comfortable, especially the pillows."

"If you need any more pillows, you know where to find me," he says, keeping his mischievous eyes on mine and taking a swig of his drink.

A light tap on my shoulder takes me away from Axel's trance. Charlie stands behind me. "Oh!" I say, jumping from my seat to greet him. Axel does the same.

Charlie brings his hand to his forehead close to his ear and moves it outward and away from his body.

Unsure what he is doing, Axel does the same but says "hello" out loud. I follow his lead, hoping I'm doing the right thing.

Charlie proceeds to use a combination of hand movements and expressive facial expressions. I hold my breath, wanting to understand what he is saying, but feel a bit shaken that I may offend him.

"He wants to thank you for helping him on the ship," Axel says with a reassuring smile. "He said his violin was very special to him but was happy to have lost it if it meant you staying safe."

Remembering he can read lips, I relax but watch Axel translate with his hands as I reply, "I'm sorry I couldn't get it for you, but I'd love to listen to you play again someday."

Charlie's face lights up and he grabs a hold of my hand, nodding and making another movement with his hands toward Axel. Watching them both communicate without a word is mesmerizing. Nile also signs to Charlie. Joy fills me, knowing he has learned how to communicate with Charlie. I hope to soon be able to do the same without relying on Charlie to read my lips.

Charlie waves goodbye and I do the same before he sits at a different table.

"Will you teach me how to speak to Charlie like you do?" I ask Axel, wanting to get an answer before finishing my food.

"Gladly. I can start teaching you every day after your ride with Nile, during lunch," he says without a second thought.

"But aren't you really busy?"

"I'll make time," he says.

Everyone finishes their meals while discussing ships, with Gus occasionally participating in the conversation. Axel talks about adding honeysuckle to the medicine so it will be a sweeter taste for the children as well as producing different types of honey that have become popular within the last few years. Sometimes, I see Carmen smiling at us in a way that makes me want to lightly knock her on the head.

Nile wraps his arm around mine and Gus's necks. "See you guys soon," he says lightly, walking toward where Charlie sits.

Gus stands up, his chair scraping against the floor. "Where are you going?"

"Charlie is going to take Nile to the ship to help him clean up some of the damage while we go elsewhere," Axel says. Elsewhere meaning my mother's grave.

"I won't be going," Gus says flatly. "I'll help with the repairs." Nile grabs his hand, and I watch them two and Charlie leave.

Axel says nothing but notes Gus's abruptness. He takes a last swig of his drink and clears his throat. "Are you ready?" he asks in a deeper voice.

CHAPTER 30

ELLE

Stroking Bertha's neck, the warmth of her coat reminds me of the mornings I'd stand at the back of *The Turbulence*, enjoying every second of the sun shining against my skin. Twirling my fingers around her long soft mane, the sunlight brings out highlights of light blonde and white. I can't let go of the feeling that maybe Bertha's hair color reminded my mother of my own. It's something to focus on rather than where I'm currently going.

How far can it be? My legs are restless, aching more with each stride. I'm ready to let my muscles relax and take a break, but at the same time I'm hoping we can continue riding until dark. If so, I can keep my face hidden from Axel. I've already caught him gazing at me a few times when he thought I wasn't looking. I silently enjoy him looking at me. My cheeks warm, and not from the heat. The concern and something else he tries to keep hidden in his eyes. But at this moment it only feels wrong to have a surge of happiness instead of sadness. Yet, I'm so spent on grieving and beaten down by my past. When he is around, somehow things are better.

In the distance I spot the two-story white house I've been staying in and the red barn, thinking we have to be close. Instead, we follow a trail down a steep hill with a small creek flowing through trees at the bottom. Thankful for the shade, my eyes close and I

197

breathe deep, savoring the coolness against my neck. Birds chirp above us and the flow of water trickling down rocks settles the tension.

The sound of Axel's horse's hooves no longer walking across the trail of dirt and rock alerts me he has stopped. He ties his horse to a tree and comes up to Bertha, his hands gentle around my waist as he helps me down. He keeps them on me when I'm back on my feet, his eyes a bit darker with worry.

"Just past those trees." He looks ahead where the tree line ends, sunlight shining past it. "Follow the steppingstones. I'll wait with the horses, Eleanor," he says softly.

Eleanor. A name my mother had chosen for me, meaning radiance and light. But I'm so far from it. Just the thought makes me feel as if I failed her by not living up to the name. A veil of darkness settles around me, dimming out any light that was once there.

A light wind rustles the trees, circling up toward the path, encouraging me to follow.

As far as I can see are acres of large rolling hills and lush green grass swaying like the waves of the sea. A prominent red maple tree stands ahead, encircled by a low white wooden fence adorned with honeysuckle vines. Adjacent to the tree is a solitary gravestone.

My chin trembles, tears threatening to fall. Instead of walking toward my mother's open arms, I'm walking toward her grave.

Grass is pressed down by the gate, indicating others have been here not too long ago. I barely open the gate before my knees give out, landing next to my mother's gravestone. My fingers gently trace the inscriptions on the stone as I read them aloud:

Gabriella "Gabby" Whitlock
A loving friend & mother.

I breathe in the honeysuckle-scented air, longing to hear her voice one last time.

I dig my nails into the ground, feeling the coolness of the earth. I wish I was able to say goodbye. To get the answers I've been wanting for so long. I rest my head on the cold stone, gazing at the clear blue sky through swaying tree branches.

The thought of carrying a child on *The Turbulence* around the filth of men and their wandering eyes . . . eyes full of lust but also a disdain for my sex. I would have done the same. I would have left.

I spent a lot of time trying to prove myself, but for what? For my father to decide he was done with me.

Nile will not witness the violent deaths encouraged by his father. Or have to worry about not being enough. To compete with others in order to be acknowledged.

I resolve to ensure that Nile will not experience the same loneliness I have felt over the past eight years.

I stand and observe my surroundings, paying close attention to the various colors and scents. It is different from the sea, yet equally beautiful. Ground to create anything I desired. A home to call my very own. A garden. I have been given a chance to start a new life. I guess I can call it the last gift from my mother. A gift to finally be free.

But one thing gnaws at me. Illira. She's my friend, but I used her for my father's ploys. I need to call her. I'll never ask anything of her again except to be my friend.

I shut the gate as if closing a chapter of my life. "Goodbye, Mom," I whisper, turning and walking down the stone path.

With each step, a fragment of the darkness enveloping me dissipates until I am merely steps from Axel.

CHAPTER 31

AXEL

I desperately want to follow her. To assure her she won't be alone again if I can help it.

I have so many stories to tell her that I know she would enjoy, but I also saw jealousy and sadness in her eyes the last time I brought up Gabby.

It pains me to see her feeling like her mother didn't want her as a daughter. Countless times I thought the same with my father. So, I'll take it slow.

My stomach aches, thinking of how I almost lost her on *The Blazing Star*. I remember my arms wanting to give out but the screaming thunder pounding in my ears was as if Gabby was telling me to hold on to Eleanor's limp body, to never let go. So, I let every muscle and tendon stretch and wear out until the storm was no more.

Hopefully she'll consider staying in Glendora. Gus, too. If he leaves, I'm not sure what Eleanor will do. I kick around dirt, waiting for her to return. When she's around, I feel more myself. Wanting to act more my age instead of someone soon to be running a whole island. I love Glendora and its people, but the pressure can be overwhelming.

Whenever Orson brings up that he can see my father in me, I

want to smash everything in sight. Even though deep down, I know he's not wrong. The tendency to strive for perfection or at least maintain a semblance of control, to persistently confront any challenges that arise, or almost choose to remain at my office longer rather than having dinner with Nile.

The horses start to get restless, prancing back and forth, ready to no longer be standing and back out to pasture. I agree with them but hold my ground, wanting Eleanor to have all the time she needs. Time she never had.

In some ways, I regret all the years I had with Gabby that Eleanor never did. I wasn't meant to have that time. She helped me grow into a man I hope my own mother would be proud of, but it also caused heartache and pain for others.

The want and need to know Eleanor burns like a fire within my very soul. But I know I should disregard these feelings that smother my every thought. The promise to the council of me finding a wife, specifically a protective political option, nags at me.

It is not that I do not desire to find someone. But I'd prefer to find them on my own terms. I've already had several dinner meetings with some of the women that the council and Orson have encouraged me to see, but nothing has sparked any kind of interest. Not until . . . my mouth goes dry, swallowing the thought.

I kick a small rock across the ground, up toward the stepping-stones leading out to the open. The trees sway gently with the light breeze, giving the impression that they are signaling someone's approach.

Eleanor appears, slowly walking back down the path, her loose hair flowing behind her like an elegant flower. As she approaches, I observe that her eyes are somewhat red and her cheeks flushed. Her green eyes soften as I smile. However, there is a distinct change that I can't quite pinpoint. Almost like a lightness off her shoulders, the way she carries herself.

"Are you ready to go back ho—?" I nearly say 'home' but stop myself.

Eleanor strokes Bertha's long white mane. "I'm ready but I'd like to stop by the sea first," she says faintly.

By almost saying home, did she immediately think of the ocean? I almost forget to reply as my gut cramps, bombarded with thoughts of why it causes me so much concern. I untie her horse and help her back on Bertha.

We both stay quiet as she follows me to a secluded place I visit on my own when I want some privacy. I'm supposed to be back for a meeting late this afternoon with my uncle and father, but Carmen knows what I'm doing. She can easily handle it without me. I contain a smirk, gripping my reins tight, knowing that Orson is secretly intimidated by Carmen's strong outspoken voice.

The path isn't long, but the terrain quickly changes. From lush green grass and rolling hills to rocks and cliffs. I catch Eleanor's expression shifting from contentment to awe as we ride between two large limestone cliffs, the ground shifting to sand.

I point toward the top of the cliff high above us. "It's called 'Where lovers unite.'" I stop my horse right below, wanting her to see how it looks like two hands are reaching out for each other. "See where they almost touch?"

"I do. Do you come here often?" she asks, gazing above her.

"Not as much as I'd like to," I say, nudging my horse forward, hoping we can catch the sunset. We ride a few more strides before the sound of waves hitting against the coast are heard. "We can tie the horses here. It's past this small cave."

She follows closely as we walk through the cave, water creeping around our feet. It is slightly dark inside but as we step out, the sky bursts with color. The sun peeks through a few stray clouds, pinks and oranges illuminating the sky, the ocean glowing, mimicking it.

We walk on to the sandy beach, and she stops. Eleanor closes her eyes, smiling. A smile I have been hoping to see, one that shows she's happy. She takes a deep breath, as if she is erasing every toxic memory and releasing it out into the sea.

"Do you have a favorite place?" she asks while her eyes are still closed, her blonde hair blowing all around her.

"Yes, we're actually here. It's more isolated, a place I can stop and think. What about you?"

She sighs, opening her eyes. The setting sun brings out the green and gold.

"My favorite place was, in a way, like yours. It was on the back of *The Turbulence*. This little slab of wood that seemed to be made perfectly for my size, where none of the men could fit. It was a place where I could sit and just watch the sunset, my feet dangling above the waves. It was my little escape." She pauses, turning toward me. "But this could possibly become my new favorite spot." The look she gives me is as if she was asking if that was okay. "Axel," she says hesitantly, glancing down at her feet and kicking at the loose sand.

I step closer, tempted to tuck a strand of her hair behind her ear. "Yes?"

"I want to thank you. For everything. For helping me get off *The Turbulence*. For saving Gus, but also for taking care of Nile. You didn't have to do any of those things, but you did. I owe you."

The words she is saying, I can tell, are not easily said. Usually she has this demeanor like she can conquer the world, that she is strong enough alone, but little by little I can see glimpses of light ready to escape.

"You owe me nothing. I would do it all again."

She fidgets with her shirt. "If I'm going to stay here, I'd like to find something I can do. To help pay for staying here."

My heart races. "You're free to stay here, no need for payment."

"But if I'm going to make . . ." She pauses, opening her mouth and closing it. "If I'm going to make this my home. I want to contribute. To be a part of Glendora."

A sensation climbs up my spine, trying to contain my excitement and desire. "I'm sure we can figure something out," I say casually.

"One other thing. I need to call my friend but it may take awhile for her to show."

I nod as I watch her take off her boots and walk out in the waves up to her knees.

The next moment, I hear a voice that instantly captivates my every being. It stirs the sea as if it is entranced, the water glistening with a more pronounced color. Almost sparkling like a dark starry night.

I've read stories that when mermaids sing it's as if the sea stops to listen but also glistens like a bright night of stars. That they would sing for their lover on land that would never show.

Vaguely, I remember being told mermaids are private creatures but also very curious. That if a mermaid ever taught you the song of the sea, you were trusted as one of them. It is very rare and a special gift.

And Eleanor is a gift for so many, even if she may not know it.

CHAPTER 32

ELLE

I llira never shows.

The moon shines brightly, still giving enough visibility to see around me. I sing until my voice is hoarse and my feet wrinkle from being in the water for so long. My shoulders are heavy while the pit of my stomach tells me something is wrong.

Behind me, Axel sits patiently in the sand. His stare lingers on me, creating goosebumps up my arms. "I was hoping she would come," I say as my voice carries through the starry night sky.

"We could wait a bit longer," he says, gazing behind me toward the dark ocean.

I have a feeling he's not ready to go back and I'm not ready to get back on a horse. I sit next to him, my shoulder slightly touching his before leaving space between us.

"You always seem to amaze me," he says, focusing out ahead of him.

"In what way?"

"I've never met anyone who knows the song of the sea. She must be a close friend of yours to share that with you."

Guilt nags at my stomach. "I'm lucky enough to have her as a friend. She's done a lot for me, more than I deserve."

"You may say that, but I bet you she would say the same thing about you. Real friends are willing to do many things without a second thought and never keep a record of it."

I curl my toes in the sand, enjoying the warmth around them. "Would you say that about Carmen?"

Axel laughs out loud, his smile as bright as the moon. "Carmen is a friend anyone would be thankful to have. She has stuck with me through thick and thin and is never scared to tell me when I need a reality check or a whack across the head."

I nudge his shoulder and he playfully returns it. "I would be happy to help her with that."

He places his hand next to mine in the sand. So close I can almost feel the heat from his fingertips. "I'm sure you would be first in line," he says with a quick wink.

I like him teasing me. It's never insulting or degrading and instead makes me feel like an equal. Like I can freely speak to him about anything without judgment. "Do you ever tire of governing Glendora?"

Axel takes a deep breath, his lips pinching tight for a split second. "Sometimes. It's more the weight of making sure everyone is taken care of and not disappointing anyone."

"You're not always going to please everyone. If you put such a high expectation on yourself, you will only doubt yourself when you fail." I bite my tongue after the words come out. How could I say that when I've been doing it almost my entire life?

He kicks some sand with his feet. "You are right. It's just easier said than done."

"Maybe that's something I could do. Help take a load off your shoulders."

As his silence lengthens, I wonder if maybe I overstepped my bounds.

"Would you be interested in making sure the shipments are all set and ready to dock? My uncle usually does but I think fresh new eyes and your experience would be a load of help."

I burst out laughing. "By experience you mean by being a pirate and stealing goods?"

"No, I saw you on the ship. You're a leader more than you may think, and a hard worker. I'd have complete faith you would make sure it would get done and . . ." he pauses. "And if you want to be part of the shipping crew, you can."

"What about Gus?"

"He is just as welcome," Axel states.

My body tenses. The thought crosses my mind that my father is somewhere out at sea waiting to find me, planning his revenge. Maybe he has figured out where I have gone, and I fear that somehow he will learn about Nile.

"You don't have to give me an answer right now."

I shake my head. "No, it's not that. I'm worried my father will come here. That he will find out about Nile. I'm afraid about what he might do," I say, that sick feeling building in my stomach, wondering where Illira is.

Axel faces me, his jaw tight. "I have had a few troops and watchers patrolling the island. But one thing I can promise you is that I won't let anything happen to Nile."

It is a promise that still gives me doubt, though I love hearing it come from his lips. I know he will do all he can, but he doesn't know my father.

"Hey," he says, his fingertips rest against mine in the sand. "It will be okay," he says with a stern but caring voice.

A sigh of relief loosens the built-up tension in my chest. Instinctively, I lean into his palm, enjoying his warmth and grasping hold of it before it can leave. His intense light blue eyes bore through me as he leans in, his broad shoulders blocking the moonlight.

We're nose to nose. His breath heats my lips, tempting me. But just as I think we will kiss, he draws back. His face is hard to read in the dim moonlight. Though his stance is withdrawn, his eyes tell a different story. Is he upset? Or was it more a glimpse of sadness?

"It's getting late. Nile will probably send a search party if we don't get back soon." He helps me up from the sand without directly looking at me.

A foreign feeling starts to build. I can't quite decipher it other than it stings. It's uncomfortable, like a splinter you can't get out of your skin.

I follow him back to the horses and an uneasy silence surrounds us as we ride back to the house. Silently, I fight the urge to scream.

When we arrive back at the stables, he politely bids me good night, leaving him to unsaddle my horse, noting he keeps his horse saddled while I walk back to the house. I have never needed to catch a man's eye and now that I want to, I'm questioning every-thing about myself. Perhaps, as always, I'm something someone doesn't want.

CHAPTER 33

ELLE

Repeatedly going over what transpired last night leaves me with a headache. If I could stay in bed all morning, I would, but I don't want Axel to think it has anything to do with him nor miss any time with Nile.

Even though my legs and bum are sore from being on horseback most of yesterday, I force myself into my riding gear. I catch myself looking in the mirror multiple times, making sure my hair is in a clean braid and pinching my cheeks to bring more color to them. I pause when I realize what I'm doing. "Elle, stop. You're better than this," I say aloud.

A note slides underneath my door, and I hope whoever left it didn't hear me.

Don't forget lunch and sign
language lessons at noon.

See you soon.
Axel

"Son of a honeysuckle biscuit!" I say, glancing at the mirror once more.

Before I make it to the barn, the morning heat has made sweat trickle down my back. Gus is already there, glowering as Nile trots around him with his horse. Rather than join, Gus still refuses to ride and leaves me with Nile, claiming he needs to go in town. As he leaves, he reminds Nile to be careful. The small show of Gus's protectiveness makes me smirk. Gus barely looks at me as he leaves and a tightness forms in my chest, wishing he would tell me what is wrong.

Nile focuses on teaching me how to ask Bertha to go faster in small increments. He's hopeful we'll be able to race each other soon. With a promise that I will soon, I rage within at my lack of confidence. There's no way I can ride a galloping horse when I'm holding my breath for so long I fear I might topple off Bertha due to a shortage of oxygen.

Nile is all smiles this morning. Dibs and Doolah have been teaching him how to read maps and tie ropes. He puffs out his chest. "I want to travel someday and work on a ship, like you."

The thought of him being out at sea makes me anxious. If I can help it, I will never let him go until I know my father is dead. Bertha moves uneasily underneath me, sensing my worry.

"Dibs has also been explaining why it's so important to swab the deck."

"And why is it?" I ask, eyeing him like he may not actually know the answer.

"Because saltwater both prevents the deck from growing mold and helps the wood swell so the deck won't leak."

"Sounds like you will be a pro soon," I say, biting my tongue and wanting to tell him it's safer to be on land. Though a part of me wants him to find something more interesting, I know that deep down being a part of the sea is in his blood as much as it is in mine.

"You should see *The Blazing Star*! It's almost all fixed up! I've been helping!" Nile says proudly.

The usual urge to be on a ship doesn't rise within me, but I agree anyway, glad to see Dibs and Doolah again.

As we arrive at the port, I look around cautiously, waiting for an old crew member or the captain to appear from within the shadows. Instead, Dibs rushes toward us, her gemstone green eyes bright with excitement.

"Dibs!" Nile yells, jumping off his horse and into her arms. "Can I help you with anything?"

"Sure, mate. Go find me some more nails, will ya?"

Nile nods and runs toward the ship, passing Doolah as she approaches.

I barely have time to tie the horses to a post before Dibs is hugging me. "We're so sorry we haven't come by to check on you. We've been working tirelessly to get this ship back in order."

I squeeze her back. "You don't have to explain. It's just nice seeing you two without a violent storm trying to take us."

Dibs laughs. "Psh, we had it under control."

Doolah gathers a few nearby boards, giving me a sincere smile. I know that, unlike her sister, she doesn't do hugs. "It's going to take a lot more than that to get us down."

"That's right, sis," Dibs says, nudging her with her hip.

Behind my smile, I remember the fear in both of their eyes when all of us were drenched from the waves trying to engulf us. A shiver runs up my arms, reminiscent of the coldness of the sea, splashing against me.

"Here you go!" Nile runs back to us, his hands full with a box of nails.

Doolah ruffles his hair. "Thanks, you little sea urchin."

"Hey! I'm no sea urchin, I'm a pirate," he spits.

We are all still. Dibs and Doolah look at me, unsure what to say.

"A pirate?" I ask, trying to keep my voice calm.

"Well, yeah. Just like you," he replies a bit hesitantly, eyeing Dibs and Doolah as if he said something wrong.

The tattoo on my wrist burns. How does Nile calling himself a pirate make me want to puke up my breakfast? He has no idea what a pirate truly is, that it's not some desirable future. I want to shake him and tell him it will destroy him. Why do I feel so ashamed to be a pirate when I used to take so much pride in it?

"Aren't you one?" he says, pointing at where my tattoo is partially covered by my sleeve.

"I . . . well . . ." Being a pirate only causes pain, for others as well as the ones I loved. We stole. Killed. Betrayed. I feel like a completely different person now but at the same time not.

"How about the protector of the seas?" Dibs suggests.

Nile jumps up and down. "I like it!"

I mouth 'thank you' to Dibs and change the subject. "Is there anything I can help with?"

"Actually, there is something I've been meaning to ask you," she says, digging a toe into the dirt.

I pinch my lips, trying not to laugh at how quickly Dibs's demeanor changed from a confident woman to a scared little mouse. Doolah rolls her eyes and grabs a hold of Nile's hand. "For goodness' sake. Come on, Nile. Let's nail these boards to the deck while they talk girly things."

"What is she talking about?" I ask, intrigued by what Dibs is so nervous to ask me.

"I'd like to find a dress for the ball, but Doolah refuses to go with me. She plans to wear her same clothes and says everyone will have to get over it, but I wouldn't mind dressing up, just for the night."

"I don't think I'm the best to give dress advice."

A couple days ago, I felt the same as Doolah, not wanting to wear anything other than the clothes I'm used to. But I do secretly enjoy wearing the green dress that was given to me. It's feminine and beautiful. It felt wrong only because a dress was never needed, and I once looked down on the women who wore them. Those women, to me, made their whole life about looking pretty and being the perfect dutiful wife. Perhaps dresses made them feel good and, in some way, empowered. Funny how some of us can make such a big deal on what we wear.

"Have you picked yours out yet?" Dibs asks, sounding more herself again.

"No, I haven't given it any thought. I barely know anything about the ball."

"I was sure you'd have heard a ton about it since you're staying at Axel's. It's not for a couple of weeks, so we can help each other find one."

We both agree that she will meet me at *The Blue Flask* after I have lunch and my lessons with Axel while Doolah keeps Nile busy working on the ship.

I spot Axel's horse already at *The Blue Flask*. Strangely, I'm happy he is waiting for me rather than the other way around. Several tables are full, and others arrive behind me, quickly finding seats. Carmen and Axel are locked in what appears to be a serious conversation, their low voices unheard over the din. Carmen leans against the table, her shoulders tense, shaking her head while Axel stares down at his drink.

My foot snags on a chair leg, bumping it into their table. Carmen's eyes dart to me while Axel stands, putting on his business smile. I know it means he's trying to hide something from others. And me.

"Am I interrupting something? I can come back later," I say.

Axel pulls out the chair next to him, inviting me to sit. "No. You should know this, too. We spotted a ship that stayed far enough out to sea that we couldn't get a good glimpse. It never came to the dock."

I stand a bit taller, and my hand instinctively goes to the blade on my thigh, ready to leave and find Nile.

"I doubt it's *The Turbulence,* but we are still taking precautions. I've asked all who work the ports across the island to report if they see or hear anything suspicious."

In no way did that make me feel any better. "That won't do anything if it's too late and they are already here," I blurt out.

"I agree. That is why I have sent out a smaller vessel to patrol around the island throughout the day and night. They will signal if there is any reason to worry. Besides, every ship that docks here must report to me."

I take a deep breath, telling myself that there is only so much we can do. The ship could have just been fishing and went farther back out to sea, but it leaves an eerie feeling in my stomach.

I flinch when Carmen grips my arm with a reassuring squeeze. "I'll get you something to eat. Now sit and enjoy your lesson."

Lunch only eases some of my anxiety. Most of it is tied up in being unsure how I should act around Axel. He hasn't said anything about last night. Our conversation revolves around my day and how my ride was with Nile.

Once we both finish with our meal, he scoots closer, facing me. "Are you ready to learn sign language?"

I swallow hard, feeling a radiant spark flickering in my chest as he moves closer. I turn toward him, our knees brushing.

He moves his hands in various gestures, mouthing words as he does. I do my best not to focus on his lips and instead put full concentration on his hands. "What did you just say?"

"I said, 'Hi, my name is Axel. What's yours?'"

"Please show me how to say my name!" I ask, already thinking how exciting it will be to communicate with Charlie on my own.

Axel grins from ear to ear. "Let me teach you the alphabet first and we can go from there."

He teaches me the alphabet along with 'hello' and 'goodbye.' Occasionally, he gently repositions my fingers and hands to help me better form the letters. His touch always lingers longer than I expect it to. When he fixes the position of my arms in the final portion of 'goodbye,' I don't pull back, hoping he'll look at me. I need to talk to him about last night.

"Excuse me," someone nearby grunts.

We both jump. Orson stands above us. "I've been waiting for you at the town hall. You're late for our meeting," he says, a flash of disapproval in his eyes as his gaze flickers over me and focuses on Axel.

Axel stands, using the hand that had just guided mine to thread his fingers through his hair. "Right." He signs 'goodbye' to me and I do the same, feeling more awkward than I did an hour ago.

Carmen slams into the chair next to me after Axel and Orson leave the tavern. "Okay, out with it!"

"With what?" I ask, grimacing at my water and wishing it was mead to savor instead.

"The tension between you two could split a table. So, either you're going to tell me or Axel will, your choice."

I stare at the wall behind her. "It's nothing."

She takes the drink out of my hand and downs my water. "Spit it out, Elle!"

"I don't know. We almost kissed last night but he pulled away. It's not a big deal," I whisper with annoyance.

Carmen spews water all over the table. I immediately regret saying anything, feeling like a silly little girl.

"Hey, you asked, nosey woman," I mutter, dragging the empty cup back to me so I have something to do with my hands.

Carmen wipes her lips with her sleeve. "I'm sorry. Axel's like a brother to me so it's just odd and I never thought I'd hear *that* from your mouth."

"You never will again. I can promise you that."

"Look, I'm sure there is a reason he pulled away."

I shake my head, closing my eyes with annoyance. "Seriously Carmen, it doesn't matter."

She bites her lip. "Mhm, well then just enlighten me. What do you know about the Glendora ball?"

"Only that Axel will be announcing his engagement. But what does it have to do with anything?

Carmen shifts uncomfortably in her seat. "I can't read Axel's mind but . . . well, I'm so dang nosey I shouldn't have asked you in the first place. What's between you two is none of my business."

I plan to let the subject end, but wanting to know more gnaws at me. "It's a little late for that. Speak, Carmen."

She blows air out her nose like a fire breathing dragon. "It's obvious you two have something but he has to think of his future and Glendora."

The thought of not being good enough charges back at me like a thousand waves. "What does kissing me have to do with that? Doesn't mean it has to be anything serious."

"Axel isn't the type to kiss for fun without it meaning anything. My guess is he knows he has a decision to make soon, and he doesn't want to be confused when it comes down to it."

I sink into my seat. "So, he has to marry someone even if he barely knows them or . . ." I can't say love; I don't believe in love. It's a silly word that's tossed around too much. "Sounds ridiculous."

"Tell me about it."

"Can he not fight it?"

Carmen retrieves a bottle of gin, filling my glass full and another for herself. "He has. I don't know if you've noticed but we don't have a squad of people trained to protect this island. Uniting with another kingdom will help keep his people safe. So, you see, he is putting your feelings first before his own. He is being the man Glendora wants instead of what he may really want. Damn him." She gulps down her gin all at once, slamming it onto the table. "Unless you have an army he can have after marrying you?"

"I've always said I'd never marry," I mumble, unsure if those words are completely true anymore.

"Well, try not to take it personally." Carmen stands and heads behind the counter. "Here." She throws a bag of coins onto the table. "Find a dress that fits you for the ball."

Testing the weight of the bag, I'm in shock that she would give me so much and for what? "I can't take this."

"It's payment for helping on *The Blazing Star*."

CHAPTER 34

ELLE

I 've never seen Dibs so giddy. As we walk into a shop called *Blazing Dresses,* her green eyes light up, touching every colorful fabric she passes. Soon she has multiple dresses in her arms. I take my time, unsure what I should even be looking for, or if I should attend the ball.

An older woman with white hair in a bun approaches us. "Want a room, dear?" she asks in a light, scratchy voice.

Dibs giggles childishly. "Yes, please," she says, practically on the woman's heels as they head to the dressing room.

Each fabric I touch is smooth as silk, soft like a rabbit's foot, or fluffy like the clouds outside. A few of the dresses look horrendous with sleeves that are as big as my head while others seem to not have enough fabric to cover a body. I find others with colors so loud they can easily wake me up every morning without a sip of coffee.

My mind keeps going back to thinking which dress would be the best to move around on a ship or fight in. I glimpse at one with a long slit that reaches the hip, picturing my dagger fitting perfectly with it for easy access. I snort. Why am I thinking this? It's a ball!

Dibs hums and I recognize the tune about a lost sailor that falls in love with a mermaid. Thoughts of Gus and Illira pop into my mind, wondering if Illira is near.

"Find one yet?" Dibs hollers, apparently not caring that everyone in the shop can hear her.

"I'm not sure." There are so many to choose from. It's so much easier picking out a pair of pants and shirt.

Dibs steps out, beaming. She is wearing a deep red dress with a V neck that flows elegantly down her long legs to her feet. "It's stunning on you!"

She twirls around in the mirror, her smile bright and contagious. "This is the one."

"But it's the first one you tried on."

"When you know, you know. Now hurry and find a few you can try on," she says, staring in the mirror and gliding her hands down her hips.

I pick a blue dress and a green dress hanging next to me and try them on. The first one is way too tight around my bust, pushing them out for everyone to see. The other is comfortable and fitting but doesn't feel like me. I study myself in the three mirrors, thinking maybe I should just buy it.

"The green one really shows off your back side! I'd pick that one," Dibs says nonchalantly. "But you have to love it, and I don't think you do."

A high-pitched laugh echoes through the shop around the corner. "Mother, what do you think?"

"Natia, you look dazzling!"

"You think Axel will love it?"

After sharing a look with Dibs, I peek around the corner. A young woman around my age twirls in a champagne-colored dress that fits perfectly around her warm skin and enviably toned body. Her dark black curls flow to the middle of her back that anyone would envy. She is, no doubt, dazzling. Any man would find her attractive. Including Axel. The pit of my stomach cramps, wondering why she spoke as if they already knew each other.

A familiar male voice steps in front of her. "I think Axel won't be able to take his eyes off you," he says kindly. "It should be a great day for all of us."

Orson. His bald head could be recognized a mile away when light hits it.

"Dearie, is that the dress you have chosen?" the shop asks from beside me, making me yelp out loud and catching the attention of Orson, Natia, and her mother.

I fake a smile, silently wishing I could run back into the dressing room.

"Elle, what brings you here?" Orson asks, stepping toward me, gaze snagging on the green dress I'm wearing.

"Dibs and I are looking for a dress for the ball," I say, gulping at the heat of Natia's judging eyes and turning to the shop owner. "No, ma'am, I don't think this dress is the one."

Dibs puts her hand out to shake Orson's. "Hello, sir. I don't think we have met. I work at the docks and will soon be helping with the next medicine shipment."

He slowly shakes her hand. "Oh, yes. You have a twin sister, correct?"

"Yes, sir," she says with her typical care-free demeanor.

"I heard you two used to be popular ballet dancers, what made you decide to work on a ship instead?" Orson asks, tone turning more judgmental with each word. "I'm sure there is a lot more elegance to ballet than working out in the sun all day."

He obviously doesn't know their back story. That their parents were killed in a carriage crash, leaving them both penniless and Doolah with a scar across her face. If it wasn't for Axel seeing them dancing on the streets in Osteria and offering them a job, I wouldn't have Dibs, my friend, standing next to me. Does Orson have any idea who these people are that work for Glendora? I squeeze her hand, when I feel her go rigid.

But when she speaks, her voice is strong. "We are very happy with the jobs Axel has given us. It may not be elegant or as lady-like as some would prefer," she says, glancing behind him, raising her chin a bit higher. "But we take pride in whatever we do, no matter if it's dancing or working on a ship."

"I see," he says, taking his pocket watch out and checking the time before putting it away.

"The time is getting ahead of me. Elle, I have been meaning to see you and give you a tour around town. I still have a few shops to go to; would you care to join me?"

Dibs fidgets with the dress in her hands. "I've found my dress, but Elle hasn't. Don't you want to keep looking?" she asks, pulling me back toward our dressing rooms.

To be honest, I don't want to try anymore dresses. Orson leaves so many mixed signals. I'm not sure if he is a man to trust or not. Axel seems to trust him, so why shouldn't I? Natia's sharp glances linger, leaving a sour taste in my mouth, noting how out of place I am.

I'm ready to leave.

"It's okay, Dibs. I think I could take a break and come back another time."

Dibs presses her lips together, obviously wanting to say something but turns her gaze to Natia before nodding her head in agreement. "Okay. You better invite me when you do."

"Promise," I say, swiftly changing and meeting Orson at the front. He eyes the dagger around my thigh before opening the door. An eerie chill washes over me. Maybe I made the wrong decision to leave.

Even though it's getting close to late afternoon, the streets remain busy. Children run around playing games, laughter filling the air. Giddiness fills me, enjoying the noise. I picture myself and Gus at that age doing the same, wishing we could have had the peace these children have. If my parents had found Glendora instead of being drawn to the heart of the sea. *How things could have been so different . . .*

A slight nudge catches my attention; Orson holds his elbow out for me to wrap my hand around. Others pass by doing the same and I follow his lead. I guess it's the proper way to stroll through town.

"Are you enjoying your stay?" Orson asks, nodding toward

others as we walk.

"Yes. Glendora is different than any other island I've been to."

"It is. We are very fortunate to have an island like this one. Axel's ancestors and father worked very hard to create such a *safe* place." He says, eyeing my dagger again with a slight tilt of his head. "Do you always keep that with you?"

I run my thumb along the hilt of my dagger. "It's become a part of me. Most of the time I forget it's even with me anymore."

"I see. There really is no need for that anymore," he says, tugging against my arm as we resume walking. "At least while you're here."

My hand lingers on the dagger, wondering if he is right and if it makes others uncomfortable. I focus more on the people we pass but not once do any of them glance at the dagger. Though its design screams 'pirate,' it was a gift from Gus. Besides, I consider it more of a tool than a cause of violence.

Orson takes us toward a white brick building with the name *Williams's Flowers* in an elegant script across a yellow and blue sign. "I'd like to show you the newest shop. It's been very popular for most of the women here." As we step in, bundles of different flowers are scattered throughout, all strategically placed in groups of the same color. It reminds me of a vibrant rainbow after a storm. I take a deep breath, savoring the different fragrances of lilacs, roses, lilies, and peonies.

"Find anything that catches your eye?" Orson asks, following close by with his hands behind his back.

A glimpse of a different type of rose shouts my name from across the room. I've never seen anything so breathtaking. The roses are a light blue turning into a bright yellow with a tinge of pink on the ends.

"Ah, yes. It's called Gwendora, a new flower created here on this very island by the Williams family."

"Gwendora?" I bring one to my nose, inhaling the rose's scent. It reminds me of sunsets and kisses.

He chuckles underneath his breath. "You said it right. It's

named after Gwen Williams who produced it. She's a very talented and well-educated young girl. She's been raised to the best of standards, I may say. I always thought Gwen and Axel would be a perfect match."

I return the rose to its place, uneasy about his comment. I can't help but feel like he is looking down on me for not being as well educated as this Gwen girl.

He plucks a couple of the Gwendora roses, taking them to the register. "We are very lucky for them to have traveled far to live here. Gwen's father Theodore is a talented soldier who trains our men but, as you know, that's not enough to keep this island protected from others." I hold my tongue, knowing he means pirates. "It's too large and we need more."

A male voice brings me back to reality, making me jump slightly. "Good day, miss." His dark hair frames a handsome face plastered with a welcoming smile. He gestures for the roses, wrapping them after Orson hands them over. As I watch, I begin to guess that this store is popular with women for a far different reason than just flowers.

"Ah, here is one of the Williams. Elle meet Troy, the son of the family. Troy this is Elle, she's visiting Glendora."

Troy shakes my hand, leaving some dirt on mine. "Nice to meet you, Elle." He notices the dirt left on my hand. "Ah, sorry about that. I swear I can never keep anything clean." He tugs a cloth from his back pocket and wipes my hand off.

"It's no big deal. And I'm not just visiting. I'm staying here. Permanently," I say, catching a glimpse of Orson's shoulders tense. That will show him for speaking for me.

"You won't regret it," Troy says, tying the paper wrapped around the roses so they create a small bouquet. He hands them to me with a twinkle in his eyes. "Are you planning to be at the ball?"

"She is. You two should share a dance!" Orson says in an over-exaggerated voice.

"I'd like that," Troy says. "Maybe I'll see you around before then. I'm usually here if you would like a tour of the gardens sometime. I'd show you today, but we will be closing soon."

I'm a bit uncomfortable with the way Orson is eyeing me and Troy, but I wouldn't mind learning more about the flowers here. There is something more about Glendora and how everything produced here is so perfect. It almost like magic. "I'm sure I'll stop by again sooner or later."

"I'll be looking forward to it," he says, giving me a slight bow. "Good day, Orson."

We bid goodbye and head out the door. The sun is starting to set, the streets quieter than before with a few finishing their shopping. "Thank you for the flowers but it is getting late, I probably should head back."

"Time has gone faster than I thought. I'll walk you back to your horse."

"There really is no need," I say, walking a bit faster.

"Nonsense. It would only be proper," he says, holding out his elbow again.

How easily could I roll my eyes by the way he says '*proper*,' but I contain it by taking his arm.

"I'm sure you have heard how important the ball is this year for Axel?" he asks in a more direct voice.

I roll my neck preparing myself for him to say something I'm not going to like. "I have."

"Good. Then I'm sure you know Axel has many responsibilities and the choice he makes at the ball will be one of the most important decisions for Glendora."

"And for Axel," I retort. Holy kraken, how much further to the dress shop? I wish I had the ability to whistle to signal for Bertha to come to me.

"Yes, right. He deserves to find someone who can be supportive with high standards. A lady I'm sure he will find at the ball, and I don't want any distractions before then." He stops and faces me. "Wouldn't you agree?"

I grit my teeth, withdrawing my hand from his elbow and clenching the rose stems so I don't throw them in his face. "I understand. I'm sure he will make the right decision when the day comes." My chest heats. "I can find my way. Good night." I rush back to Bertha.

Tears fill my eyes as I ride back to the house. Thinking about what Orson said makes me want to scream. I'm well aware of who I am. I pause. But who am I anymore? I'm no longer a pirate but I'm also not an educated woman racing to be married. No matter where I go, I feel as if I can't be my complete self. On the ship I was too much of a woman and here I'm not enough of one.

By the time I make it back to the house, it's dark and a light rain prickles against my skin. I'm sure Nile and Axel have already eaten and are getting ready for bed. I head to the stables, unsaddling Bertha, and letting her back out into the pasture.

"There you are," Axel says behind me, making me jump.

"Sorry. I lost track of time." I hasten past him, trying to keep away from the light of the lantern he is holding. All I want is to rest in my bed.

He steps closer to me as I take a step away from him. "I went to the docks. Dibs said you were with my uncle."

"Yes, he took me to *Williams's Flowers*." I raise my hand holding the bouquet of flowers. "He bought me these Gwendora roses but I'm unsure what to do with them now."

"I can put them in a vase for you," he says, and I let him take them from me. His eyebrows narrow.

"It's been a long day, and I should get some rest," I say briskly, catching my breath. I feel my throat tightening and turn away before he can say anything else.

CHAPTER 35

AXEL

The sound of Clarence's hooves galloping against the barely seen path matches my heart jarring against my chest. My shadow follows as moonlight shines between trees and toward the house I'm approaching. An owl protests loudly in the distance as I scare his prey into hiding.

Once I'm at the gate of Orson's house, I barely get Clarence to a complete stop before jumping out of the saddle. I have one purpose this late evening and that is to figure out what Orson said to Elle, though I already have an idea. She can't fool me. Once she told me Orson took her to *Williams's Flowers*, I knew exactly why.

I bang on the door. Silence. I bang again and turn to see Clarence is back to eating grass after I interrupted his meal earlier.

A candle flickers through a side window. Orson's bedroom. I bang louder, not letting up. The door opens slowly, his head poking out, sleep in his eyes. "Boy, why are you waking me up in the middle of the night? You should be happy your aunt can sleep through anything," he grumbles.

I shove the door open. "What did you say to her?"

Orson's eyes widen slightly. "To whom?"

My head shakes automatically. "Don't play dumb with me, Uncle," I reply, my breathing increasing with annoyance.

He sighs and puts his hand on my shoulder. His eyes are stern and serious. "I only want the best for you, Axel. You and Elle are no match. I see the way you look at her, but she is not what you want."

I shrug his hand off. "You have no right to say who I should and shouldn't be with. You barely even know her."

"I know enough. She hasn't been raised like you. You need someone who can be the wife you need while you take care of Glendora. She keeps a dagger on her person, for flying sakes."

"Yes, for backstabbers like you!" I blurt. My thoughts fill with the few memories I have of my mother. My father did love her in his own way, but neither she, nor I, were ever put first. I want a wife by my side who is willing to speak up and join in the conversation of the business. Someone who will take charge when needed while also loving others before herself.

I swallow, making sure to choose my words carefully. Looking square into his eyes, I say, "I have done everything demanded of me, that I have been trained to do my whole life. I'm even choosing to marry someone I may barely know." I take a deep breath. "But if you love me like a son then I ask only one thing of you. Be happy for me with whoever I choose. Elle is Nile's sister and that means she will always be a part of my life, wife or not, I never want a bad word about her to come out of your mouth again."

"But what about Natia? She would be a perfect fit for you, including what her father has offered. It's truly more important than ever before to keep Glendora safe. Elle can't—"

"Not another word about her, Orson," I say, making a sharp motion with my hands as indication for him to stop, my shoulders tight.

Orson's eyes soften and he leans against the doorframe, the lines of his aged face appearing deeper in the moonlight. "I do want you to be happy, and I promise you that love can come later after marriage. Just remember that. Think wisely before making a lifetime decision. Not just for me, but for all of Glendora."

That is the best answer I'm going to get from him and so be it.

I have nothing else to say and take my leave. Mounting Clarence, I trot off without looking back.

Desperately needing a drink, I head toward *The Blue Flask*, hoping Carmen is still there. She always seems to say the right thing; I'm hoping she will do that tonight.

"Well, looky here, prince charming has arrived before the stroke of midnight," Carmen says while locking the door. Her hair is a mess, clearly ready to rest in her own bed. I smile sheepishly, hoping she will rethink closing.

She groans and waves me in. "I was hoping to get some shut eye, but you look like you need a drink."

I head straight toward the bar, thumping the weight of everything on my shoulders into the chair.

"That bad, huh?" She asks, already putting a drink in my hand and, just as quickly, I gulp it down. Warmth slides down my throat, expanding into my chest. "I don't know how I'm going to do it, Carmen."

"Do what exactly?" She refills my glass.

"This whole time I have known I'm going to be engaged soon, and I've barely taken any initiative to get to know these other women. Now it's only two weeks away and I . . ."

I eye her and hesitate. She leans on her elbows, egging me to continue. She wants me to say it.

"I think it's always been her. It's like I have been waiting for her."

"For whom?" Carmen asks with a mischievous look.

"Eleanor! Carmen, Eleanor!"

"Okay, okay, sheesh, you don't have to yell. I just wanted you to admit it. Finally."

I groan and take another swig of my liquor. "We have barely had any time alone, and the last time we did . . . I screwed up." I take another swig, trying to black out the memory of my lips barely touching hers. "I don't want her to feel rushed. She's been through enough."

"So, give it a chance. You have two weeks. Tons of things can happen within that time."

"You act as if this is so simple, but it isn't. So many things are at stake."

"Appreciate the moments you have with her. Don't allow the council nor your father to stop you from missing out on the best thing that can happen to you."

I take a deep breath, shaking my head and contemplating what Carmen is saying. I can't allow my feelings for Eleanor to get in the way of me marrying another. *For Glendora*, I repeat in my head. *For Glendora. For Glendora.*

Carmen slowly smiles, to the point it's comical.

"Why are you smiling like that?"

"Because you're so cute when you're in love," she says smoothly.

I choke on my drink.

She smirks, picking up a rag, cleaning off the table. "What?" she asks, as if stating I was in love was just another daily conversation.

I wipe my mouth and focus on the drink I'm holding, not sure If I have the guts to look at Carmen. "I said nothing about love."

The mood in the room changes. My chair squeaks as I shift nervously in it. I can feel Carmen's fierce knowing eyes on me, waiting for me to fess up. That I'm being a complete fool.

Carmen leans on her elbows and moves closer to me. "You literally just said it's always been her. If you want it, fight for it. Maybe she's been waiting all this time for you, too."

CHAPTER 36

ELLE

The warm sunlight signals a waking world, yet my body wants sleep despite my mind's all-night resistance. I hate myself for allowing Orson to take any more sleep from me. That I can't push away the thought that maybe he is right.

I sink deeper into my soft covers, wanting to forget any feelings I have for Axel.

A long time ago I promised myself I wouldn't allow any man to get in my way. But deep down, I know why Axel is making me question myself. He isn't just any man. I groan loudly and put a pillow over my head.

The door swings open, banging against the wall. Nile jumps onto the bed, Gus following closely behind as I try to sit up. "Wake up, sleepy head!"

"Breakfast is downstairs," Gus says softly. "It's getting cold."

"I must have overslept," I say, rubbing my eyes. Nile grabs my arm and pulls me out of bed while I pretend my limbs are heavy.

"You need to hurry. I think Axel wants to take you somewhere."

My body jolts and I stand up straight. The thought of being alone with Axel makes my palms sweat. "But are we not riding together this morning?"

"Well," he plays with the sheets. "I was going to tell you at dinner last night, but Gus is going to take me fishing and he said this is the best weather for it."

My heart swarms. "I see. That's very nice of him."

Nile perks up. "So, you're not mad?"

"Of course, not. We have plenty of time to ride together again, silly."

"Good." He hugs me and jumps off the bed. "Hurry, Axel's waiting for you." Nile is already out the door, his loud footsteps trailing down the stairs. Gus gives me a faint smile, turning to follow.

"Wait! Can we talk for a moment? I know it's been a bit hectic, finding out that we have a brother and that—" I pause, unsure if I should even bring up our mother. The last time I did, he was short and left in a hurry with Nile.

"Our mother is dead," he finishes my sentence with a hint of anger in those words. He shuffles his feet, looking at the carpet. "I really don't want to talk about it."

"Please, Gus."

"This is new to me," he says lightly. "Living under a roof in a soft bed, having a brother that I'm already completely protective of, but also"—he looks up at me his eyes with a hint of more warmth—"seeing my sister laugh again." His comment makes me stop.

"I laugh," I state with hesitation, pondering why I'm lying to myself. Wondering why I allowed myself to be so miserable on *The Turbulence*. Only hoping for things to get better when they never did.

I can tell he is still keeping something from me. "Do you want to leave?"

He scratches his head and shakes it. "No, I could never leave Nile nor take him away from all the people that love him but it's not that. You are living like *The Turbulence* is in the past while I can't seem to let it go. I'm envious that you can so easily do that."

If only he knew that our father still lingers in the back of my mind on a daily basis.

He clenches his hands into fists and then straightens his fingers. "I would have died if it wasn't for you," Gus clears his throat. "He was going to let me die. He had the means to give me the medicine, but he didn't. I lived my whole life trying to be the best son for him and it meant nothing. Now I have no clue what I'm supposed to do." He laughs faintly.

I slowly walk toward him. It's odd to hear my brother speak of his feelings, but it all makes sense to me. He loved our father, and it hurts when you don't get it back. Hesitantly, I put my arms around him and squeeze. I can't remember the last time I hugged Gus. He does the same. I close my eyes, wishing we spoke more freely, but this learning curve will take some time. "We lost him a long time ago, Gus. He can't hurt us anymore."

He pulls back. "You know he won't forget what you did. We need to take precautions. That's one of the reasons Nile and I are going fishing. To view the beaches, see where he may be able to breach the island."

"Axel has this whole island being patrolled," I state. But knowing our father, that won't keep him away.

"Have you seen Illira? Or spoken to her since we got here?"

"She didn't show when I tried to call for her. But I will try again," I say. An uneasiness builds in my stomach, upset with myself for not calling for her again sooner.

"Let me know when you see her and have fun today," he says, giving me a childish wink and shutting the door.

What is that supposed to mean?

Unsure exactly what Axel has in mind for today, I put on my riding pants and boots. Instead of braiding my hair, I let it flow freely. I stop and glance at my dagger next to the dress stand, remembering Orson's distasteful look. With a smug smile, I strap it around my thigh.

Hungry from barely eating anything the night before, my stomach grumbles when the scent of bacon and eggs reach me.

Axel stands abruptly as I walk into the dining room. His radiant smile is contagious. His cheeks redden but when he catches sight of my dagger, his smile turns approving.

"I heard we're going somewhere this morning," I say while piling eggs on to my plate.

"Yes," he says, sitting back down. "It's a surprise."

I raise my eyes from my food. "A surprise?"

A smirk tugs at the corner of his mouth as he takes a drink of his coffee. "Mhmm. It will take most of the day, so we won't be back until dinner. I packed lunch for us."

Though I wait for him to say more, he stays quiet, his eyes mischievous.

We head east toward the cliffs, and I think we are going to his favorite spot until we ride past the cove, toward the center of the island.

"It's not far from here, just between those two trees. We can tie our horses there," he says, bringing his horse to a trot. I focus on the two giant trees that are probably five ship lengths away, and the large boulders behind them. It is an odd place for giant rocks to be surrounded by rolling hills of green grass. Like they were placed there instead of naturally occurring.

Axel rides closer to me and I'm hyper aware his leg almost touches mine. Why is it whenever he gets close to me my body draws to him? Like his skin has a secret and the only way to find out that secret is by touching him.

"Want to race?" he asks, holding Clarence back. His horse prances like he knows what the word *race* means.

My stomach rumbles thinking about going faster and my voice is lost trying to keep my composure as I shake my head, with a soft "okay."

Axel speeds to a canter, and Bertha increases her speed to stay with Clarence. I grab the horn for a split second, questioning if I can do it but take a deep breath and move with her.

"Just stay with me, I know you can do it. Nile has been saying for a week now that you're ready. I'll let you decide when you want to go faster," Axel says.

Underneath me I can feel Bertha wanting to go faster but patiently waiting for me to squeeze my legs for more speed. Axel stays next to me, his chestnut hair blowing across his eyebrows every time he turns to check on me. He gives me a reassuring smile and for a second I forget about the fear of losing control and squeeze a bit more.

Bertha goes faster, leaving a stride ahead of Axel. The sound of our horses' hoof beats hitting the ground sounds like thunder rolling against the sky. I keep my eyes ahead of me, my heart beating in my chest, and I focus on keeping in rhythm with each step.

"Come on, you can go faster than that!" Axel yells, galloping ahead of me. His shirt billows with the breeze.

I inhale and squeeze harder. Bertha doesn't miss a beat, and we burst forward, my hair flying behind me. The grass looks like waves of the sea as we travel faster. My heart wants to jump out of my mouth but at the same time my adrenaline is urging me to keep going. I lower the reins and lean forward, touching the top of Bertha's mane.

And I let go.

I let go of the fear that has been hiding inside of me since I was a little girl. The thought of not being good enough. The thought of being alone. The wind blowing against me takes all my worries and gusts them away.

My body feels light and free as I move with Bertha like we're one. We catch up to Clarence and Axel and pass them. A flash of my mother doing the same thing makes my vision blur for a second. *No wonder she loved this.*

I take a deep breath. "I trust you, girl," I say, spreading my arms out like I have wings. I lean my head back and laugh. Tasting complete freedom. Like a bird flying against the wind.

Axel catches up to me. He looks like a natural atop Clarence, moving like he is a part of the horse. I never thought a man could look so good on horseback but the sight of him makes my lips tingle. He smiles charmingly, his dimple quickening my heartbeat.

We approach the two giant trees, and I relax. Bertha follows my every movement until we reach a complete stop. I laugh, thinking how silly it was for me to take so long to ride faster. Ready to do it again.

"I could do that all day," I say, sliding out of the saddle, giving Bertha a kiss on the cheek before tying her to the tree.

Axel dismounts and tosses one of the saddlebags over his shoulder. He holds out his hand, silently asking me to take it. Our fingers intertwine as I follow him through the trees.

The two giant boulders before us block whatever is behind them and I wonder if we are meant to walk around them.

"One second." Axel disappears between the two boulders by sliding around a corner I didn't think anyone could fit through.

After a few minutes, he comes back without the bag. "Close your eyes."

I give him a funny look.

"Trust me." He holds out his hand for me to take again. I hesitate but close my eyes as we slither between the two rocks, his strong grip guiding me.

The sounds of birds singing and water flowing catch my attention. "Don't open them yet," he says, bringing me to a stop. His hands move around my hips, urging me to turn. "Now, open."

A swarm of colorful butterflies are flying everywhere I look. There must be at least a thousand, maybe more!

"They migrate here every year before they go farther north," he whispers in my ear. I can barely speak as I put my hands in the air letting the butterflies dance all around me. They land on my arms and the tips of my fingers. In addition to the butterflies, there is also a galore of vibrant flowers growing all around. Sunlight peeks between the trees, creating a shimmering array of colors when it hits the water that flows from one of the boulders. It's as if I'm in a whole different world. A small paradise. I have never seen anything so enchanting, almost like it was gifted by magic.

"Has anyone told you that when a butterfly lands on you, it's a sign of good luck?" Axel asks as he moves within the group of butterflies, holding out his arms for them to land.

"Looks like you're good luck as well," I say with a light giggle.

He looks at the few fluttering close to his ear. "I am pretty lucky," he says, looking back at me, giving me a smile that only makes him even more handsome. My cheeks burn as if his look alone can warm every inch of my skin.

He slowly walks toward me, and the butterflies open a space for him to come closer. The gaze he gives me creates invisible butterflies in my stomach, fluttering around wildly.

"Why did you bring me here?" I ask softly.

He stops when his toes almost touch mine. His eyes are sincere and glimmer with a shade of concern and seriousness. "You need to know I believe nothing Orson said to you."

I bite my lip, unsure what to say. I didn't want to believe what Orson had said but in some ways he was right. I am who I am, and nothing can change my past. This is me.

"I see those gears moving in that head of yours." He glides his hand up my cheek, threading his fingers through my hair, and leans closer. "You are beautiful just as you are, good luck."

Every word he says sounds truthful and honest. It's refreshing and pure.

"You need to understand. Soon I will have to make a decision and this—"

"I know," I say, stepping close enough our chests graze each other. I don't want to hear about the ball or the politics or stipulations. I just want to be with him without the outside world telling us what we should be doing. "Can we just take this moment?" I whisper, tilting my head slightly. "And forget everything else, even if it's only for today?"

There is no need to say more. Axel's lips are soft as they firmly touch mine. My body shakes, like it demands more of him. His tongue finds mine, unlocking my very soul. He tastes like freedom and salt, like he's made by the sea. How can a kiss be so good? I want to somehow be closer even though there's no space between us. I feel like I'm out of air, but I don't want him to stop. Just his simple touch breaks me.

Axel splits away, his blue eyes locking onto mine. He grabs a hold of my hips and pulls me up to his chest. My legs wrap around him, placing me between him and the closest tree. His hand laces through my hair, sending shivers racing down my spine. I already miss his lips and move in, but he turns, brushing his cheek against mine. His hot breath is warm against my ear. "Don't ever change," he says before grazing his lips against my neck and back to my demanding mouth. Oh, how could I devour him every day, every night.

I told myself I'd never get attached to a man, but I can already feel the threads slowly breaking one by one with each longing caress. Feelings rise to the surface that I can no longer ignore.

I'm unsure how long we stay intertwined before Axel lowers me to the ground. He leans his forehead on mine, both of us catching our breath. My stomach grumbles loudly.

"I think it's time for lunch," he says, kissing my nose.

He sets out a blanket next to the small pond where we can watch the waterfall flow into it. I sit and take in the complete paradise that surrounds me. Even the water is the clearest I've ever seen, the bottom full of small colorful rocks shimmering like crystals.

Axel hands me a sandwich and puts a bowl of fruit out for us to share. I take a giant bite, hungrier than I thought and finish within a few bites. Axel smirks before taking a bite of a strawberry. I lick my lips and tell myself to let him enjoy his meal before devouring him once again.

"What is this place?" I ask, studying the surroundings so I won't be distracted by wishing I was the food near his lips. "I never would have thought something like this could be concealed by two boulders."

"I wouldn't have either, but it's always been here. Only my ancestors, my father, Orson, and . . . now you, know about it." He pulls some of the grass next to him by the roots, a sapphire color glows at the end of them. "We believe it's the center of life for this island. Something about this soil here makes everything grow abundantly and strong. We also believe this is why we can produce medicine that cures almost anything. It's still a mystery to us but it's important for this place to stay secret."

My eyes widen as Axel places the grass into my hands. This is amazing. It makes so much more sense why everything seems so alive in Glendora. The things this soil can do for so many . . . the profit but also the demand. I stop and place it back into his hand. "What made you decide to share the medicine?"

Axel sighs. "Because I cannot in good conscience hold back from helping others. And yes, it will also bring questions. Questions that will lead to demanding answers. Answers that could lead to it being taken by force." He runs his hands through his chestnut hair. "But if questions arise, so be it. When that time comes, I'll do my best to keep Glendora protected." There is a silence lingering between us, not voicing what we both know, what he must do to keep Glendora safe.

"Why are you telling me this?"

"Because I trust you," he says firmly. "I want you to know why Glendora is so special but also why Orson is so . . ." He pauses, moving his neck side to side like he's deciding how to finish his sentence. "So protective."

"It makes sense," I say, choosing not to add what I think of Orson.

"I'm not giving any validation for what he said to you. These shipments have made him a bit greedy and overpowering but that is why I think he should take a break and help me elsewhere while you and Gus take his place. I've already spoken to my father about it, but we haven't spoken about this since we were at the beach. Are you still interested in helping at the docks?" He swallows like he's hesitant to continue. "Are you and Gus planning to stay in Glendora?"

My cheeks redden, thinking of our almost kiss back on the beach. I never would have thought only a few days later we would be here. "Yes," I reply.

Axel smiles wide, his dimples appearing, making my heart race and wishing he didn't have such an effect on me as he did.

For the rest of the afternoon, Axel shows me the small patch of paradise while he keeps his arms around me as if cherishing every moment before it has to end.

CHAPTER 37

ELLE

The next two weeks go faster than I have wanted. I ride with Nile almost daily and Axel makes a point when he can to join while Gus watches close by and still refuses to get on a horse. All of us together brings up a swell of emotions I try to ignore. It's almost like we're a little family, but I push the thought away. It isn't going to stay this way.

Axel hasn't been able to teach me sign language as much as he was, stating he has meetings to attend. We both don't acknowledge his *meetings* are dates with women from the other kingdoms, but their pristine ships can't be ignored when they arrive at port. I know he has a decision to make and the time we spent together isn't confirmation that we would be together in the end. We were enjoying ourselves, that is all.

"You barely touched your food," Nile says next to me during our usual lunch stop at *The Blue Flask*.

I blink away my thoughts and take a swig of my water. Axel left the table after a short sign language lesson. I clench my hands, still feeling the warmth of his hands on mine from moments ago. I've been able to show Charlie what I have been learning and seeing his genuine smile makes me more determined to learn.

"Sorry, Nile. I was thinking about all that needs to be done at the shipyard," I state.

Nile veers his eyes toward the entrance door to where Axel stands with Orson. Discussing the ball, most likely. No matter where I go, everyone talks about the Glendora ball, constantly reminding me of it. "Mhmm," Nile says, rolling his eyes and shaking his head.

Can this eight-year-old boy notice what is really on my mind? I'm starting to learn I can't trick Nile. He is quite observant.

Carmen walks by with two plates of desert. "Nile, I made your favorite: chocolate cake."

A familiar loud laugh echoes across the tavern. All three of us turn toward the sound and I spot the girl from the dress shop, Natia, speaking to Axel. Standing a little too close.

I fidget with a loose thread on my chair, watching Axel converse with her. Orson beams from ear to ear next to them. The room is too warm, my cheeks burning. My gut wants to explode. Axel's eyes find mine for a second and I focus back on my food.

Carmen pats my hand. "You know he isn't trying—"

"I know, Carmen."

I peek behind me only to see them all leave. Soon he is going to be engaged and most likely to *her*.

Gus and I will have to find our own place once Axel gets married. And what about Nile? Who will he stay with? Axel or us? Thinking about it all only makes my head hurt.

Dibs walks to the table with alarm in her eyes. "Someone at the docks is asking for you. He won't speak to anyone but you."

My chair skids as I stand up, my hand going to my dagger. I relax my muscles, not wanting to scare Nile, whose face is full of chocolate cake. "I'll be right back."

Carmen stays with Nile as I leave for the docks with Dibs.

"Does he look familiar to you?" I ask, thinking there would be no possible way for anyone from *The Turbulence* to arrive without being stopped first.

"No, I've never seen him. He doesn't look to be a pirate either, more of a tradesman."

When I spot his ash-brown hair and the blue feathers in his hat,

I already know who it is. You could say he was the closest acquaintance of Gus's when we were younger on *The Turbulence* before leaving to do the captain's bidding elsewhere. Dorr turns toward me, puffing out his chest as he looks down on me.

A knot grows in the pit of my stomach already hating how little he makes me feel. I raise my chin, plastering a fake smile. "Dorr, you always have a knack for fashion, but this," I say, taking an exaggerated step back and pretending to admire his lavish black boots and blue dress shirt that coordinate with the familiar blue feathers on his black hat. "How many times did you have to lie and cheat to get it?"

He sneers with one side of his mouth, which tips his chest-length beard to the side. "I'd have to ask you the same," he says with similar scrutiny of my appearance. "It seems you found a man to feel pity for you and dress you with decent clothes."

I swallow back the burning hate of his words, readying a barbed reply when Dibs steps closer to me, her mouth tight. Dorr eyes Dibs with annoyance, flicking his eyes as a silent suggestion she leave. She crosses her arms, warning him that she won't.

"It's okay, Dibs. This won't take long." I nod reassuringly as she takes a few steps back to give us some privacy.

"That's all you're going to get," she states.

I hold back a smile, appreciating her determination to stay nearby. "Shouldn't you be elsewhere."

He spits next to my feet. "As should you." He looks around, eyebrows hunching into a full unibrow. "Nice place. A little too nice for you, wouldn't you say?"

"What do you want, Dorrance?" I ask, my voice deepening.

"Rude. I haven't seen you in years and this is how you treat me?"

My hand hovers near my dagger, my mouth flat with disdain.

Dorr shrugs. "Have it your way. I'm here to warn you. The captain you so lovingly betrayed wants you to follow through on what you promised him."

I tighten my jaw, grinding my teeth. "I owe him nothing and if he ever tries to step foot on Glendora or come close to any of their ships, I will kill him myself."

He snickers, flicking his nose up in the air. "You seem to forget what blood runs in your veins. Don't think just because you're on this island that you're safe or that you're ever going to be like any of these people." His lips curl as a couple walks past. "A pirate is always a pirate. Even a filthy female like yourself."

I swallow back the rage that boils in my stomach, wishing his words didn't hurt like they did. "It's time for you to leave," I say, stepping forward.

"Don't say I didn't warn you. I'll be sure to tell your mermaid friend hello for you."

My mouth falls open, dread crawling up my skin. Is he baiting me or has my father captured Illira?

"Ah, now I have your attention."

My whole body shakes as I try to contain my composure. "What does he want?"

Dorr lowers his head, keeping his voice low so only I can hear. "Bring the medicine to his favorite spot. He won't wait long. I don't think your friend can last much longer either," he adds before his eyes move toward a boy now standing next to me.

"I've never seen feathers like that before." Nile says next to my hip and pointing toward the blue feathers on Dorr's hat. My eyes widen and I hear Carmen distantly yelling Nile's name in frustration.

Dorr leans down, obviously assessing Nile. "And who's this?"

"I'm Elle's brother, Nile," he says, grabbing a hold of my hand and leaning into me.

Dorr's dark eyes squint in thought. "You have another brother?"

A gust of air blows past me and next I realize, Gus is standing above Dorr, who is sprawled in the dirt, blood trickling down the side of his lip.

"You're not welcome here!" Gus growls.

People around the docks stop to watch the commotion. Dibs and I pull Nile back, shoving him into Carmen's arms so she can take him back to the tavern despite his loud protests.

Dorr picks up his hat and stands back up with a grunt, wiping the blood off his chin. "So, you're alive. I was wondering if you were hiding. Just as you always did behind Velis."

Gus clenches his fists. "That's the only warning I'm giving you."

Dorr puts his hands in the air. "I did what I needed to do." Dorr winks, pulling down his shirt and flicking off dirt. "Enjoy the ball and tell Nile it was nice meeting him."

We watch him walk back to his ship before Gus turns to me. "What did he want?"

I shift my weight, preparing to lie, something I've never been good at doing. "Nothing. You know him. He is most likely here for some trading."

Gus shakes his head. "No. This was no coincidence. You know he still conspires with our father. And now he knows about Nile! We need to leave."

I hear Dibs inhale sharply, like she wants to say something.

My voice lowers as I tell Gus, "If you're right, then the best option is to stay here on land. Not out at sea where he has eyes everywhere and you know that. Besides, we can't just take Nile. His family and friends are here."

"We're his family!" Gus rolls his neck. "Nile is *our* brother. If we must leave, we will." He pushes past Dibs and I, his steps heavy against the ground as he walks toward *The Blue Flask*.

I'm ready to scream. How long has Illira, my friend, been in the hands of my father? Sniffling, I press my fingers against my eyes to stem the tears and offer Dibs what I hope is a reassuring smile before heading back to the tavern to make sure Nile is okay.

If anyone leaves Glendora, it will be me. I did this and I'm the one that will end it between me and my father. I have already lost my mother, and I don't plan to lose anyone else I love even if it means I may not return.

Making up my mind on what I will do to get Illira back repeats over and over in my mind as I help load boxes of the new honeysuckle medicine onto *The Blazing Star* for the next shipment. Carmen, Dibs, and Doolah eye me with concern throughout the afternoon as I mainly keep to myself knowing that I'm soon going to betray them. That I will be taking this ship to my father. *To save Illira.*

Wanting rest, I remind myself to enjoy the time I have left with Gus and Nile. Though Axel is, once again, absent from dinner, I join my brothers. Gus surprises me by telling me he will be going to the ball but only because Nile relentlessly pleaded with him. Then Nile talks about his favorite fish and how he wishes he could breathe underwater. I contain a small laugh by his comment but sadness dwells behind it, thinking of how Illira and Nile would have so much fun together. Gus eyes me and I note how tense his shoulders are. He hasn't spoken to me about what transpired earlier but I can tell by the fierce determination in his eyes that he has a plan brewing in his mind.

"Can we please check the fishing lines tomorrow?" Nile begs.

Gus shifts in his seat. "I told you; you need to stay inland tomorrow. Because of the ball, remember?" Gus's voice is deep and stern.

Nile shrugs his shoulders. "But I'll take a bath after. I promise I won't smell like fish before the ball. I can even go check on them in the morning by myself, I know what to do."

"The answer is no. We can go another time," Gus replies.

Nile turns to me, silently begging me to change Gus's mind. "You need to listen to your brother. It's a very important day tomorrow," I say, hoping the sadness in his hazel eyes will dim but instead they focus back and forth toward me and Gus.

"Can we not go because of that man from early?" he asks.

The candlelight flickers from the light breeze flowing through the dining window. Gus's fork clangs against the porcelain plate as he gets up to shut the window, leaving me to answer the question.

I shake my head, placing my hand gently onto Nile's arm. "You don't need to worry about that man. It was just a misunderstanding between your brother and him, that *should* have been dealt with differently," I say, side eyeing Gus whose jaw clenches before he takes a bite of his stew. "We have a lot of new visitors coming from many different lands to visit Glendora and it would be best if you stayed closer to home while they are here."

Nile heaves a sigh, like a weight has been lifted off his shoulders. "Very well." He takes a cinnamon honeysuckle biscuit and wraps it in a napkin. "Can I be excused? I'd like to read some before bedtime." I nod in agreement and give him a kiss on his forehead before he scoots out of his seat.

"Wait, Nile," Gus walks toward him and he gets on his knees before bringing him into a hug. Nile hugs him back, his small arms tight around Gus's neck. An ache of sadness looms at the tender interaction, wishing Gus and I could have had the same relationship growing up.

I wait to hear Nile's bedroom door shut down the hallway before daring to speak more about what just transpired as Gus resumes his seat and continues his meal.

"You know you can't keep him away from the shoreline forever," I state. "He is obviously shaken up about Dorr."

Gus leans his elbows onto the table and leans toward me, eyebrows narrowing. "And I know you're not telling me everything, Elle. Dorr wasn't just here for the fun of it. He plays games just like our father. What did he say and what are you planning?"

I take a sip of my drink, hoping to keep my facial expressions neutral instead of showing any inkling about the plans that have been running through my brain. "Like I said, it was nothing."

Gus shakes his head, his eyes weary with concern. "I thought we were done lying to one another," he says softly.

I can't bear to look at him and start to pick at my stew, not wanting to see his disappointment. "Fine, don't answer me," he says. His steps are heavy on the wooden floor. "Don't wait up for me. I'll be at Theordore's for some combat training."

Illira, please be okay, I whisper to myself as I slowly head to my bedroom, reminding myself that it's only for the best I don't tell Gus what my plans are. If I did, he'd go with me and leave Nile without a brother or sister.

I slither into my bed sheets, wanting to embrace my comfortable bed one last time but a loud knock at my door interrupts it. I hesitate before another knock, and I drag myself out of bed. Before I make it, the door swings in front of me and almost hits my nose.

"Geez, Elle, you're so slow," Dibs says, carrying a giant white box in her arms. A giddy Carmen is on her heels.

"I was trying to sleep. If you haven't noticed, it's late," I say before checking to see if there's any light coming from Axel's bedroom before closing my door.

"Sleep can wait! We have a surprise for you," Carmen says, eagerly rubbing her hands together.

Dibs places the box on my bed and opens it. "When I saw this, I knew it would be perfect for you." She pulls out a long dress the color of soft violet.

Happiness and guilt rush through me equally as I adore the beauty of the dress. "I wasn't sure If I was going to go," I say, running my hands down the silky-smooth fabric.

"Nonsense!" Carmen says, helping Dibs lay the dress out on the bed. "Now undress so we can help you put this on."

I know I won't win this argument, so I give them both an eye roll before turning around and taking off my long night shirt. They giggle behind me as they tug the dress over my head. They tie the lace tight behind my back and shuffle me toward the full-length mirror.

The dress fits *perfectly*. Never have I felt so beautiful and elegant in all my life. Attached to the corset top are sheer sleeves that are partially sewn on the bodice, leaving my shoulders bare. The corset tapers into a soft 'v' shape, guiding the eye to the waves of fabric flowing delicately to my feet. Carmen grabs the necklace my mother gave me from the dresser and clasps it around my neck.

Dibs claps and jumps up and down with an ecstatic squeal. "I just knew it! It's simply perfect."

My throat constricts, feeling cherished by this small act. "You guys really shouldn't have," I whisper, worried I can't tell them how thankful I am to have them in my life without getting teary-eyed.

Carmen rests her chin on my shoulder, studying me in the mirror. "As I've said before, that's what friends are for." Dibs goes to my other side and gives me a squeeze.

I never thought this could be real. A life with real friendships that I can openly talk to, with whom I feel safe and loved. I never even thought I'd enjoy hugs so much.

After they leave, I turn my back toward the mirror. One of my scar marks peaks past the corset. Tears run down my cheek, the slash marks reminding me of who I am and what I'll soon be leaving behind.

CHAPTER 38

AXEL

My hands ache from clenching them underneath the table for the past hour. The meeting Orson organized at his home is taking longer than I expected. But King Toradian and his daughter Natia are not to be ignored. This is another one of his ploys for me to agree to a marriage before the ball has even started.

I've barely eaten any of my meals or attuned to what my father, King Beris, or Orson have been discussing. Tomorrow I will be making an important decision but all I can think about is Eleanor. The day we kissed replays in my mind. What I wouldn't give to go back to that moment, to savor the sweet taste of her lips. My promise to not let my feelings linger for longer that day, for them not to interfere with my impending engagement, have failed greatly.

How am I going to make a choice tomorrow? I want to slither into a hole rather than play nice with the Toradians.

Orson clears his throat. "That sounds like a great proposition. Don't you think, Axel?"

Theodore sits next to me and nudges me with his foot. I blink away my thoughts and focus on Orson. His eyes widen, warning me to answer while my father sits next to him with a suspicious frown.

Without thinking, I push out of my seat, bumping against the table and making wine slosh from my glass. "Please excuse me," I say, needing to get some air.

"I'd love to show you Orson's garden! I'm told you haven't seen it since it's been updated," Natia says, already standing and grabbing a hold of my arm.

"Yes, yes, delightful idea my dear," her mother says, grinning conspiratorially while King Baron grumbles under his breath.

Natia's arm wraps around mine, pulling me toward the back door.

"I could create a contract the day after tomorrow," Orson says as I walk out. I hear my father reply but can't catch what he says.

I grit my teeth, wanting to turn around. It feels like my choice has already been taken away from me.

Natia rests her cheek against my shoulder as the sea breeze flows through the night air, the sound of crashing waves reminding me how close to shore we are compared to my home that's more inland. Farther from Eleanor.

Candlelight streams from lanterns hanging on multiple tree limbs to light up the area. Natia's hand glides seductively down my arm before grasping my hand and pulling me toward the luscious garden. No one can deny that she is eye-catching, but the first thing I notice are her delicate hands. Hands that have probably never had a hard day in their life.

The wind blows Natia's dark black hair, wafting the scent of jasmine in my face. My body aches for a different smell; honey-suckle and sea salt. Instead of Natia's violet eyes, I picture a set of emerald green with slender strands of golden-brown lighting up with fierce determination and hope.

I tell myself Elle isn't an option. I know she was raised by harsh men, but I have hoped she could see since she's been here that not all men are the same. I want to kick myself for not mentioning the possibility we could make things work. That every moment I have spent with her has made me feel more alive. As if I can conquer any obstacle as long as she is by my side.

"Do you like them? It's a new breed of roses, I've been told," Natia says. She's standing in front of rose bushes that have multiple different colors. A light orange to a yellow and then to a red.

"The Williams's family planted these here?"

"Yes." She clears her throat irritably. "As I was saying, this soil is amazing. Glendora's land is quite magical."

I focus more on its beauty, knowing very well that this is the start of Glendora becoming more popular.

"Gwen's brother stated before they came here that they had tried to cross breed roses before but it became so easy here. They have even produced a different type of lily that glows at night.

"I can't imagine what else this land can do. Just think of all you could sell, how much coin you would make!"

I flinch, knowing others will soon want to find why this island produces so well. Natia put it into the best of words: it's like magic. My stomach clenches at the thought of others wanting a part of this island. Greed can change people.

We need a strong army for protection, to patrol the sea around Glendora. And Natia's father has one. But at what cost?

Natia cuts a flower and brings it to my nose. The aroma is strong, reminding me of my guilt but also a future for Glendora and all the people I love.

"It's lovely," I say, giving her a smile I wish to give to someone else.

At the entrance to the gardens, Theodore clears his throat. Barely any emotion is on his face, but a slight movement of his jaw tells me he isn't enjoying whatever conversation has been happening at the dinner table. "Axel, can I have a word with you?"

Natia pulls on my arm and raises her nose to the dark sky. "He's busy at the moment."

I lightly remove her hand from my arm. "I shall be back when we're done."

She grunts, stomping back to the dining room and leaving Theodore and I in the gardens.

Theodore's stance reminds me of a bear. While his eyes are gentle, they also possess a type of hardness reminiscent of the strong warrior he is. "You may regret that later," Theodore states.

"Probably," I say, kicking a piece of gravel across the dirt. "You seem to have something on your mind. No point in holding it back now."

"You don't need to go through with this," he says flatly.

"I do," I say dejectedly, wishing this was coming from my father rather than Theodore.

"But you don't, Axel," he says more sternly. "I have seen other kingdoms fall due to loveless marriages. Where they turn their backs on one another and destroy their own people's lives while they destroy their own. I have been here long enough to know you don't love this woman nor any of the others. There can be other arrangements with these kingdoms for protection. Your father hired me to train you, but also to protect you. And I'm telling you there are other ways."

I take a deep breath. "Is my father aware of how you feel?"

I wait for any glimpse of emotion transpire across his face but only his grayish eyes blink before answering, "He's aware."

That gives me answer enough that even from Theo's point of view my father still disagreed with him.

"I don't go back on my word, Theodore."

He puts his hand on my shoulder. "You don't have to make a choice that will ruin your happiness. Gabby would be telling you the same. Trust me. Life's too short. I will stand by your side on whatever choice you make but that choice can be what's good for you and for Glendora." He pats me on the shoulder and walks back into the dining hall, leaving me even more conflicted than before.

Gabby would be upset with this whole situation, but all my life I've been told I will have to make sacrifices for the good of my people and this is one of them. The kingdoms of Osteria, Nurehmia, Florencia, and Toradian are here, hoping their daughter's hand will be the one I choose and soon one of them will be considered part of my home.

CHAPTER 39

ELLE

It's only midmorning, but I can hear faint music from the town, no doubt practicing for this evening of events. This is supposed to be a joyous day for everyone, a celebration for all, but for me it's a countdown for when I leave. The council hall, which I can barely see from my room, is receiving its final touches before holding the ball tonight.

I have barely seen or heard from Axel since I last saw him leaving with Orson and Natia at *The Blue Flask*. His distance makes my skin crawl, and I wish this day would fast forward. My stomach tightens and my breakfast threatens to come back up whenever my mind thinks of every different scenario that could happen tonight.

I keep fighting this inner voice demanding I tell Axel how I feel about him because it may be my only chance. But what is there to say? I can't even sort out this rush of adrenaline whenever he is around. It won't matter after tonight. I will be gone, and he will be engaged to some other girl.

I'm ready to do anything to keep my mind busy and find myself knocking on Nile's bedroom door.

He opens it looking to be ready to leave, swinging a small bag over his shoulders.

"Would you like to go for a long ride today?" I ask, wanting to enjoy what time I have left with him.

"I would, but I'm meeting Gus at Theodore's. He said I could watch and maybe learn a few things."

My shoulders slump. "Just don't be late, you need to be back in time for the ball."

He gives me a silly look, moving his head up and down like he already knows. "I haven't forgotten. I'll be there," he says, pulling an apple from his pocket and putting it in his bag.

I nudge him. "Either way, you silly boy"—I kiss on the top of his forehead—"Better be cleaned up as the perfect date for Carmen."

"Yeah, yeah. I promise," Nile says, giving me a hug before heading down the stairwell.

With Nile out of the house, it's too quiet and makes me more anxious about the ball. Worry gnaws at me when thinking of leaving everyone I've come to love. Everyone is most likely putting up the finishing touches to the decorations in town, cooking food, or cleaning up before the evening. I should be contributing in some way instead of standing alone in this giant house.

It reminds me that I should go to the port and make sure the ship is loaded to set sail and hide a bag of clothes and weapons in one of the barrels.

For the rest of the day, I'm loading and taking inventory of all the medicine bottles, making sure they are snug and tight before carrying them onboard. When that's done, I sweep and mop the deck.

"Seems to me someone's procrastinating," Carmen says behind me.

I turn around, noting the sun is lower than I remember. Carmen stands with her hands on her hips. In the distance, a hint of a storm catches my eye.

"I'm not procrastinating."

Carmen grabs the mop. "It's been good for the last hour. Axel shouldn't be late and you—" She sniffs the air. "Stink."

She's not wrong, the humidity has made me sweat more than usual. "Could you not join us?"

"You know I have to close up *The Blue Flask*. Besides, Nile will be meeting me here to help him get ready."

I roll my neck around, feeling it get tighter. "Why don't I stay with you and wait for Nile."

Carmen sighs loudly, putting her hands on my shoulders. "Elle. Dibs and Doolah will be at your place shortly, if they are not already. This night is going to happen either way so let's just try and enjoy it."

"Okay, okay. But please find me once you get there with Nile. I want to see him in his cute outfit."

"You will be the first one I look for," Carmen says lightly as I turn to leave, hoping she doesn't see the dread on my face.

Dibs and Doolah are already in my room, fully dressed. I lean against the door, enjoying the two siblings bickering with one another about who they should dance with first. Dibs has her hair up in braids and her V-neck red dress looks daring but fitting. I hold back a giant grin as I watch Doolah put on bright red lipstick. Her coal black spaghetti strap dress flows nicely down to her ankles.

"Seize the day, is that a dress, Doolah?" I ask while wiggling my eyebrows. Doolah releases an exaggerated sigh and focuses on applying her lipstick.

"Where have you been?" Dibs says, pushing me toward the bathroom.

"It won't take long to put on a dress. I can use a washcloth to get this grime off my face."

Dibs stands in the doorway, shoving me further into the bathroom. "You need to take a bath and then we will do your hair and makeup."

I try to push past Dibs's strong arms as she holds tight against the door frame. "It's really not needed."

"I swear on the sea gods if you don't get in that bath, I'm going to drag you in myself."

Dibs isn't kidding and even Doolah stands behind her with a hint of determination in her eyes. "I'm not going to be late," she says, folding her arms.

The bath is cold, making me quickly scrub away the day's work.

Doolah sits me in a chair in front of the mirror and starts playing with my hair while Dibs picks up some makeup, bringing it close to my eye. I flinch.

"We're either going to do this the easy way or the hard way. I'll tie you to the chair if I must," Dibs says. I roll my eyes before she starts brushing something against my cheek. "There she is," Dibs says with a smile.

Standing in front of the mirror, I admire the lavender dress and how my curled hair has been pinned atop my head. The eye makeup is a dusty gray that brings out the emerald green in my eyes. I grab a hold of my necklace, wishing my mother could be here to see this. I strap my dagger around my thigh ready to leave.

Doolah comes up from downstairs. "Ready?"

I nod, ready to face the night.

"Wait. I almost forgot." Dibs pulls a few honeysuckle flowers out of a vase and weaves them into my hair. "Now, you're ready."

Axel stands below the staircase, waiting. The sight of him is breathtaking. He wears a dark purple tailored suit with a perfectly fitted deep purple vest that accentuates his broad shoulders and hips. The white dress shirt underneath brings out his tanned skin and my mother's pendant is visible on his collar.

His ocean blue eyes never waver from mine as I take the last few steps down the stairs. He glances at my bare shoulders and down my hips, making me feel like he is touching me with only his sight. I bite my inner cheek, feeling a rush of heat.

"Doesn't she look radiant?" Dibs asks as we follow her and Doolah toward the carriage.

My eyes widen, wanting her to keep her mouth shut but she only tilts her head, giving me a smug look.

"More radiant than the blazing stars," he says, placing his hand out to help me into the carriage. There's an electric spark between us when we touch and I quickly drop into my seat, wondering if he felt it, too.

He sits beside me, his knee and thigh brushing against mine

while Dibs and Doolah sit across from us. They talk about the food and drink they can't wait to taste. I watch Axel from the side, his shoulders tense as he looks out the window. He seems distant even though he's only a touch away.

"Who do you plan to dance with first, Axel?" Dibs asks cheerfully.

His knee brushes against mine as he turns toward me. "Eleanor, I'd love for it to be you, if you would have me?"

If you would have me echoes through my mind. The thought of his arms around me one more time makes me blurt out a "yes." For a person who once hated the word *love,* I'm itching closer toward a reality I don't want to face.

He nods and focuses back out the window while Dibs eyes me with confusion. I slightly shake my head, hoping she will go back to talking about the food. Thankfully, Doolah makes a point to keep conversation going as both Axel and I remain silent.

Gwendora flowers intertwine around the two bannisters that lead up to the council hall, reminding me of a sunset before dawn. Orson paces next to the entrance, his black top hat sliding to the side of his head as he rushes over to the carriage. "Axel, you're late! Your father has been patiently waiting for you inside."

Axel sighs. "I will be there shortly," he says as he steps out of the carriage before helping Dibs, Doolah, and I. Orson grunts and rushes inside. Behind me, Axel walks slowly toward the entrance, fidgeting with his sleeve for a second and then stands tall. His face is stern and determined. I ache to squeeze his hand for comfort but continue walking with Dibs and Doolah, leaving Axel to walk inside alone.

The council hall is decorated from top to bottom with bundles of purple blazing stars scattered throughout the giant room while gold-colored ribbons twirl between hanging lights of enclosed candles looking as if they are floating mid-air. The room sparkles and creates an illusion of being outside with the stars shining brightly. It is romantic and elegant.

A crowd full of smiling faces face us, waiting for Axel. All the different colors of dresses in the room remind me of wildflowers. Axel enters and the crowd claps, many hollering his name. The smile he offers the crowd as he bows to us all doesn't reach his eyes.

Orson and another man, one that more strongly resembles Axel, stands beside him. Gerald Ardanian, the ruler of Glendora. For a king, you would think he would be wearing a more ostentatious suit, but instead he presents himself with a more refined grace. His crisp blacktail coat with golden colored buttons helps elongate his older taller silhouette and complementarily paired with matching black flat-front trousers and a vest.

The room falls silent, waiting for the king to speak. "I want to thank every one of you for being here tonight. I can't express enough how enchanting you have made this day, you all have outdone yourselves with the decorations, food, and music. I am truly proud to be able to call this my home. I also want you to welcome our neighboring kingdoms for they have travelled a great distance to visit us. Let us unite as one and cherish our new friends."

A round of applause quickly dissipates when Orson raises his hands and gestures toward Axel. "As tradition goes, we will ask our ruler's son, Axel, to start the dance."

He cues the music, and Axel is already next to me, holding out his hand for me to join him on the white marble floor. With well over three hundred people watching, I take a deep breath and glide with him as we take each step. I can feel every eye on us but once we start to dance, I forget they exist. His attention is completely on me, not missing a step.

He leans forward and his breath tickles my neck as he says, "You truly take my breath away. You're beautiful, Eleanor."

A shiver runs down my back. "You as well," I say lightly.

His laugh is deep and low. "I look beautiful?"

"You know what I mean," I say, rolling my eyes and making

him smirk.

He pulls me a tad closer. "I need you to know . . ." He clears his throat. "I've enjoyed every moment with you."

I laugh nervously, trying to control whatever is bubbling inside me. "Even the times when I've yelled at you?"

His blue eyes shine a bit brighter. "Especially those."

The rhythm of the music fades. It's like ending a chapter I never want to finish. I glimpse into the crowd and see Natia watching, her face tight while she taps her foot impatiently.

The music ends. Axel squeezes my hand and steps away, taking his bow. I can still feel the warmth of his arms lingering on my skin. The light in his eyes darkens as Natia stands next to him, like she is already his. I curtsy slowly and walk away, hoping no one notices the pain jolting through me.

I force myself not to watch them dance to the next song and search for Carmen and Nile, hoping Gus will be with them.

"You seem to be on the run," a deep familiar voice says behind me. King Lucas Divian stands in a dark blue jacket edged with gold. He is taller than I remember, almost towering over me.

"I'm looking for someone, but they don't seem to be here yet," I say, my feet antsy to move instead of standing in one place.

He holds out his hand. "I believe you owe me a dance."

Across the room I spot Dibs and Doolah by the pastries, laughing with a few men around them, obviously enjoying the company. Carmen promised she would find me once she arrived. I'm desperate to have that final moment with Nile before possibly never seeing him again.

I take Lucas's hand and let him guide me toward the dance floor. Charlie, the evening's violinist, is already in the middle of a song. When Lucas wraps his arms around me, it's not the same sensation as Axel's, but it's still warm.

"Did your sister Blaire come after all?" I ask politely.

He twirls me around. "She did but only to meet the other princesses. I thought it would be good to meet other girls that are in the same position. But I didn't bring her for an alliance, if that's what you're asking. I have other ideas for that," he states, leaving me wondering what he means.

Axel circles around us, Natia still in his arms. He is close enough to see the flush of his cheeks and the tightness of his expression. But I blink and it's gone, leaving only the smell of peppermint and musk behind.

Lucas notices my gaze following Axel and twirls me the opposite direction. "You don't hide it well, you know," he says with a smirk.

"Hide what well?"

His carefree laugh echoes through the grand room as if it's part of the music. "I thought the way you two look at each other wasn't anything except friendlessness, but now . . ." He shakes his head. "It's a pity. I was hoping to invite you back to Yurma, but I already have too much respect for Axel and his father. Have you noticed they don't wear crowns nor like to be called king?"

I almost stop moving my feet, never truly noticing it until now. "I didn't."

He smirks. "I'm too forward and asked Gerald why and his reply was he doesn't want to be considered more supreme nor a royal over his people. For why call him a king when it can only separate himself from his people. The only difference is he's been given a responsibility to care for them as if they are his own family."

"I've never thought it that way," I state, liking Axel's father more.

Lucas barrels another laugh, "Neither have I. It's made me ponder why a crown of gold is needed to be to a ruler."

The song ends and he bows politely before I can reply. With a sly wink, Lucas says, "You seem to have caught another fish by the hook."

Troy, the man who wrapped the rose bouquet at the flower shop, is bowing to me and requesting a dance. Still no Nile or Gus. I was hoping they would be here before I have to leave.

"How's the flower business?" I ask, feeling like I should say something as we step to the music.

He gestures at the bouquets adorning the surrounding tables. "It's been popular and very busy but it's only temporary for me. My sister Gwen has always been fascinated with flowers; I've just been a helper. I'd like to make my own path soon, just not sure what that is yet. Glendora seems to have many opportunities."

Before I respond, Axel passes by with Natia still in his arms.

Troy notices my gaze following Axel and twirls me farther away from the middle. "I knew your mother, Gabby," he says, quickly catching my attention.

"You did?"

He looks behind me into the crowd surrounding the dance floor and back at me. "Yes, she used to bring muffins to our house when my mother was sick. I swore every time my mother ate one, she felt better, little by little."

I smile, loving to hear anything about my mother. "I think her honeysuckle muffins had that effect on many."

He grins, giving me the idea that he is happy to have my concentration back on him. He glances behind me, and I turn to see Orson and Natia's mother standing together, focusing on us. Orson nods approvingly while Natia's mother smiles as though she's hiding a secret.

My feet stop. "Did they ask you to dance with me?"

He flinches and tries to move us forward, but I keep my feet firm to the ground. "Orson only encouraged me to, but I was going to ask you either way."

My chest heats, flinging my hand out of his. "Excuse me." I rush toward the closest hallway, wanting to escape the piercing eyes burning on my back. Footsteps follow me. "I swear, Troy. I have a dagger and know how to use it."

I'm yanked into a dark room and the door slams shut behind me. A flash of light from outside shines through the window. The storm I saw earlier must be moving faster than I thought but that is not my current concern. Axel is standing in front of me, his chest heaving as he leans with one arm above me while the other is close to my side. I face him with my back flush against the door. "You should be out on the dance floor with . . . whoever."

Lightning strikes again, bringing out the tight features of Axel's face. "I can't," he says bluntly.

"Why not?" I demand.

His blue eyes shine fiercely. "Because when I saw those other two men holding you, I wanted nothing else but to beat them to a pulp."

"You can't stop it just as much as I can't stop you being in someone else's arms."

He leans closer. Too close. His forehead almost touches mine. "Whose arms would you rather be in?"

I focus out the window, tilting my head away from his. "It doesn't matter."

He sighs, gently bringing my chin back to face him. "Say it, Eleanor. I need to know. I'm the idiot that thought I could only have you for one day and that be the end of it. One day to enjoy your lips is not enough. I should have spoken up sooner and told you exactly how I felt but I didn't want to scare you. But you need to know."

"Know what?" I whisper breathlessly.

"That you are the radiant light I've been waiting for all my life. Every time I see you, you make the world shine a bit better. That I'm deeply in love with you," he says, enunciating those last three words.

My eyes widen. I'm positive my mind is playing tricks on me.

"I promise I will never burden you with this again if you don't feel the same, but I need to know."

"Burden?" I question while still trying to catch up on Axel saying he loves me. Can what I have been feeling this whole time be love? This undeniable pain when he isn't near, like I'm missing a part of me. Every morning waking up to him being my first thought? Being willing to sacrifice anything, including my own feelings, for him to marry someone else thinking it's the best for him?

The urge to touch him intensifies. I move forward, wanting to devour him, but he takes a step back.

"I need to hear it. I know what tonight is, but we can figure this out together."

"What about Orson?" I ask, knowing his uncle will go ballistic about this.

"Forget, Orson. I want you. I can figure everything else out when it comes."

A loud bang against the door makes us both jump.

"Leave us!" Axel demands.

"Axel!" Carmen shouts, banging against the door again.

"One second!" he yells.

"You and Elle need to come out, now!" She pushes open the door, her eyes red and cheeks flushed. Dibs and Doolah behind her, their faces full of concern as Gus paces back and forth still in his training outfit. Carmen chokes on a sob. "Nile is missing."

Axel and I both frantically move out of the room

"Have you checked the docks?" I ask, thinking maybe somehow she had missed him, ignoring the confused faces as we all exit.

Carmen nods her head. "Yes, the docks, around the port, the stables, Axel's estate, everywhere!"

I stop. A faint familiar voice drifting from the shoreline catches me off guard. A voice I have been waiting to hear.

Illira.

CHAPTER 40

ELLE

The still night air crackles as lightning and thunder build above us. Illira's voice rings weak as if she hasn't used it in weeks. I regret having a dress on but pick the bottom up and run toward the shore, toward Illira's call. I don't look behind me to see if the others are following, jumping over bushes and anything in my way to get to her faster.

I know why Nile is missing. Hearing Illira's call confirms my deepest fear. I picture his young face in terror of his own father. A father that doesn't deserve a moment with him. *If he touches one hair . . .*

Bile rises up my throat, knowing I should have killed the man when I had the chance.

The gleam of moonlight shines through patches of the dark clouds, directing me straight to Illira. She's close to one of the docks, the wind carrying her voice like its music against my ears. My legs burn as I quicken my pace. Her green glowing hair catches my attention, her tail flapping against the waves. "Elle!" she yells.

Seeing her, I bite my lip, holding back the tears that want to break free. She is alive. I want to jump off the dock into the water and hug her. So many things I want and need to say to her. Instead, I fall to my knees not caring that I've slit my dress on the wooden pier, reaching my hand towards her. She grabs a hold of it, our gazes locked as we catch our breaths.

"Is my father here?" I whisper, thinking maybe I'm wrong since she is here.

Her simple "yes" creates a storm of turmoil and anger within me that builds even more as I notice Illira's arms are no longer the color of porcelain but red and blotchy. The scales that travel up her neck flake as if they have been dried out. "Did he hurt you?" I croak. Her silence is answer enough. "Illira, I promise I was coming to you. I was going to take the ship and deliver the medicine to get you back. I was going to leave tonight. I'm so sorry I didn't come sooner. I should have known."

She shifts back as Axel appears next to me, Gus on his heels as he says, Illira's name with such sweetness it makes my heart ache.

Axel's not looking at me, his jaw rigid, nostrils flaring with his heavy breathing. *Did he hear my confession to Illira?*

Before I learn an answer to my question, Illira blurts out, "He has a boy! He wants the medicine and wants Elle to bring it to him."

A faint whimper comes from Carmen as she Dibs and Doolah join us. The twins cover their mouths in shock.

"Where is he?" Gus growls.

"Not far, just around the island by two giant cliffs that look like hands," she says shakily.

"*Lover's Touch*," Axel says. "Carmen, find the patrol and—"

"It's too late for that!" Illira says in a gruff voice. "We need to go now, or he will leave if he sees any signs of others."

Adrenaline rushes through me, giving me the strength I'll need to get my brother back. My gaze focuses on the people behind me who love Nile as much as I do. It is my turn to be the pirate I should have been all along.

"This is my fault," I say. Axel's shoulders visibly tighten. "I forgot who I was, what I risked staying here."

Gus steps forward, his eyes fierce. "Don't you blame this on yourself. You are not alone in this. We stick together," he says, gesturing at those around us.

Dibs and Doolah link arms next to him, their faces serious with a glint of love showing behind their eyes.

"You will never be alone," Doolah says.

I swallow past the tightness in my throat. I believe them but knowing only Axel and Gus have combat training worries me. Rain soaks through our dresses, and a rumble of thunder draws our attention to the cliffs, as if pointing us toward our destination.

"My father never plays fair. He will do anything to get what he wants. And his goal right now is to hurt me. So, I need you all to focus on getting Nile off that ship. Let me keep my father's attention on me."

All except Axel nod their understanding. A muscle spasms in his jaw and his hands clench into a fist. I know he doesn't like the idea of me being my father's main target, but this is my doing. I need to fix this, and I will.

Gus, Carmen, Dibs, and Doolah find a small enough rowboat to keep them well hidden and follow Illira through the dark sea toward *The Turbulence*. Axel refuses to leave me as we travel on horseback. A bag of medicine that was once stored on *The Blazing Star* now lays across my saddle ready to be delivered to my father.

Rain pelts us as we ride silently toward the unknown. The wind whips against us, the clouds moving fast above, like it's close to the finish line.

"You were going to leave. Just disappear. Axel states gruffly, making me wince at the truth of his words. I can barely see him through the darkness but every time a gleam of moonlight pierces through the clouds it highlights the hurt and worry in his blue eyes. "I knew you all would follow me if I did. I couldn't allow that."

He doesn't reply as he looks straight ahead. The rain slowly dissipates, droplets of water dripping down his chin. His once elegant attire is now adhering to his skin, exposing his muscular arms as he firmly holds the horse's reins.

His silence pulls more words from me, a halfhearted attempt to explain my actions. "I'm sorry I was going to take *The Blazing Star*—"

"Damn the ship, Eleanor. You are what's most important to me and you are right; I would have followed you. I would do anything for you. What I hate most is knowing you thought you had to do it alone," he states still not looking at me. The shifting clouds allow the moonlight to shine down our path. Coldness travels down my back as I watch his usual strong stature deplete; his shoulders now slump as if the rain itself weighed him down. "And what's worse is I have broken my promise to you and Gabby that I'd keep Nile safe, but I swear we will get him back. He will be in your arms again, even if I . . ."

"Axel, don't," I say, not wanting him to blame himself.."This is between me and my father. This is how it's going to end. Either him or me but never, never will it be you. Save Nile. Leave me to deal with this monster that should have been dealt with years ago." I turn back toward the path, unable to look at him any longer. Anxiety builds in my chest, making me shake while thinking of what can happen very soon. It is almost too much but I force myself to continue. "Don't blame yourself. You gave an honest promise, but you also don't know my father. You didn't fail; I did. I failed at becoming a pirate. I failed to save my brother, and I failed to find my mother. Now . . ." I shake my head, unable to finish.

Axel grabs my reins and pulls back, making Bertha stop. "I won't lose you. Not today. I won't allow it. Don't act as if you're already at death's door. The woman I fell in love with is stronger than that. If anyone failed you, it was your father. It will only end with him at the bottom of the sea and then you will forever be free of him. Free to stay." He pauses. "Free to leave."

I'm quickly reminded we both didn't get to finish our conversation from the ball. To hear those words that he loves me fills my body with warmth and dread. Dread knowing I may never get to enjoy the full extent of his love. When I deeply want it. And only from him.

I want to tell him now, but this is neither the time nor place. I instead lean forward shifting some of his wet hair that's laying across his eyebrow to one side. "Thank you for teaching me that not all men are like the ones that I grew up with."

Axel leans farther and lightly kisses my cheek before letting of my reins and continues riding toward the cliffs. As we get clo to *Lover's Touch,* I jump off Bertha and tear a slit in my dress u to my knees to allow better access to my dagger.

"You shouldn't come with me. This is most likely, a trap," I say flatly, hoping he will change his mind.

Axel straps his own dagger around his shoulder and chest "Like I said. I'm not leaving you. We're finishing this together."

I swallow, nervousness creeping up my neck as I swing the bag of medicine over my shoulder. For the last eight years it's just been me and Gus. He was the only one that I cared about on *The Turbulence.* The only one I felt the need to keep safe. But now the weight of fear clings to me, knowing I can't protect everyone. So many others I now care about are going to be in my father's territory. A territory I never want to be part of again.

The rain has completely dwindled as we walk between the cliffs, but the lingering thunder and lightning seem to warn us to turn back. I cringe at the sound of our feet walking across the sand, realizing how easily it can alert anyone within earshot. We both search for anyone near but see nothing other than an unrecognizable ship not far from shore. It's not *The Turbulence* but a smaller fishing vessel. A hint of pleasure fills me, hoping my father lost the ship he was so proud of.

"I've had eyes on you," a snide familiar voice says as he walks out of the deep shadows of the nearby cave. The step of his offbeat wooden leg sends a shiver up my spine. The moonlight brings out the creases of his skin, highlighting the darkness underneath his eyes. He looks as if he's not slept in days. "To think that my own daughter could be enjoying herself on land. Maybe enjoying herself too much," my father says with a hint of hostility as he glances at Axel. "Pity. You have been fooled into thinking love exists."

"As if you would know what love is," I say, scowling at him.

He snickers. "It only exists for ones who want to be defeated by their own stupidity. Love is a lie."

ₜween you and my mother?" I blurt, asking

ᵥe always feared to hear him answer.

ₒ, his stance becoming a bit more frigid. "You know

don't speak of her," he growls. "But it seems as if she

ₐd left me a son. Maybe, this one will be better than the

ₑe whistles loudly, looking toward the ship that's anchored

ₐe dark shadows of the sea.

A commotion of boots is heard travelling from the top deck of the ship as Nile appears. He's thrashing back and forth in Gyn's tight hold. Another crewmate follows, carrying a lantern for us all to see as Gyn pushes Nile toward the edge of the ship. Lightning flashes, illuminating my younger brother. His hands are tied behind his back and he's screaming Axel's name. I clench my fist, trying to control the burning flame inside of me as Axel growls, his forward step halted by my raised hand.

I must figure out my father's plan, or else I risk Niles' life. What I do know is my father wants a reaction. So, I stand quiet, controlling the blood boiling in my veins.

A smaller boat rows toward the shore with a familiar crew member, the youngest boy that was on *The Turbulence* appears. Sam's red hair is in a fray and his clothes hang loosely upon him as his brown eyes stare blankly at me.

"Get in," my father says sternly.

Axel steps in front of me and points his dagger at my father's chest. "She won't be doing that."

"Oh, but she will." He whistles again. "Maybe I don't want this other son as much as you think I do."

Gyn shoves Nile closer to the ship's edge, his toes hovering far above the water as my father's first mate threatens to push him overboard. Even in the distance I can picture Gyn's cold grin as a few of the other crewmates behind him laugh. "Choose wisely."

"Stop!" I scream, taking a step toward the water that separates me and Nile. But my father takes that moment to pull his narrow blade out, swiping Axel's out of the way and pointing it at Axel's neck.

"The clock is ticking," the captain says, flicking his blade at the boat. "Now get in with the medicine."

I climb into the boat, trusting that Illira and Gus are nearby, hoping that my father will take his sword away from Axel's neck. With a slight flick, he moves it away. A bead of blood drips from Axel's throat. I hold my breath until my father steps into the boat with me. "If you follow us, boy, she won't be breathing for long."

"Go," I whisper to Axel. He shakes his head, but I turn away from him as we row to the ship where Gyn still holds Nile close to the edge.

"This looks hideous on you," my father says gruffly, lifting a piece of my now stained lavender dress with the tip of his sword.

I grind my teeth together, telling myself to keep my breathing steady. To be ready to do whatever I have to do to get Nile off this ship. We reach the ship, and I climb up the ladder to the top deck as both my father and Sam follow behind me. I fight the urge to slam my foot into my father's teeth but my focus lands on Nile, his tear-stained face looking back at me. "Elle!" he whimpers, his gaze straying to the dark waves beneath his toes.

I swallow back the lump in my throat but firmly say, "Everything is going to be ok. Don't forget you are the protector of the sea, not a pirate." He shakes his head and his whole body follows. *He needs off this ship, now.*

My father laughs loudly, before leaning down and hacks on his own spit. "Don't be telling him lies, he is a pirate. It runs in his veins." He grabs a hold of the medicine bag that lays across my shoulders and tears apart the bag, pulling out one of the bottles. He wipes away a trace of blood from his lips and swallows the medicine in one gulp like a thirsty animal.

Gyn grabs my wrists and ties them behind my back, leaving Nile with another. His stench almost makes me gag; not all is well on this ship. There are only four other crewmates. Far less than before. "Looks like the great Captain Velis has lost his edge," I say sarcastically.

Gyn punches me and my vision goes hazy. My teeth cut open the side of my tongue. I spit blood on his face and dodge his next

...ny own feet and land on my knees. Gyn rais-
...iake his next move into the side of my stomach.
...ny father demands. He comes forward carrying
...dden beneath a small cloak. As he lifts the cloth his
...c the sapphire glow that shines from the jar containing
...y body stills, aware he has found the secret Axel wants to
...ect. A secret that has been hidden for generations is now held
...a my father's hands.

My father brings the jar closer to me, taunting me with it before handing it to Sam. "Take this below the deck with the others you collected. It seems you tricked the man to trust you enough to take you to the very spot that proves Glendora is not *any* island. But a source that will give me all the power and riches."

He gives me a sinister grin. "Doesn't seem I have lost my touch, has it?"

I stare back at my father, already noticing the medicine taking effect. His stance is taller and his skin is no longer tinged with yellow.

This isn't happening. Knowing I have been watched this the whole time and giving my father everything that can destroy Glendora makes me want to vomit.

Sam emerges below the deck, breathing hard. "The rest of the jars are gone!"

But then I hear a crack of bones as the man behind Nile flops onto the deck like a dead fish, Gus now standing in his place.

"Get him!" my father yells, raising the hair on my arms while the rest of the crew rushes toward him with their weapons drawn.

Gus wraps his arms around Nile and looks back at me before disappearing into darkness, only a splash can be heard from below.

"Search the ship and kill anyone on sight!" my father growls as he leans against the railing, searching for any sign of Gus or Nile.

I force myself to my feet even as my wrists burn behind me, "You have lost."

He whips toward me, lips curling with a gleam of insanity shining in his eyes.

Now this ship will burn.

270

CHAPTER 41

ELLE

"Set the sail!" He spits in my face. "Gyn, remind her whose ships she's on."

The captain heads below deck, taking the jar from Sam and swinging the bag of medicine over his shoulder before warning him, "If you don't find the rest of the jars, it will be your head" and disappears below.

Sam looks around him frantically with a noticeable tremble. The realization that he, like Gus and I, has been merely following the captain's orders to survive fills me with guilt.

Gyn grabs my bound wrists and throws me against the side of a barrel, "I've been waiting to do this for a long time."

My back burns from the hard impact but I quickly get on my knees, knowing the next blow is only a few seconds away. "If you want a fair fight, how about you untie me, you coward," I say, ignoring the pain in my ribs. My legs tremble when I try to stand, but I'm tugged back into the barrel as if I'm stuck. I try to shift away, but my wrists are pulled back again.

"You and your mouth are always getting you into trouble," Carmen whispers behind me. I stop and realize the rope around my wrists has been loosened. Hearing her voice brings comfort and a sharp sense of dread. She shouldn't be on this ship.

Before I can respond, I curl up, ready for Gyn's next blow, but instead I hear him grunt, landing on his back next to me.

"Don't touch her," Axel growls, breathing hard as water drips down his clothes. Gyn snarls, pulling out his long dagger and swinging it at Axel's pelvis. But Axel jumps out of the way, blocking it with his own.

Carmen grabs me, tearing my sleeve as she helps me stand. "We need to go. Axel can take care of him." She directs me toward the edge of the ship to jump. But we can't just leave. My father will return. He will destroy Glendora after sharing with others what he found hidden in their soil. She tugs harder with an urgent, "Let's go!"

Two familiar pirates run toward us, men that I barely spoke to but always knew to keep a close eye on when I was on *The Turbulence*. "They can't swim," I yell as Carmen and I separate. Using the rope that was once around my wrists, she wraps it around one of the men's necks and flings him toward the open sea.

The other swipes his dagger toward my shoulder. I duck and kick him between the legs, making him howl at the moon as he falls onto his knees. Carmen joins me and we both pick him up by the arms, vomit trickling down his mouth as we throw him overboard, ignoring the screams from below.

Axel groans not far from us, blood trickling down his arm as he blocks Gyn's blade.

"Go!" Axel demands as he slashes his sword across Gyn's waist and punches his nose, knocking him out cold onto the wet deck.

Carmen takes my arm again, but I shrug it away. "No, I'm finishing this!" I yell, running toward the stairs and grabbing a lantern, skidding to a halt when my father reappears from below.

The gold in his green irises flash as he glares at me, pulling his long sword from its scabbard.

With each stair he climbs, I step back.

"It's over," I say, raising the lantern above my head. In my peripheral vision, I see Axel and Carmen fight off another. Gyn is still unconscious.

272

"It's not over until I say it's over," my father says, pointing his sword at me. Axel and Carmen yell for me once more to leave but instead I slam the lantern between us, keeping them at a distance. Axel screaming my name carries through the flames, followed by him begging me not to do this. Fire blazes along the deck, burning everything in sight. "Go! I've got this," I holler back. Both of their silhouettes disappear in the flames.

Fire glints off my father's blade as I draw my dagger to block it, the force of his blow jarring my bones. Barely keeping upright, I push back as he snarls in my ear like a fierce animal. There is a reason why my father is so feared. Never once have I stood up to him and now that I am, terror needles up and down my skin.

Metal grinding upon metal rings in my ears. He comes closer and closer to my chest as my arms shake, trying to hold against his strength. "No woman is going to defeat me," he snarls into my ear.

His words awaken something in me. Something that has been growing inside of me, ready to be released.

I scream and release all my pain, hurt, and failures. Instead of pushing harder against him, I let his weight fall toward me and right before his sword impales my chest, I nudge my shoulder to the side, making him lose his balance. His sword misses my chest and cuts across my shoulder instead. Blood rushes down my arm as I twist away and ram my elbow into his neck. He catches himself before landing face first on the deck and turns to swipe away my blade coming right at his heart.

Both of us breathe hard as smoke creeps into our lungs. Sweat trickles down my face. He staggers away from the fire, closer to the edge of the ship. Soon we will be consumed in flames.

My eyes burn as I fake a strike toward his chest and jam my right knee where his wooden leg and thigh connect. His fake leg cracks, forcing him to lean against the railing, losing his grip on his weapon. I point my dagger at his throat, ready to end him.

My hand trembles as I lean in, blade pressed against his skin until a small amount of blood trickles down his neck. I growl in frustration, knowing I can't do this. I can't make the final blow. To end all this. I don't want to be a killer like him. Even if he deserves it.

"Can't do it, can you? All this time, and you still can't follow through. You have failed me once more," he says, coughing out a deep laugh, blood smearing his teeth.

There's a flap of a tail below us, glowing green eyes moving within the water. I swallow and lower my dagger. "No, you have failed me."

His brows narrow in confusion before a deep haunting vibrato shakes the ship, calling my father's name. *Velis. Come.*

His breathing slows and his eyes glaze over. I watch as he plummets into the water, arms flailing as if trying to grasp air, but Illira's arms wrap around his torso and pull him down. His cold dark eyes slowly disappear into the deep wanting sea.

The ruthless pirate known as Velis is gone. Never to sail the seas again.

My heart is pounding. My sweat-drenched clothes cling to my skin as the heat rises from the flames. The stairwell to access below the deck, where the jar of Glendoran soil was taken, is now covered in flames. There's no way for me to get to them. I sheath my dagger and prepare to jump into the water.

Pain sears through my legs as I'm thrust onto my back. "You're not going anywhere," Gyn snarls as he wheezes out of his mouth. His nose is black and blue from Axel's doing. I try to thrust my knee into his groin, but he blocks it with his thigh. "Not this time." Drool drips out of his mouth as his weight smothers me.

"I never understood why he kept you alive for so long. You were always bad luck. Always bringin' the storms. Always causin' trouble. You filthy female," he says, pushing his fingers into the cut on my shoulder. I scream in agony, feeling every movement as he digs in deeper. "You deserve to die on this ship, not I," he hisses.

"And you deserve more than death," I spit out, feeling faint from the blood seeping out of my shoulder. I flail my uninjured arm at him. He grins as I hit him as hard as I can in the face. A blade from his hip appears, ready to plunge into my chest but I catch hold of his wrist, though my arms are losing the strength to hold him much longer.

The tip of the blade moves closer and closer. *This is it*. My hand slips from Gyn's wrist as the tip of his blade draws blood from my chest but then he stops.

The smell of burnt flesh fills my nostrils. Gyn screams in agony as his sleeve catches fire, burning his skin and hair. He drops his blade and rolls, trying to smother the flames. A crack echoes above us. The main sail leans toward where we lay. I take hold of Gyn's blade and pin his palm to the deck with it. He wails trying to pull it free. But I know it's too late for him as the sail plummets on top of him.

Weak, I roll forward and sprint toward the edge of the ship, practically flinging myself off the rail and into the ocean waters. The coldness of the sea soothes the heat on my skin, but the salt also burns my wounds. I watch the ship go up in flames, half of it already underwater.

"It's over," I whisper, almost not believing it. The waves pull me to the shore as I float on my back, using my uninjured arm to direct me. Once I touch sand and can stand, I tear a piece of my dress and wrap it around my wound. It is all I can do before I collapse from the pain and fatigue.

I listen to my own breathing as I lay on the sand. The storm clouds are gone, and the stars shine freely above me.

My name echoes in the distance. I scramble to my feet and look across the coast, staying as still as I can. I hear nothing but the sound of the waves hitting the shore, the crackle of the fire burning in the distance. I'm about to sit down and rest when I hear my name, closer this time.

"Eleanor!"

"Axel," I breathe, my throat tight. I see his silhouette running toward me in the sand. The stars and moon seem to shine brighter as he gets closer. Warmth radiates through my chest.

I force my legs to run toward him, needing his arms around me. Never wanting to be separated from him again. When I'm close enough, I jump into his arms, tears streaming down my cheeks. He runs his hands up and down my body like he couldn't believe I'm truly here.

"You're alive," he croaks. "Gods . . . I thought you were gone." He kisses my forehead and cheeks, wiping away my tears. "You're hurt!" he says looking down at the silly excuse of a bandage on around my shoulder.

"It's okay for right now but, I need you to know. . ." I bite the inside of my cheeks, the words on the tip of my tongue.

"What is it?" he asks with concern in his eyes, moving my wet hair away from my face.

"I love you. I should have said it sooner but—"

His lips crash against mine, drawing every tingle and sensation up through my body. It is a kiss of longing and passion. A tenderness that makes me feel safe and wanted. A kiss that confirms love does exist.

"Alright, love birds. Get a room," Carmen says, making us both jump.

"Carmen!" I say, opening my arms to hug her. I curse, noting her injuries from fighting on the ship. She gives me a lopsided smile; her lip is swollen and one of her eyelids is darker than the other.

"Don't worry, the other one got it worse," Carmen jokes.

"Where are the others?"

"Gus took Nile on the smaller boat into town so he can be looked at and to have Theodore and his men sent out here."

"And Dibs and Doolah, why are they not with them?"

Carmen shifts her feet. "Because at the moment they are both trying to convince a frightened young red head boy to come out of the cave."

Sam. My eyes widen. I had completely forgotten about him. Not once did I see him on the ship after it began to burn. My stomach twists, hoping he won't cause too much trouble for the twins.

Carmen gestures toward the dark waves. "I think someone is waiting for you."

Water ripples around Illira as she flaps her tail and swims toward the shore. I squeeze Axel's hand reassuringly before walking over to have a moment with my friend.

The water is knee deep as I lower myself to embrace her. My adrenaline-given strength is waning, but I have waited long enough to see her.

"How's the boy, your brother?" Illira whispers nervously.

"He's safe." I take a deep breath, my ears ringing. "'I've missed you so much," I say, leaning my forehead against hers. "I'm so sorry for everything."

Her body tenses and she leans back, nudging me with her shoulder. "I missed you, too."

"I wasn't a good friend. I used you in the past to help my father, but I promise I will never do anything like that again," I say, wishing I could turn back time. She risked her life to be close to me despite my father. And in the end, she's the one that ended it for us both.

Illira curls into a seated position. "I never thought of you as a bad friend, but I do know that you will always be like a sister to me, even without one of these," she says, splashing her tail out of the water, creating a slight smile from me. "But you need to tell me about that man over there with those lovestruck eyes."

I smooth my torn-up dress and face Axel standing on the beach, my ears now ringing. "He's . . ." Another wave of dizziness makes me feel off center grabbing a hold of Illira to anchor myself.

Illira steadies me as I lean into her. "I think you have lost too much blood," she says. Axel is already next to me, cradling me in his arms.

The next thing I know is I'm in a saddle and Axel's holding me up by my waist, his chest hard against my back. Consciousness drifts in and out to the rhythm of horse's hooves beating against the ground as the sun threatens to peak above the hills. Axel whispers into my ear, "We're almost there."

CHAPTER 42

ELLE

My mother's laughter can be heard in the distance. A sweet sound that, like the welcoming scents of honeysuckle and cinnamon, has never completely left. Gliding my hands up the rail, I follow the fragrance to the top deck. As I step into the wide-open air, the sea breeze whips against my blonde hair, and I savor its soft touch.

Gus and my mother are dancing, moving to the beat of the waves. As I approach, my mother opens her arms wide, gesturing for me to join. We all join hands and skip in a circle, Gus sticks his tongue at me, and I do it back.

"I have a surprise for you both," she says, pulling something out of her pocket.

She pins a pendant shaped like a moon with two stars onto Gus's lace up shirt, kissing him on the forehead and whispering a secret in his ear. He looks at her sincerely and nods before inspecting his pendant.

She pinches my cheek, rubbing her nose against mine, and making us both giggle. "Turn around," she says. A necklace is placed around my neck, the same shape and design as Gus's pendant. Mother leans in and whispers, "Eleanor, my radiant daughter. So full of light. Let this be a reminder that you will never be alone.

That someone will always love you."

A gasp of air fills my lungs, shooting me forward out of bed. I try to move my hand to wipe the sweat from my forehead, but it is being held. Gus leans against the wall next to my bed, asleep. His golden-brown hair sweeps across his face.

My hand squeezes his, reminding me that he is right here with me. Sitting right next to me. Alive. I remind myself I'm no longer going to hide how I feel. To not hide from emotions I always thought were a sign of weakness. To cherish every moment I have with the people I care about.

His hazel eyes open lazily, his lips lifting in a small grin. He squeezes my hand back. "Good evening, sleepy head."

"Looks like you're the sleepy head," I say, happy to hear his voice. "Snoring and drooling all over the place."

"I'm not the one that's been sleeping for the last two days," he says, focusing on the bandage around my shoulder.

I move my right arm, and a stabbing pain runs up my shoulder. I push away the image of my father's face as he fell into the ocean and was taken by Illira. "It could have been worse," I reply, hoping I will someday be able to completely forget him. "Most importantly, why are you not in bed?"

He huffs a low laugh. "I've had my rest, considering I'm not the one that got stabbed."

"Just in the shoulder," I shrug. "You were right about our father. I should have known he would find Nile."

Gus sits gingerly on the bed beside me. "It's in the past now and all I want to do is move on."

Though I know it will take time for our pain to heal, I can't ignore the thought that my brother is still trying to protect me. "But if you want to talk about it—"

"I'm not ready, Elle," Gus whispers shakily, looking away from me and squeezing his eyes shut. I bite my lip to keep quiet, brows furrowing as Gus smiles wryly. "I do need to figure out what to do with Axel, though." He rolls his neck. "I've barely been able to get him out of this room. I had to get Nile to coax him out of here and get something to eat."

My cheeks warm. "You used our baby brother?" I say giggling.

"Hmf. Baby brother. It's still weird to say those words. But yes, I did. I think I'll need to talk to Axel more about what exactly his intentions are."

I roll my eyes. "I promise you he is nothing like the men on the ship." I pause, smoothing the blanket over my legs. "He's a gentleman."

"A gentleman. My sister is in love with a gentleman."

"Who would have thought?" I say with a soft chuckle, hoping the man I love will soon show his face.

After a soft knock on the door, Axel walks in with a plate of muffins and places them on the dresser. His face lights up when he sees me sitting upright in my bed. "You're awake," he says, his one dimple showing as he smiles.

Gus stands and straightens his shirt. "That's my cue to go." Before he can walk away, I grab a hold of his arm, wanting him to look at me. "You mean more to me than you know."

A glint of something builds in Gus's eye, but he quickly turns, wiping it away. "We will talk soon," he says, clearing his throat. "And Axel, thank you for taking care of her."

"Always," he says softly, bowing to Gus before the door shuts.

My heart races as Axel steps closer. Happiness surges against my chest when he sits next to me on the bed, his hand brushing my cheek. "How are you feeling?"

I lean into his touch, missing his gentle hands on my skin. "Better."

"Better enough for some food?" he says, kissing my forehead. I'm sure he's talking about literal food though my only thought is devouring his enticingly close sweet lips. A loud grumble emanates from my stomach.

Axel kisses me for a short second before getting up from the bed. "I'm guessing that's a yes." He takes the plate off the dresser and puts it on my lap. The smell of honeysuckle greets me.

"How's Nile?" I ask before taking a bite.

"He's doing a lot better than I thought he would after meeting his father but

he's been more concerned about you." He pauses. "He has also been helping Dibs and Doolah with the young boy from the ship. I don't know if you know but they found him in the caves carrying a jar of Glendora's soil."

I perk up, putting my food down. "He had it?"

He takes a deep breath. "Yes. He is very cautious but said he didn't want to fight anymore. That he wanted to do the right thing for once and give back what was taken."

My breathing stops for a short second, aware of what the boy has done.

"It seems as if our secret is still safe."

I shake my head in disbelief. "He could tell others."

"I don't think he will. If he meant to cause harm, he never would have returned the jar, but time will tell," he says, grabbing my hand and sitting in the chair beside my bed. "Which brings up another matter."

Axel stares at me, searching my face. "You knew your father had stolen those jars of soil. You were not just there to save Nile, but you also risked your life for Glendora."

"Yes," I say bluntly. "This place has become my home. I wasn't going to let him destroy it."

He rubs his thumbs against my palm. "Orson and my father are aware of what you did." His uncle's name makes me fidget in bed, unsure if that is good or bad. "And yesterday we had a meeting with the council regarding me leaving the ball without making a decision." I bite my lip, wondering how this has anything to do with what I did. My stomach sours when thinking of him being with Natia.

"I've chosen to join the alliance with King Divian. He asks nothing in return other than providing medicine and other goods commonly created on Glendora until he can get his land back in order and, in return, he will send more ships and men here to keep Glendora safe."

I lift myself so I'm sitting taller, my back now firmly against the bed frame.

"So, what does that mean?"

Axel leans toward me and puts his forehead on mine. "That means we have the rest of our lives to be together, Eleanor. If you will still have me," he says warmly.

Hearing my full name from his lips makes me feel more alive than ever. As if he can truly see me and who I've always been.

"Yes," I whisper before my lips join with his.

ACKNOWLEDGEMENTS

I began writing Against All Waves almost five years ago during COVID. It started as a dream and is now a reality. For any writer that works a full-time job on top of other responsibilities, I'm here to say you can do it! It may take longer than you were hoping, but it's all worth it. To think I'm finally close to the end mark is extremely heartwarming but also sad to know I will be saying good-bye to my characters . . . at least for now.

First, I would like to thank my husband for his continuous support and encouragement throughout this journey. You have given unwavering support even during my moments of self-doubt. I love you so much.

I'd like to give a shout out to my critique partners, The Writing Whimsies: Cristen, Holly, Jenn, Brittney, Jess, and Jessika. All your input has helped me become a better writer. All of you are very talented and it's been a joy to get to know you all.

A huge thank you to my editor, Cristen Cagle, for both being patient, supportive, and willing to answer all my publishing questions. Also, many thanks to Miblart and Nearly Novel Book Design for assistance with formatting and enhancing the appearance of my book.

I can't forget to share my love toward all my friends and family who have been with me every step of the way.

Additionally, thanks to Vivien Gintner, Flourishing Fables, and Adamszkiart for their artistic contributions. You all three are chef's kiss in the artist world.

And, finally, thank you to all who have helped me with my book cover reveal, Hidden Hollow Book Tour, and all the readers who have given my book a chance. I'm so happy to finally share Elle and Axel's story with you all! I hope you love them as much as I do.

ABOUT THE AUTHOR

Chelsea Ray is a hopeless romantic who is addicted to iced lattes and all about happily ever afters.

She writes fantasy adventure with swoon-worthy banter and heroines who persevere, which you will find in her debut novel, *Against All Waves*.

When she's not writing, you will find her training horses, playing with her corgi, or spending time with her husband on their small Kansas ranch.